A LOVE THAT LEADS TO HOME

What Reviewers Say About
Ronica Black's Work

Freedom to Love

"This is a great book. The police drama keeps you enthralled throughout but what I found captivating was the growing affection between the two main characters. Although they are both very different women, you find yourself holding your breath, hoping that they will find a way to be together."—*Lesbian Reading Room*

Snow Angel

"A beautifully written, passionate and romantic novella."—*SunsetX Cocktail*

The Seeker

"Ronica Black's books just keep getting stronger and stronger. …This is such a tightly written plot-driven novel that readers will find themselves glued to the pages and ignoring phone calls. *The Seeker* is a great read, with an exciting plot, great characters, and great sex."—*Just About Write*

Flesh and Bone—*Lammy Finalist*

"Ronica Black handles a traditional range of lesbian fantasies with gusto and sincerity. The reader wants to know these women as well

as they come to know each other. When Black's characters ignore their realistic fears to follow their passion, this reader admires their chutzpah and cheers them on. ...These stories make good bedtime reading, and could lead to sweet dreams. Read them and see."
—*Erotica Revealed*

Chasing Love

"Ronica Black's writing is fluid, and lots of dialogue makes this a fast read. If you like steamy erotica with intense sexual situations, you'll like *Chasing Love*."—*Queer Magazine Online*

Hearts Aflame

"Sleek storytelling and terrific characters are the backbone of Ronica Black's third and best novel, *Hearts Aflame*. Prepare to hop on for an emotional ride with this thrilling story of love in the outback. ...Along with the romance of Krista and Rae, the secondary storylines such as Krista's fear of horses and an uncle suffering from Alzheimer's are told with depth and warmth. Black also draws in the reader by utilizing the weather as a metaphor for the sexual and emotional tension in all the storylines. Wonderful storytelling and rich characterization make this a high recommendation."—*Lambda Literary Review*

"*Hearts Aflame* takes the reader on the rough and tumble ride of the cattle drive. Heat, flood, and a sexual pervert are all part of the adventure. Heat also appears between Krista and Rae. The twists and turns of the plot engage the reader all the way to the satisfying conclusion."—*Just About Write*

Wild Abandon—*Lammy Finalist*

"Black is a master at teasing the reader with her use of domination and desire. Black's first novel, *In Too Deep*, was a finalist for a 2005 Lammy. ...With *Wild Abandon*, the author continues her winning ways, writing like a seasoned pro. This is one romance I will not soon forget."—*Books to Watch Out For*

"This sequel to Ronica Black's debut novel, *In Too Deep*, is an electrifying thriller. The author's development as a fine storyteller shines with this tightly written story. ...[The mystery] keeps the story charged—never unraveling or leading us to a predictable conclusion. More than once I gasped in surprise at the dark and twisted paths this book took."—*Curve*

"Ronica Black, author of *In Too Deep*, has given her fans another fast paced novel of romance and danger. As previously, Black develops her characters fully, complete with their quirks and flaws. She is also skilled at allowing her characters to grow, and to find their way out of psychic holes. If you enjoy complex characters and passionate sex scenes, you'll love *Wild Abandon*."—*MegaScene*

"Black has managed to create two very sensual and compelling women. The backstory is intriguing, original, and quite well-developed. Yet, it doesn't detract from the primary premise of the novel—it is a sexually-charged romance about two very different and guarded women. Black carries the reader along at such a rapid pace that the rise and fall of each climactic moment successfully creates that suspension of disbelief which the reader seeks."
—*Midwest Book Review*

In Too Deep—*Lammy Finalist*

"Ronica Black's debut novel *In Too Deep* has everything from nonstop action and intriguing well developed characters to steamy erotic love scenes. From the opening scenes where Black plunges the reader headfirst into the story to the explosive unexpected ending, *In Too Deep* has what it takes to rise to the top. Black has a winner with *In Too Deep*, one that will keep the reader turning the pages until the very last one."—*Independent Gay Writer*

"...an exciting, page turning read, full of mystery, sex, and suspense."—*MegaScene*

"...a challenging murder mystery—sections of this mixed-genre novel are hot, hot, hot. Black juggles the assorted elements of her first book with assured pacing and estimable panache."
—*Q Syndicate*

"Black's characterization is skillful, and the sexual chemistry surrounding the three major characters is palpable and definitely hot-hot-hot...if you're looking for a solid read with ample amounts of eroticism and a red herring or two you're sure to find *In Too Deep* a satisfying read."—*L Word Literature*

"Ronica Black's debut novel, *In Too Deep*, is the outstanding first effort of a gifted writer who has a promising career ahead of her. Black shows extraordinary command in weaving a thoroughly engrossing tale around multi-faceted characters, intricate action and character-driven plots and subplots, sizzling sex that jumps off the page and stimulates libidos effortlessly, amidst brilliant storytelling. A clever mystery writer, Black has the reader guessing until the end."—*Midwest Book Review*

"Every time the reader has a handle on what's happening, Black throws in a curve, successfully devising a good mystery. The romance and sex add a special gift to the package rounding out the story for a totally satisfying read."—*Just About Write*

By the Author

In Too Deep

Deeper

Wild Abandon

Hearts Aflame

Flesh and Bone

The Seeker

Chasing Love

Conquest

Wholehearted

The Midnight Room

Snow Angel

The Practitioner

Freedom to Love

Under Her Wing

Private Passion

Dark Euphoria

The Last Seduction

Olivia's Awakening

A Love That Leads to Home

A LOVE THAT LEADS TO HOME

by

Ronica Black

2020

A LOVE THAT LEADS TO HOME

ISBN 13: 978-1-63555-675-9

This Trade Paperback Original Is Published By
Bold Strokes Books, Inc.
P.O. Box 249
Valley Falls, NY 12185

First Edition: August 2020

Credits
Editor: Cindy Cresap
Production Design: Susan Ramundo
Cover Design By Tammy Seidick

Acknowledgments

I would like thank every single person at Bold Strokes Books for taking my words and making them all shiny, pretty, and glittery, and for putting them out there for the world to read.

And thank you, dear readers from around the world, for reading and appreciating those words.

Dedication

For my family back "home."
For understanding that I will always love
and cherish where I come from.
And that I will always have that red mud
running through my veins.
No matter where my heart may lead me.
I love you all.

CHAPTER ONE

The large mass of marching teachers moved together like a formidable sea of red in their matching scarlet T-shirts as they headed for the capitol in downtown Phoenix. They were united in purpose and in voice, and Carla Sims was right there in the middle of the march, holding her homemade sign high and doing her best to continue to chant along with her fellow educators. But her voice was strained from days of protesting, and now her throat was beginning to hurt as well.

She lowered her sign and pushed up her visor to wipe the sweat from her brow. The smell of sunscreen was strong, not just from her own skin, but from the numerous others crammed in next to her. It was early afternoon and the sun was bright, baking them all in ninety-five-degree heat, an unfortunate consequence of protesting outdoors in May. Carla plucked at her shirt, trying to cool herself by pulling it away from her moist body. It did little to help. In addition to her sore throat and feeling overheated, her feet ached, and she was exhausted. But still, she wanted to press on. When she forced down a swallow to lubricate her throat, however, the stabbing pain put a stop to that immediately.

She nudged her friend Nadine, who, like her, was wearing a red visor and sunglasses. Other than those two similarities, they couldn't look more different.

"I need a break."

Nadine leaned in and cupped her ear, apparently not having heard her.

"I need a break." Carla pointed to her throat and Nadine nodded and they wove their way out of the group and crossed to Wesley Bolin Memorial Park. They found shade under a tree and sat amongst other resting protestors. Carla noticed that they too, appeared to be exhausted and overheated. She touched her own cheek, wondering if she was as pink as others were. Her face felt hot and it stung slightly beneath her fingertips, suggesting she was a little burned, despite her generous slathering of sunscreen.

She settled into the warm grass next to Nadine, crossed her bare legs, and relaxed. It felt wonderful to be still, if only for a few minutes. She shrugged off her backpack and retrieved two bottles of chilled water, thanks to her frozen cool pack, and gave one to Nadine along with a chocolate peanut butter Cliff bar.

"Ah, gracias," Nadine said, hurriedly opening both.

"De nada."

Carla unscrewed the cap on her own bottle and drank heartily, wincing as she swallowed. Then she removed her mirrored aviator sunglasses and visor and tilted her head back to douse herself with what was left of her bottle. The sensation was breathtaking as the water soaked into her hair and scalp and instantly cooled her face. She ran her fingers through her short hair, happy that she'd decided to cut it. It hadn't been an easy decision, going from shoulder length locks to a short, stylish pixie cut, but she'd finally decided she might as well go for it seeing as how she was now embarking on a new phase in her life. A thirty-seven-year-old, newly single lesbian phase, that is.

It had been seven months since she and Megan had split, but she'd done little else to forge ahead courageously into the next chapter of her life. Her friends tried relentlessly to get her to date, but she kept refusing, knowing she wasn't ready and fighting like hell to avoid the grueling process of serial dating. She believed, at this point in her life, that if love did ever find her again, it would be something that happened spontaneously and unexpectedly, not from swiping through dozens of dating app selfies on a cell phone. Needless to say, though, she wasn't holding out hope for love to find her that way anymore than she was with the process of dating.

She heard Nadine's breath hitch as she also soaked her head and face.

"Whoo! That feels so good." She dabbed herself with a hand towel she'd retrieved from her own bag, but she'd created dark smudges beneath her eyes.

Carla laughed. "Here." She took the towel and wiped her face. "Your eye makeup."

"Oh."

"Yeah, you look very Alice Cooper."

Nadine chuckled. "Not a good look for me?"

"Yeah, not so much."

"Did you know he's an avid golfer?" Nadine asked and it took Carla a second to understand to whom she was referring. Keeping up with Nadine and her random change of topics was sometimes difficult. She was chock full of useless facts about all sorts of things, especially people, and she'd blurt out something and Carla would just begin to make sense of it, only to have to jump to another topic two seconds later.

How Nadine came across such things, Carla had no clue. But she was always eagerly anticipating what little gem of useless but nonetheless entertaining trivia Nadine would share next. And she was a treasure trove.

Carla finished cleaning off the makeup and returned the towel.

"Alice Cooper a golfer? Really? No, I didn't know that."

"Max played in a tournament with him a few weeks ago."

Carla tore open her Cliff bar and took a bite.

"I knew he lived here in Phoenix, but no, I didn't know about the golf thing."

"Somehow Max still manages to play eighteen holes two or three times a week despite that job at the dealership."

Carla quickly shifted her mind to Max, Nadine's husband. "I figured he would. He really loved being a golf pro."

"I know he did, but we needed actual food on the table, and as slow as things were for him and my low income, we didn't have a choice."

"No, you didn't." Carla often had to work an additional part-time job bartending for a friend's catering company just so she could make her ends meet. Her summers and occasional weekends during the school year weren't always used for her much-needed leisure time. She cleared her throat, but it didn't seem to help with the pain or the strength of her voice.

Nadine pulled her knees up and wrapped her arms around them. "Your voice is really shot. Maybe we should call it a day."

"No, not yet."

"We've been here for hours."

Carla wanted to be there to show her support just as she'd been doing for the past several days. They were all on a mission and she wasn't about to back down because her throat hurt. No way. Teachers needed better pay. Deserved better pay. And education needed more funding.

"Let's just rest a while," she said. She thought about her students and how each and every one of them was special to her. Some loud and boisterous, others quieter and more reserved. Some overachievers, others just average. And a couple, well, sometimes she was lucky if they ever turned in a completed assignment at all. But all of them were young and vibrant with healthy, open minds just waiting for someone to care enough to reach inside and tap into them. She happened to be one of those people. She was someone who cared. And she absolutely loved it when she found a new way in and lit up their interest in science. If she were being honest, there weren't very many things in her life that gave her that kind of satisfaction.

"Think the governor's going give in and end this any time soon?" Nadine asked.

Carla shook her head. "No, I don't."

"School's almost out. Are we really going to have to strike that long? God, I hate this."

"Who knows at this point? I really didn't think we'd have to go as long as we have." Thousands of Arizona teachers had walked out on strike and schools had closed. And still, no word from the governor.

"We're only asking for what's fair," Nadine said. "If our kids don't get the quality education they deserve, that won't only hurt them in the long run, it will hurt everyone. What do they think is going to happen when these kids turn eighteen and have to work? Do they honestly think that they will be able to perform effectively in the workplace?"

She crumbled up her wrapper and did the same to Carla's and shoved them in her bag. "It scares me. It just really, really scares me."

"Me, too."

Carla took careful sips from another bottle of water she'd pulled from her backpack. Then handed another bottle to Nadine. They were both quietly drinking when Carla's cell phone rang. She slid it from her pocket to silence it but changed her mind when she saw the caller ID.

"Oh, no." Her stomach clenched.

"What?"

"It's my aunt. Something must be wrong."

"What makes you think that?"

"We usually only speak on Sundays after she gets home from church." She answered the call, heart already pounding.

"Maurine?" she rasped.

"Carla?"

"It's me, but I'm a bit hoarse. Is everything okay?"

Silence.

"Maurine?"

"It's Mama, Carla. She collapsed in the kitchen this morning and was rushed to the hospital. I've been trying to call."

Carla's heart dropped, and a lump rose to her throat causing the initial pain she'd felt earlier to literally throb.

"I'm sorry, I didn't hear it. How is she? Is she okay" She knew there was more. Knew it must be serious. Otherwise Maurine wouldn't be calling.

"She's sick." Her voice caved.

Carla closed her eyes. Maurine getting emotional meant the situation was dire. Very dire. "How bad?" Tears brimmed and burned as she waited for the answer.

She heard Maurine struggle to speak and she braced herself.

"She's not going to make it, Carla. They don't think she's got much longer. They're not even sure she's going to make it through the night."

Carla's world spun. She had to close her eyes again to fend off the dizziness. The tears that had welled began to fall, streaking down her cheeks like narrow little streams carrying the most gut-wrenching pain she'd ever felt.

She had always known this day would come. She'd just hoped she'd somehow, someway, be prepared to face it. But she now knew, as she sat totally and completely helpless under that tree three thousand miles away, that she could've never, ever been adequately prepared for the news that was just relayed to her.

"Okay," she managed to say. "I'll be there as soon as I can."

She heard Maurine break down completely as they said good-bye, and it took all Carla had not to do the same in response. She stared endlessly into the green grass, doing her best to steel herself. She startled when Nadine rested her hand on her shoulder.

"Is it your grandmother?"

Carla swallowed down the threatening sobs. She nodded.

Nadine had been her closest friend for fifteen years. They'd met the very first day Carla stepped foot in her classroom to begin her career. She'd seen her through some rough times throughout the years and she knew her better than anyone. So, she knew how much her grandmother meant to her. She knew she was like her mother; knew she had raised her. And she no doubt knew how terribly devastating this whole thing was going to be for her.

"It's bad news?"

"My aunt broke down." She looked at Nadine. "She never cries. So, yes, it's the worst kind of news." She sucked in a shaky breath. "She said she doesn't have long," Carla said. "I have to go. I need to leave right away."

But, at the moment, she couldn't move. She was stuck to the ground as if the shock had weighed her down and rooted her there.

"Of course."

"I'm probably going to miss the end of school—all of—"

"I'll take care of all of it. You've pretty much packed up and prepared everything for the last day anyway because of the strike. The rest I can handle. We can handle. You know, your friends and colleagues who adore you?"

"Thank you. I just—I'm not ready for this, Nadine. I'm not ready."

"Aw, sweetie." She inched closer and embraced her. "I know this is hard. It's probably one of the hardest things you'll ever have to go through. And I'm so, so sorry. If there was anything in the world I could do to ease your pain I would. But when it comes to something like this, there's very little anyone can do to help with the pain. So, I'm going to do what I can, which is to make sure you don't have to worry about a thing here, okay? Max and the boys will pitch in and we'll take care of the house, the mail, the yard, everything. You just go be with your family. That's all you need to worry about. That's all that matters now."

Carla wiped her tears.

Nadine was right.

She needed to pack her bags, catch the soonest flight back to North Carolina. Back to where she came from. Where she was born and raised. Where anyone and everyone who had any kind of blood relation to her currently resided.

She needed to go back so she could do the most difficult thing she'd ever had yet to do.

Say good-bye.

CHAPTER TWO

Carla rushed through Charlotte Douglas International Airport, bypassing the long, familiar row of wooden rocking chairs that welcomed visitors in a relaxed, southern hospitable kind of way. She often sat in one while waiting to board her return flights to Phoenix, preferring the gentle rocking chairs over the stiff, stationary seats at the gate. At the moment, though, thoughts of departing were the last thing on her mind. Her plane had just arrived, and she was hurrying, wanting to get to her grandmother as soon as possible.

She made it to baggage claim and paced while waiting for her luggage. She texted Nadine, letting her know she'd arrived safely and then texted her uncle Rick telling him she'd be ready for pickup soon. Another quick text, this one to Maurine, resulted in a much-needed update on her grandmother. She was still alive, but she hadn't been conscious for hours. Carla slid her phone in her pocket, the same pocket where it had rung with bad news. She hadn't taken the time to change clothes, having rushed home right away from the march to book whatever flight she could get and pack her things. Now that she was there, she couldn't seem to slow down. She was still in overdrive. She tried to breathe deeply and calm some but failed. To her great relief, the luggage carousel came to life, and with her bags in tow, she headed for the exit and stepped out into the mild night where the strong smell of jet fuel and car exhaust permeated. She waited curbside after texting her uncle and stared into oncoming headlights. It wasn't long before his early model Chevy Blazer slowed and pulled in next to her.

Rick climbed out and met her at the rear of the vehicle.

"Hey," he said in his gruff voice. He tugged on the worn brim of his Skoal tobacco ball cap and stroked his long brown beard. His jeans and T-shirt were dirty from his work at the sawmill and very typical for him, just as his calm demeanor was. He didn't appear to be anxious like Carla, despite the current situation. But that was Rick. He was laid-back with a quiet kindness that put people at ease. Even the way he moved was slow and easy. Carla had always said that if he were a whisky, he'd go down smooth. But also like whisky, he wasn't to be messed with. His gentle manner could change in a flash if he felt threatened. Thankfully, Carla had only ever seen that twice in her lifetime, and both times the men who'd tested Rick's limits had regretted it. And Rick had been easy on them.

"Hey," she said back as she was swallowed up in his tattooed arms in an embrace. He was a large man, close to six foot five, thick with muscle and big, broad shoulders. Working at a sawmill was very physical and he had the build to prove it.

But that outer strength and quiet calm apparently weren't able to protect him from the grief and sadness of the situation.

He jerked with a few body-racking sobs and the two of them pulled apart, both wiping their eyes. Rick crying wasn't something she'd seen often, like Maurine, and it took nearly all she had not to completely fall apart.

He sniffled and rubbed his face.

"Ah, let's get you out of here." He tossed her luggage in the back of the Blazer as if it weighed no more than a feather and closed the hatch. They climbed into the SUV and rode in silence for a while.

"You hungry?" Rick eventually asked, stroking his beard once again. It had become a habit, one she'd noticed during her last visit home, and she surmised it must comfort him somehow.

She thought for a moment before answering his question.

"I don't really have the desire to eat, but my body is hungry. If that makes any sense."

"It does." He stopped at an intersection and switched on his turn signal. "You want your usual?"

She sighed at the thought of having to eat and fastened her seat belt. "I guess."

He made the turn and accelerated once again. "I never thought I'd see the day when you didn't get excited about going to Bojangles."

"Yeah, well, the day has come. And it sucks." There wasn't a Bojangles in Phoenix, so she usually always looked forward to that spicy fried chicken and an ice cold Cheerwine when she arrived. But this visit was obviously very different.

"How is she?" she asked after another long silence.

"She was in and out all day until about four o'clock. She fell asleep then and hasn't woke up since."

Carla checked her watch, having already changed the time on the plane. It was after ten.

"Did she talk when she was awake?"

"Not a whole lot. She knows who we are and everything, but she just seems really tired."

"She's not in any pain, is she?"

"Oh, Lord, no. Dr. Braum says she's gonna pass very peacefully, probably in her sleep."

Carla smoothed away more tears. "That's good, I guess."

She saw his eyes begin to water again as well.

"I don't understand," she said. "Why is this happening? Is it her COPD?"

"And her emphysema. They said they can't do anything else for her."

"So, she just collapses one day and that's it? There's no warning?"

"She's been sleeping a lot lately and not getting around much. And there's been a few times when the home care nurse couldn't wake her up. She was breathing fine and all, she just wouldn't wake up. But when she finally did, she seemed fine."

"It's just too fast. The whole thing is happening way too fast."

They pulled into the drive-through at Bojangles and Rick ordered for her, already knowing very well what she wanted. She did her best to eat as they drove toward the hospital, but she could only swallow a few bites, too worried she wasn't going to get the chance to say good-bye. She was so worried about it that when they did finally reach the hospital, she had the door open and was halfway out before Rick even had the car in park.

"What room is she in?" she called out.

"Three-oh-four."

She slammed the door and hurried inside, taking the elevator to the third floor, and then scrambling down the hallway in search of the correct room number. It ended up being the last door on the right, and when she stood before it, she paused and tried to prepare herself for what she'd find just beyond it. Just like her failed attempt to stay calm at the airport, this strength-seeking moment didn't help much either. With a big breath, she pushed on the partially opened door and stepped quietly inside.

The room was large and dim, the only light coming from the first half of the room, where another bed would've been had there been another patient. She crossed the empty space toward Maurine and her other uncle, Cole, where they stood at the end of what Carla assumed was her grandmother's bed. A curtain was drawn, ending where Maurine and Cole stood, preventing her from seeing anything else.

She slowed her approach, suddenly so anxious her heart thudded from somewhere low in her chest. Maurine was dabbing her eyes with a tissue and Cole had his head bowed. They, like her, had the Sims' trademark blond hair and lean build. The only one who didn't was Rick. He had the darker hair and more muscular build that favored her grandmother's brothers. But they all did share one thing that couldn't be denied.

Their eye color.

Gold.

Like sweet, warm honey straight from the hive.

That's how her grandmother had always described it. And she should know. They inherited that eye color from her.

Carla smiled softly at that, but tears came, nipping at her throat, forcing the smile away. Cole caught sight of her and motioned for her to come over. She did, and they enveloped her in long, firm hugs. Cole shook when he held her, a lot like Rick had. Maurine did a little but it was obvious she was trying to control her emotions. Nevertheless, she clung to her long and hard before she released her.

Maurine had always been stronger than her brothers, despite being younger. Carla had idolized her for that strength as a kid and had followed her around everywhere. Maurine was only seven years older than her, and they'd always been more like sisters than aunt and niece. They'd all been more like siblings to her, and a lot of folks had often assumed they were until they were told otherwise.

Maurine finished wiping away more running tears and took her hand. She led her to a chair that sat next to the head of the bed.

"Her breathing has really slowed the last hour," Maurine said.

Carla sat slowly and squeezed her eyes tight before opening them to look at her grandmother.

"Hey, Grandma," she said, doing her very best not to fall to pieces at the sight of her. Her voice was still strained from the teacher's march, and she tried to speak louder, needing to make sure her grandmother heard her. "It's me, Carla. I'm here."

Her grandmother didn't give any indication that she'd heard her. She just kept slowly breathing, her jaw slack and her mouth open. Her cheeks looked sunken and her beautiful olive skin was noticeably paler. Her breathing, Carla soon noticed, was not only slow, but there were considerable pauses. Each one bringing about a wild panic in her for fear she wouldn't inhale again.

"Is this—normal? Her breathing like that?"

"The nurse said it happens when they're close to the end," Maurine said.

"I don't think it's gonna be long now," Cole said.

Carla held her grandmother's soft, cool hand. It felt strangely pliable and her nail beds were white. Carla kissed her knuckles, fighting back sobs as she recalled entertaining herself by pushing at the veins on the back of her hand when she was little when they were somewhere where she was supposed to be still and quiet.

Her grandmother had never complained.

Carla touched her face and noticed that she still had on her oxygen tubing. She could hear the hiss of it as it pushed air into her nose.

"She's wearing her oxygen." She looked to Maurine and Cole. "Kind of senseless at this point don't you think? Especially considering how she hated it."

Cole laughed. "She'd cuss up a storm when the cord snagged on something in the house."

"She'd be mad as hell if she knew that thing was still on her right now. At the very end," Carla said.

Cole patted her other hand from his seat across the bed.

"You ain't got to wear it no more, Mama," he said. He stood and carefully removed the cannula and cord and placed it back behind her pillow. He knelt and kissed her forehead and then resettled, taking her hand in his.

Rick appeared from behind the curtain and stood next to Maurine.

"I been on the phone. Everyone is calling wanting to know how she is." He stroked his beard as Carla stroked her grandmother's long white hair.

She looked very different from the last time Carla had seen her. She seemed to be thinner and a little feeble. She'd lost a lot of muscle tone and her hair, which had always been very thick, appeared to have thinned near her hairline at the top of her head.

Apparently, a lot had changed in the three years since she'd last seen her. She should've come back sooner. Why hadn't she come back sooner?

"I'm sorry I haven't been here, Grandma. I'm sorry."

"She missed you," Maurine said. "But she always wanted you to be happy. Knowing you were happy made her happy."

Her grandmother stirred and began to mumble.

"She's dreaming," Cole said. "Been doing that all day."

"Grandma? Grandma, can you hear me?" Carla squeezed her hand and smoothed her thumb along her brow. "I'm here," she said again. "I'm right here."

She felt a gentle squeeze from her grandmother's hand.

"Yes, it's me," she said, the tears breaking through. "It's me and I'm here and I love you. I love you so much."

She rested her head on her grandmother's chest and broke down and cried.

"I just love you so much," she whispered.

Her grandmother made another soft noise and there was a very long pause before the next breath. Carla felt a pressure on her shoulder, and she sat up and found Maurine standing right next to her, eyes brimming as tears continued to run down her face. Her uncles, looking similar, each placed a hand on their mother.

They all knew it was time.

"I love you, Mama," Maurine said.

Rick was once again shaking with sobs and he spoke, but his voice was barely audible. "I love you, too, Mama."

"We all love you," Cole said. "And we all know you love us." He, too, began to quietly cry as the woman who meant so much to them took in another breath.

"You go on and go now, Mama," Rick said. "We're gonna be okay." He struggled to speak. "Everything's gonna be okay."

Carla felt another slight squeeze from her hand and her grandmother pushed out one last breath. One last gentle sigh.

And with that final exhalation, the bright, beautiful flame that was her grandmother quietly blew out.

"I love you," Carla repeated once more, wanting her to take that with her as she crossed over.

Then she bowed her head and cried and somehow managed to say what she'd come three thousand miles to say.

"Good-bye."

CHAPTER THREE

"Are you sure you're all right?" Janice asked her lifelong best friend, Maurine, over the phone.

"I'm doing okay."

Janice sighed and sat on the bed in her hotel room and glanced at herself in the mirror above the dresser. She ran her hand through her hair and seriously considered changing out of her sleep pants and tank top and just driving back home to be with Maurine. It didn't matter that she'd just arrived for her favorite college literary conference where she would be participating in a panel and giving a presentation. Nor did it matter that this year's conference was being held on Hilton Head Island, where she'd looked forward to exploring South Carolina's Lowcountry. What mattered was that Maurine needed her. And there was always next year.

She waited for Maurine to say more, but all she heard was her breath hitch. She knew Maurine very well and knew she was doing her best not to cry over her mother's death, probably not wanting to worry Janice any further.

It made Janice tear up.

"I think I should come home," she said. Betty Sims had died, and to Janice, that woman might as well have been kin and Maurine a sister.

"No, you don't need to be doing that. We're just gonna sit here with Mama for a while before they take her and then we'll go home."

"You're still at the hospital then?"

"For now."

"And you're not alone?"

"No."

"Okay." Her brothers were probably there with her. Or "the boys" as she'd always called them. That made her feel a little better.

She wiped away tears, hurting for Maurine and also for herself. Losing Betty tore at her just as much as the passing of her own mother had several years before.

"I'm so sorry this has happened," she said. "So sorry for your loss. She will definitely be missed."

"Yes. She will." More stifled cries.

"I'm here for you. Always. You know that."

"I do."

"I mean it now, Maurine. I can leave here if need be. So, don't you dare hesitate to call."

"I won't. But right now, there's not much anyone can do. I don't want you rushing home to tend to me and miss out on something you've been looking forward to all year."

"You're more important than a conference, Maurine."

"Just please stay and try to enjoy yourself. It's what I want. I'll be okay."

"All right. But I'm not happy about this. And I doubt I'll have much fun. She was—I—" Her throat tightened.

"I know," Maurine said.

"And I worry about you and how you're going to handle this. You always try to be the strong one and you try to hold everything inside when you do that. It's not healthy."

"There's no need to worry about that, Janice. I can't even think about being strong right now." She exhaled. "It's so hard. Hurts so bad."

"I know, Mo," she said, using the nickname she'd given her when they were kids. "I wish I was there so I could hold onto you until all that hurt is gone. You did that for me, remember? Stuck to me like glue when my mama died. I wouldn't have made it without you."

Maurine cleared her throat.

"I'll be all right, Janice. Carla's here and she's gonna stay with me."

"Oh?" She pressed her hand to her face, the mere mention of her name causing a chain of involuntary reactions within. Learning that she was already there, and would be so close by, only intensified those reactions.

She rubbed her leg and attempted to keep her voice at a normal octave.

"I didn't think she'd be able to get here so quickly."

She'd thought the earliest she'd get there would be early tomorrow morning.

"I didn't realize," she said softly, more so to herself as she pictured her in her mind and grew a little dizzy. She'd been reacting to news about Carla a lot since she'd last seen her on that unforgettable Christmas day three years ago. And now, with Betty's passing, it seemed that even the direst of circumstances couldn't change the way she automatically responded. "But I'm so glad she's there with you," she added, coming back to reality.

"Having her here helps. You know how strong she is," Maurine said.

Yes, she knew. She was well aware of her quiet strength and her self-assured, yet somewhat subtle confidence.

Among other things.

She blushed.

"How long is she staying?" Her voice shot right back up to what she was sure was an ear-piercing pitch. Thankfully, Maurine didn't seem to notice.

"She said she wants to stay a while and help us get things settled with Mama's affairs."

"Oh. That will be nice. I'm sure she'll be a big help." Sure, she was going to be a big help to Maurine and the boys. But what was her presence going to do to her? Better yet, what was it *already* doing to her?

She hadn't exactly planned on seeing her again so soon.

"She will," Maurine said, bringing her back in to focus. "I'm so glad she's home."

"Me, too." Janice sighed.

Shit.

She was convinced she'd just given herself away with her reply. But again, Maurine didn't seem to notice.

"Listen, I better go," Maurine said. "They're gonna come for her soon and I want to sit with her a little more."

"Okay, darlin'. You'll let me know immediately when the services are going to be?"

"Probably around Wednesday or Thursday next week."

She'd be home well before then.

"Okay, I'll see you soon," she said. "Try to get some rest, and please, take care of yourself."

"I will."

"I love you."

"Love you, Jay-Jay."

"Night."

She pulled back the covers and crawled into the king-size bed. She reached for her book on the nightstand, usually more than eager to read the lesbian romances she'd discovered. But her thoughts kept going to Carla.

Her interest in her wasn't new, but when it had begun it had been instantaneous and surprising. It had happened during her last visit home, three years before, when Carla suddenly announced that she was gay. Janice had been there, sitting right across from her at the dinner table along with the rest of the Sims family and she couldn't forget the way her declaration had penetrated and flooded her heart. An unforeseen excitement had come from down deep inside and she hadn't been able to stop thinking about her since. Carla's lesbianism had fascinated her, and she'd nearly gone insane with the constant imaginings of her being romantically intimate with women. Those thoughts had consumed her and eventually led her to an exploration of sorts. The freedom of living on her own after her divorce had made her secret quest for information quite easy and she'd learned some very interesting things about herself since.

Some very, very interesting things.

But what it all ultimately meant, she didn't know. For the time being she'd just been enjoying her exploration and allowing herself to dream without the complication of deeper or further contemplation. And until now, living that way had worked. Now, however, the subject of those thoughts and dreams was back, and soon Janice would have to interact with her.

"My God, I have to stop this." Frustrated, she tossed the book on the nightstand and switched off the light. "What am I going to do?"

She had to make being supportive of Maurine and the Sims family her main priority. She couldn't be caught up in herself and her attraction to Carla. But that's exactly what she was worried about. The woman she'd been fantasizing about for three years was going to be right in front of her, in the flesh.

How am I going to feel? React?

Think?

Will I be able to control any of those things, and more importantly, hide them from others if I somehow can't?

This was what happened when you lived in the moment and avoided thinking about anything beyond it. If she had, she would've reined in her imagination, or at the very least, kept it better corralled, knowing that someday soon Carla would eventually return. That would've been the wise, cautious thing to do. Under any other circumstance, that's what she would've done. But this had been different. It had thrown her for a loop. And she'd felt like, for the first time in her life, she deserved to feel good, without any rules or concerns about the future. After all, no one knew, so what was the harm?

This is the harm.

Carla was there and someone dear to them all had died. Completely unexpectedly. A hard punch to the gut.

She was not prepared for either.

Somehow, she was going to have to face them both together.

I need to think.

Just calm down and think.

She breathed long, deep, and slow, and soon she began to relax.

Carla's image seeped into her thoughts like a sneaky liquid elixir. Too quick and too euphoric to fight, though she knew, somewhere down deep, almost too deep to even comprehend, that she should. But her mind and body were limp with the sedation of anticipated dreams.

Blissfully helpless, she stared up into the darkness just as she'd done so many nights before and freed her mind, letting it go to where it wanted to be most.

To Carla.

Chapter Four

Carla sat with her head in her hands on Maurine's couch. The sofa was relatively new, and the deep maroon went well with her recently redecorated living room. Or so Carla had been told anyway. And according to Maurine, so did the newly reupholstered armchair with the flower print. Carla took her word for it. Maurine's creativity and pension for decorating were what made her such an excellent floral designer at their great-uncle Floyd's flower shop. It seemed, however, as Carla glanced around, that her compulsion to decorate and arrange knew no bounds.

Carla sighed. Even if she had been into decorating like Maurine, she still wouldn't be a fan of the new sofa. The damn thing had been doubling as her bed, and her backache and stiff neck were what she had to show for it. A good night's rest had yet to pay her a visit. But her discomfort was really the last thing causing her concern.

She glanced at her watch, the one her grandmother had given her when she'd graduated from Arizona State. She'd been so excited on that warm desert day when she'd handed her the small wrapped box. Carla had opened it slowly, wanting to cherish the moment, so touched and grateful that her grandmother had made the trip out west for her special day.

"I hope you like it. I already set it to Arizona time. Since I know this is where you want to be. Where you're the happiest."

She closed her eyes and forced the memory from her mind. She couldn't cry again. Not right now.

"Maurine, you about ready?" What was taking her so long? Though Maurine was borderline obsessive about the appearance of her home, she'd never been overly obsessive with her own appearance. Carla had always assumed it was because she simply didn't need to primp. Her beauty was all natural. Carla almost asked her what the hold up was but she stopped herself, the answer already apparent.

They'd all been dragging their feet today because they knew very well what they had to face. Carla had eventually kicked in and showered and ironed her black slacks and matching form-fitting blazer. She even took extra care when putting on her makeup, which she hadn't worn since her arrival, and checked herself in the full-length mirror several times before deciding that she should button all three of the buttons on her blazer. She ran her fingers down the collar to the cream-colored camisole underneath, still worried about whether or not she looked nice enough. Realizing she didn't have time to fuss with her outfit regardless, she refocused on her watch.

"Maurine!"

Damn it.

They were going to be late for the funeral. She couldn't seem to light a fire under anyone's ass. The only one who seemed to have any concern for the time was Travis, Maurine's husband. He'd already left for the church to meet with the other pallbearers. Carla was glad he was finally home. He was a long-haul trucker and had been on a run across the country when her grandmother had passed. His being home had made a big difference in Maurine. Whether she wanted to admit it or not, she needed Travis. He was her love and support. A truly good guy who was the yin to Maurine's yang. Maurine didn't know how fortunate she was to have someone by her side like that.

Carla felt that sickening dread that kept recurring just when she thought it was finally gone for good. It came on the coattails of the reality of her loss, the loss she'd endured before her grandmother's death. The one that had been preceded by betrayal. It was a loss, she now knew in thinking about Maurine and Travis, that included more than just her relationship with Megan. It also included the hope she'd once had in having someone by her side for love and support.

"Give me a damn minute!" Maurine shouted, causing Carla to jerk.

Maurine sounded like she was still in her bedroom. Still getting ready.

Carla groaned, completely exhausted, but more so, frustrated. She was just as tired as everyone else, having to meet and greet dozens and dozens of family and friends the past few days. She'd shaken hands, given hugs, and accepted kisses. She'd laughed and she'd cried. She'd comforted and consoled. And she'd made sure everyone was fed and hydrated with the relentless attention she'd paid to the enormous amount of food people had brought on their visits. They had so much she knew if she hadn't kept it organized, first labeling and then rotating the dishes in and out of the fridge, and then cleaning up those that weren't touched or already devoured, both Maurine's and her grandmother's house would be in a state of chaos with mountains of food everywhere. As it stood now, she'd even had to take multiple dishes to store at the neighbor's homes.

And then there had been the other issue with space.

The people.

Family and friends she hadn't seen in years had driven in to pay their respects. She'd met people she didn't even know were kin or that they even existed at all. They just kept coming and there hadn't been room for them all in Maurine's house or her grandmother's, and they weren't about to turn them away. Thankfully, the family's long-time preacher, Douglas Kirby, was one of the first to stop by and he'd made a phone call, and an hour later, vans and pickup trucks pulled in and people unloaded and set up all the folding chairs and tables the church had. Carla had almost cried as she watched those kind folks do their best to make sure her family and friends at least had a place to sit when they came to visit.

She'd given Douglas one of the biggest hugs she'd given thus far, and he'd only patted her on the back and reassured her that the chairs and tables were surplus and stored in the church basement and that there was no hurry to return them. They already had enough to accommodate everyone at the funeral.

Moments like that made her appreciate where she came from. Made her so grateful that she had been raised around such good, kind people. People in that town considered everyone to be family and they treated them as such. Things had been that way for generations, and the families that were by her side today were the same ones that had been by her family's side decades ago. There were, of course, those who weren't so kind, and they'd let her know how they felt about her sexuality. But they weren't the majority and she didn't allow them or the town gossip and serious lack of privacy, keep her from appreciating where she came from.

There was a knock at the door, and she hurried across the living room of the modest farmhouse to answer it.

Cliff Buford, whom she considered to be the oldest living man in America, as well as the owner and manager of the town's only funeral home, stood wearing one of his trademark dark suits and a somber smile.

"Miss Carla," he said in his gentle manner. "I'm here to escort your family to the church." He spoke with such grace and elegance, and Carla had always wondered if that was just who he was or if it was because of his job. Or perhaps it was a little of both.

She pushed open the squeaky screen door and gave him a hug, even though she'd seen him the night before at the private viewing up at the funeral home. She was still reeling and trying to recover from that. Having to see her grandmother one last time and give her a final good-bye had absolutely torn her heart out. It had torn all of their hearts out. And Cliff had teared up too. He'd known her grandmother from birth, having lived down the road from her family when she'd been born. He'd told Carla that he could still remember that day because she'd been breech and his father, who had been the closest thing to a doctor nearby, had rushed to their home and helped deliver her.

She'd never known that before, and it had been nice of him to share that with her. He probably had a story like that for nearly everyone in town, and she contemplated just how difficult it was for him to bury the people he knew so well.

She pulled away and he held her hand in both of his. At last, Maurine came out behind her and she was softly cussing and fumbling in her purse for a mint, no doubt so her breath would be pleasant when interacting with folks at the funeral. Tending to tiny, nonsensical things was what Maurine did when anxious. It was her version of beard stroking.

"Miss Maurine," Cliff said with a polite nod.

"Hey, Mr. Buford."

"Shall we go?" He offered them both an elbow, forever the gentlemen.

They walked down the porch steps and crossed the lawn to where her uncles waited next to the limousine. They'd gotten ready at her grandmother's house, where they'd been staying since her passing. They looked very nice in their suits and ties, dressed in their Sunday bests to lay their mother to rest.

They rode to the church in silence. Maurine sucked on her mint and dabbed her nose with a tissue. She, too, looked nice in a long, floral print dress. She'd refused to wear black because, as she'd said, "Mama loved color and flowers" just like she did and she would've rather seen her in something like that. She messed with it the entire way, smoothing it down with her palm, over and over, as if thinking about her mother, until Cliff eased into the parking lot and headed slowly for the front entrance.

The Sims family church was Southern Baptist, just like all the churches nearby, but it wasn't as large as some of the others and didn't have near as many members. It had history going back more than a hundred years, however, and loyal, devoted families that went back generations. Carla had always thought it a bit majestic with, not only its placement atop a hill, but its decorative stonework and steeple that seemed to soar into the sky. As a child, she'd often pretended it was a castle, and she used to love to just stand and gape up at it.

The limo stopped and Cole opened the door, not realizing that Cliff was waiting to do it for them, none of them used to being waited on. They climbed out and gathered at the front entrance where the big doors were propped open. The gentle sound of gospel music enveloped them, along with the familiar smell of the church interior. Something Carla would recognize blindfolded. A few other family members joined them at the entrance, mostly her grandmother's remaining siblings. When they walked inside, they went two by two, and Carla was overwhelmed at the mass of people in attendance. The church was packed full and they all stood for them as they entered, and Carla, who was so moved she teared up, questioned for the first time whether or not she'd be able to make it through the eulogy.

She looked upward and said a silent prayer as they were led to the pews in the front. Her knees bounced as she sat waiting, only able to half listen to Preacher Douglas as he spoke. The eulogy she'd written was crinkled from being folded up in her pocket, and it shook in her hand. She closed her eyes, and suddenly, there was a hand squeezing her shoulder.

She opened her eyes to find Cole looking at her.

"It's your turn," he whispered.

Preacher Douglas was looking at her too from his position next to the pulpit. She stood and walked up to the steps on numb-feeling legs. Her hands tingled as she placed the eulogy on the stand and glanced out at the crowd. Faces blurred and meshed into other faces. She knew nearly every one of these people, yet she couldn't focus well enough to recognize anyone. She scanned the pews, looking, searching, needing to see a familiar face. Someone who would look back at her and nod, letting her know she could do this.

She cleared her throat, hoping it wouldn't seize up, and that's when she saw someone. Right there in the second pew. Just behind Maurine.

Janice.

Janice Carpenter.

A woman she'd known her entire life.

A woman she had nothing but the utmost respect for.

A woman who had always been there for her family.

Now she was there once again. This time for her.

She was staring directly at her, holding her gaze, and she looked so kind and understanding and empathetic, like she wanted to stand alongside her and hold her hand as a pillar of silent support.

As if confirming that she was indeed willing to be that pillar, she gave Carla a single, encouraging nod.

Thank you.

Carla looked down at the crumpled paper and began to read. She spoke loud and clear, and her voice, which had thankfully recovered from the week before, seemed to carry very well. She was still a little shaky at times, and her voice wavered with emotion, but she carried on, sharing bits of her grandmother's life and who she was as a person. She shared treasured memories and humorous moments that caused people to both wipe away tears and laugh heartily. And as she did this, she continued to glance up and lock eyes with Janice Carpenter. For she was her anchor and the only soul who was keeping her from being engulfed and tossed about by the stormy sea of grief and sadness that lingered close by.

But as Carla came to the last sentence, the one she knew by heart, she had to pause. She closed her eyes and swallowed. Her throat was tightening, betraying her. Tears were mounting. She inhaled and her breath shook in her chest.

She opened her eyes and focused on Janice who had her palms pressed together beneath her chin like she was in prayer. Maybe she was. Maybe she was praying for her.

Carla could only hope that her prayer would be answered.

She spoke, made it through two words, and her voice caved. Preacher Douglas came to her and placed his hand on the small of her back. He asked if she was okay.

She continued, forcing the last line out and into the ears of all who loved her grandmother. It didn't come out pretty and it wasn't loud and clear. But she got it out.

And then, as she finally tore her eyes from Janice and Preacher Douglas began to lead her away, she did what she'd been trying so hard not to.

She broke down and cried, succumbing to that lingering sea of sadness.

Chapter Five

Janice nodded politely at Mrs. Jenkins, her former first grade teacher, as she carried on about her grandson and his prowess on the basketball court. According to her, he was so good he was Carolina bound, which was what she'd always hoped for seeing as how she was a former Tarheel herself. She seemed to think Janice should be just as proud of him judging by the way she was carrying on and looking hopefully at her.

Janice feigned interest with raised eyebrows and nodded. She sipped her Sun Drop from a Styrofoam cup and tried to keep paying attention as they ate the buffet lunch the church had provided. Mrs. Jenkins was a wonderful woman and one of her favorite teachers. And considering how proud she was of Janice and her position as a professor of English literature, she felt she owed her that at least.

She was having a great deal of difficulty though, her mind continuously straying to Carla, worried whether or not she was okay after her touching eulogy. She was as moved by her evident grief as she had been by her appearance when she'd first entered the church. Janice had audibly gasped at her androgynous new look. She'd cut her hair. Now wearing it very short in an edgy, stylish cut that accentuated the beautiful contours of her face and brought even more focus to her ever-alluring eyes. And she didn't even want to start thinking about how gorgeous she looked in that black fitted suit. In fact, if she hadn't seen the heartache on Carla's face a split second after her initial arrival had floored her, Janice probably would've embarrassed herself by either passing out or making some sort of wanton noise of desire.

But Carla's sorrow had been more than obvious, and Janice had gone from wanting her to wanting to comfort her in an instant. When she'd stood to give her eulogy, Janice had stared directly into her, willing all the strength and fortitude she had to somehow reach Carla to help her get through a very difficult moment. It seemed to have worked, because Carla had seemed to sense her energy, having looked up and locked onto her gaze. She'd visibly steeled herself then, like Janice had pressed a supportive hand into the small of her back and whispered kind words of encouragement in her ear, thus enabling her to give the most beautiful eulogy Janice had ever heard.

Their silent connection had been palpable, and though Carla had managed to finish her speech, she'd nearly collapsed in Preacher Douglas's arms and Janice had stood, highly alarmed and intent on getting to her. But the boys beat her to it, hurrying to meet her at the steps, where Preacher Douglas handed her off to be escorted from the church.

Janice had never seen Carla so distraught and she'd just wanted to get to her to do something, anything, to comfort her. That strong need had continued all through the graveside service. But even when Janice did get a chance to be with her one-on-one, she wasn't sure what sort of comfort she could provide. She would, of course, hug her and offer her condolences, but other than that, what could she do? More importantly, what would Carla allow her to do? She was just as strong-willed and self-reliant as the rest of the Sims clan, and she might not want much in the way of help or comforting. Maurine hadn't been very open to her affections since she'd arrived home from her conference. She just kept insisting she was fine when it was more than clear she was anything but. Carla could very well respond to her the same way, but Janice hadn't seen her until she'd walked in the church an hour before. She'd been out running errands the two times Janice had stopped by, so she truly had no idea how she would react to any sort of offer of comfort.

"But I guess those college scouts can't talk to him until his junior year," Mrs. Jenkins said, still talking about her grandson. She seemed to be clueless to Janice's wandering mind.

Janice blinked to refocus on her, intending to engage, wanting to engage with her. Unfortunately, she just couldn't tie her thoughts down enough to discuss basketball. Everyone around them seemed to be able to properly converse, so she should be able to as well. What was her deal? Why was this so difficult? Was it the venue? They were in the large activity room of the church's second building, where the offices, daycare, and Sunday school classrooms were. The space was crowded, regardless of its size, with many people still waiting in line at the buffet. But large crowds and loud noise had never bothered her before.

She refocused yet again and found Mrs. Jenkins looking at her with her wide eyes, probably waiting for her to respond to something she'd said.

She scrambled for words, a bit panicked. "It all sounds so exciting. You'll have to be sure and keep me updated." She smiled, anxiously waiting to see if her hurried response had been sufficient.

Mrs. Jenkins nodded and returned the smile. "Oh, yes, you bet I will."

She seemed pleased and took a bite of macaroni salad while Janice pushed at the unwanted deviled egg on her plate with her plastic fork. The potato salad was good and so were the baked beans, but she couldn't finish them. Instead she sipped her Sun Drop and panned the room, still anxious to see Carla.

She entered at that very moment, walking in from the adjoining kitchen as if she'd sensed Janice's thoughts again. She carefully wiped her cheeks as if trying to make sure she looked presentable. She'd cried all through the graveside service. Janice had been behind her, but she could tell by the way her head was bowed and her shoulders shook. Cole had kept his arm around her, and he'd tried to soothe her by rubbing her back. It seemed to do little to console her, and when they'd walked back for the buffet, Carla had promptly disappeared, and Janice had assumed she'd wanted some privacy and a quiet place to gather herself.

Janice watched her bypass the enormous spread of food, waving off Maurine who was holding up a paper plate and speaking to her, obviously trying to get her to eat. Instead, Carla crossed the room and sat with Ms. Starnes, who was alone at a nearby table. She had been one of Betty's closest friends and Janice was surprised to see her. She'd last heard that she wasn't faring too well with her health. But there she was, dressed in her best, gray hair set, and makeup on. Only…she was crying. Not in any real noticeable fashion. She just had tears glistening in her eyes. And Carla, despite her own pain and anguish, held her delicate face and gently smoothed those tears away for her as they fell. She then took her hands in hers, said something more, and stood to kiss her forehead. Ms. Starnes smiled warmly up at her, and Janice realized that witnessing their heartfelt interaction had left her breathless.

She'd seen Carla do things like that countless times over the years, but there was something about that particular moment that struck her. It could've been the gentle way in which she'd held the older woman's face. The soft, kind way she spoke to her. Or the deep affection Carla had shown for her with the kiss. But Janice suspected it was the selflessness that had gotten to her.

Carla had taken the time to sit and comfort a sad, grieving soul when her own sadness and grief was so strong, it kept overwhelming her.

In fact, she'd probably had to do her best to hold back even more tears as she'd comforted Ms. Starnes.

The whole scenario moved Janice profoundly, and when Carla left Ms. Starnes and headed for the exit, Janice stood and collected her cup and plate.

"Would you excuse me, please? I need to go catch Carla."

"Okay, sugar," Mrs. Jenkins said. "You give that girl a big hug for me."

Janice assured her she would and then quickly threw away her trash and followed Carla out the door. But much to her dismay, Carla was nowhere to be seen. Janice shaded her brow, trying to locate her amongst the various people mulling about, talking and embracing.

Where had she gone? Did she leave?

Then Janice saw movement from behind a far tree and she homed in on the stark blond hair. She crossed the vast lawn and tried to come up with something to say. Nothing came by the time she rounded the tree and quietly approached her from behind.

Carla was standing with her hands in her pockets, staring out across the church's property to where the cemetery was near the edge of the woods. Janice followed her line of sight to the mound of red dirt that now topped Betty's grave. Carla appeared to be taking that in and no doubt trying her damndest to accept what she was seeing.

Janice came to a stand next to her and stared along with her, not wanting to disturb her but too concerned to leave her be. She could feel the heaviness of her sorrow and the intensity of her thoughts, like she was sensing and understanding Carla in a way others couldn't see or comprehend.

The silence between them stretched for a long moment before Carla spoke.

"She would've hated all this," she said, her eyes still trained ahead. "She loved everybody and would've been touched that so many people cared, but all this...attention, she wouldn't have liked it. She was too humble and introverted for all this."

"She was, wasn't she?"

"I'm glad I put my foot down about having a public viewing. She would've haunted me for years had I allowed that."

Janice studied the side of her face and saw a hint of a smile at what she'd just said. It made Janice's heart flutter.

"Granted, she'll probably still haunt me," Carla continued. "Just for mere shits and giggles."

Janice laughed and Carla glanced over at her then. Her eyes looked like liquid gold, and Janice blushed at their intense searching of her. But in an instant, that powerful seeking stopped, leaving Janice confused and off balance, like the thick, tight chord that had been between them had snapped.

Carla looked back toward the cemetery, apparently not nearly as affected at the loss of connection as she was. She wondered what those shimmering eyes had seen in her. If they'd found what they'd been searching for. Carla's demeanor gave away nothing, however.

"I'm not really sure how to do this," she eventually said.

"Do what?"

"Grieve."

"I don't think there is a knowing how when it comes to grieving. Everyone does so in their own way."

"You've always been so insightful," she said. "It didn't matter what the situation was, you always had the answer or knew what to say."

Janice had never known she'd felt that way. She was almost moved to tears to hear her say it.

Carla looked at her again, her gaze full of emotion. "Thank you."

"For what?"

"For everything you've ever done for my family. And for... what you did for me back there during the service. I don't think I could've made it through without you."

"You don't need to thank me, Carla."

But everything you're saying is making my heart sing.

"Oh, but I do. I'm not exactly sure what it was that happened or exactly what it was that you did. All I know is that you helped me. You were there. You. Your face amongst dozens of others. Why did you stand out and others didn't? I don't know. Why did I look up at that very moment to find you? I don't know. I just know it felt like— even though I knew it was you—it felt like you were different. Like I was seeing you for the very first time." She rubbed her forehead. "I know that doesn't make any sense."

"Actually, it does," Janice said.

But she seemed too lost in her struggle to make sense of things to have really heard her.

"I can't help but wonder why," she said.

I think I know.

"You're still you, right?"

Janice forced an odd sounding laugh. "I guess so." She struggled to continue, completely unsure as to what to say, or what she even *should* say. "I mean, you know there are some things that have changed, but—"

She watched as Carla winced while massaging the back of her neck.

"Your neck bothering you?"

"It's that damn new couch of Maurine's. It's like sleeping on cement."

"You're sleeping on the couch? Why?"

"She's got all that stuff in the spare bedroom."

"Oh, right." The boys had moved a bunch of boxes and furniture out of Betty's basement and into Maurine's house because Maurine was insisting it be gone through before being given away.

Janice hated the thought of Carla going without a bed, especially now when her grief and exhaustion were at their peak. She knew she hadn't been eating much, Maurine had informed her, and she did look a little gaunt. But it was the way she was carrying herself that really bothered Janice. She seemed to be weighted down with circumstance and emotion, and her need to intervene and somehow take it all away overcame her.

"You're more than welcome to stay at my place," Janice said. *What am I doing? What in the world am I doing?*

She was risking everything, most notably exposure, by inviting Carla in. But she couldn't help herself. Taking that risk, she had to admit, excited her a little, along with the realization that she'd get to spend a lot of time with Carla and have her all to herself.

"Your place? Really?"

"You'd have your own room."

"What about peace and quiet?"

"There's an abundance."

"There's just been so many people and it's been nonstop."

"I can imagine."

"But I don't know. Maurine obviously wants me there and she needs me right now. I'd be hesitant to leave."

Her heart fell and she got upset at herself for getting so excited to begin with.

"Well, the offer stands. You're always welcome."

They looked at each other for a long moment, and Janice had the urge to reach out and touch her. Carla spoke, though, interrupting her intention.

"Thank you."

Janice smiled. "Like I said, there's no need to thank me."

"There is." Carla stepped up and embraced her, and for the second time that day, Janice gasped. The warm, firm press of her body against hers took her breath away, as did the scent of her tantalizing cologne.

"You okay?" Carla had pulled away, but seeing her face so close to hers made Janice's head spin.

"Mm. Why?"

"You—gasped. I thought maybe I'd hurt you or something. Or that maybe—"

Her heart pounded.

"Maybe what?"

Another wave of what appeared to be sadness visibly washed over her, and Janice almost panicked.

She knows. Oh, my God, she knows.

"Nothing."

"No, tell me." She had to know now. She had to know what was going on and where she stood with her. She'd go crazy not knowing.

"I thought you might be uncomfortable with my hugging you."

Janice blinked, trying to make sense of what she'd said. She couldn't.

"I don't understand."

Carla released her and squinted into the sunshine. "You never really said anything to me after I came out. So, I've wondered off and on if maybe you had a problem with me now. With my being gay."

What?

"Oh, my God, Carla no. I never—there's no—how could you think that about me?"

"Because you went silent on me. You didn't even come to tell me good-bye when I left after that."

"I—"

Couldn't.

"Whatever," she said. "It doesn't matter. You feel how you feel, and you think how you think."

"Carla, I don't feel that way. I don't think that way. I…"

"What?"

"Adore you."

This time Carla blinked as if she were surprised. And Janice looked away into the sunshine.

"Hey! You two!" Maurine was shouting at them and waving them over. "There's dessert and I'm not letting either one of you turn it down."

Carla waved at her to hold her off.

"I guess I was wrong, then," she said. "I apologize if I offended you. It's just—well, let's just say there are some people who do have a problem with it."

"Well, fuck them, then."

Carla appeared shocked and then she laughed. "Okay then. I wasn't expecting that."

"Seriously."

Maurine called out, demanding their presence, and Carla stepped up to her again and leaned in. She stared into her eyes and then lightly, like a touch from the wings of a butterfly, kissed her cheek.

"Thank you," she said one last time as she backed away. "For everything. For always."

Janice grew so hot and dizzy she stumbled for balance.

"You coming, or what?' Maurine said to her, Carla having already reached her.

Janice did her best to right herself and then walked on air toward her best friend.

Chapter Six

It's so good to see ya'll," Carla said as she stretched out her legs and leaned back on her hands. The brightly covered blanket she was sharing with her younger cousin Erica was soft and warm from their bask in the sun. "Just wish the circumstances were different. And I wish I would've come back sooner." The last sentence had been hard to say, and she hoped Erica, who had always looked up to her, hadn't heard the quaver in her voice.

"Don't do that to yourself, Carla. We're all here and that's all that matters. You know that's all that would've mattered to Grandma. And if you think about it, she's once again the one who brought us together, just as she always did. One last little secret ploy on her part, I reckon."

"When did you get so grown up?" Carla asked, impressed by her insight. "Weren't you like twelve day before yesterday?"

Erica chuckled and picked a few blades of grass from her leg. "Hardly. I'm twenty-nine. Thirty's just around the corner."

"Oh God, why did you say that? That makes me feel absolutely ancient. Where does time go?"

"It's a tricky son of a bitch, I'll tell you that. I remember when I was a kid I used to beg and plead for time to pass quicker. And the more I wanted that the slower it seemed to crawl. It was torturous. Now, though, with the boys, it just flies by and I find myself begging and pleading again, wishing it would slow. But it doesn't. The hands on the clock keep spinning out of control and the boys keep growing and changing on me, sometimes literally overnight. There's just no stopping it."

"I suppose all we can do is just buckle up and hang on for the ride." Carla smiled as Erica's three sons splashed and played in the creek that ran the length of the Sims property. It was just down the hill from Grandma Betty's house. "You especially," she said. "With those three little guys, you're going to need to cinch that seat belt real tight and probably wear a helmet as well. Because your ride is going to be a bit bumpy."

"Oh, I'd be happy with bumpy. I'm afraid I'm in for more of a rollercoaster type deal at this point. Deep dips and crazy loops."

"If anyone can handle it, it's you. You're a wonderful mother. And the boys…they are beautiful."

"Quit," Erica said, tossing bits of grass at her. "I done enough crying this past week."

"Ya'll stop it!" Denny, Erica's oldest, yelled at his two younger brothers. "You're scaring away the crawdads!" But his brothers continued to play and screech, and Denny picked up his fishing pole and pulled the line from the water. He threw up his hand in obvious frustration when he saw that his hook was void of bait. Again.

"Carla, will you put more bread on for me?" he asked as he carried his rod to her.

"Sure, Bubba," she said, calling him by the endearment his mother and brothers used for him. She opened the bag of white bread and tore off a small piece. "You don't need much, see. Just a little piece. Then you just roll it up into a ball and stick it through your hook." She demonstrated.

"Are you sure bread's gonna work?"

She smiled. It was their first time fishing for crawdads, and he'd been confused when she said they didn't need typical fishing bait.

"Oh, it will, I promise." she said. "Bread is all I ever used as a kid and I caught all kinds of crawdads. And fish, too." She'd promised the boys she'd take them fishing for crawdads upon their arrival from Asheville a few days before. Needless to say, that's all they'd talked about. Somehow, she and Erica had managed to put them off until after the funeral.

"*Fish?* In this creek?"

She smiled again, amused by his disbelief.

"You bet. Quite a few, actually."

"You probably mean those little tiny fishes, huh? Those don't count."

"No, I'm talking some pretty good sized fish. In fact, I lost three poles in this creek to big fish."

Denny's eyes widened and his two younger brothers, Victor and Val, who were twins, came up beside him, having overheard the story.

"Really? How big were they?" Victor asked.

"Huge. They got hooked on my bait when I left my pole on the ground and then they flew down the creek, dragging my pole along with them."

"What did you do?" Val asked.

"What did I do? I ran after my fishing rod! All three times. But I wasn't quick enough, and those dang fish took my poles with them, right on down the creek. I never saw those fishing poles again."

"For really, Carla?" Victor, who was only discernible from Val by the small freckle below his eye, asked in his four-year-old fashion.

"Yes, love, for real. But after that third time, I sat my butt down, sat real still, and I held my pole. Because Grandma Betty made it very clear that I wouldn't be getting another one."

The boys looked at one another.

"We better hang on to our poles," Victor said.

They returned to the creek, grabbed their poles, and sat promptly on the ground. Denny, however, turned and gave her a big, toothless smile.

"Thanks, Carla," he said.

"For what, Bubba?"

He cupped his mouth and whispered. "For making them sit still. Now maybe I can catch something."

He sat next to his brothers and they looked like three little towheaded urchins, sitting side by side.

Carla leaned back on her hands once again.

She and Erica soaked up the sun and the silence.

"I'm worried about Daddy," Erica eventually said, referring to Cole. "He ain't said very much since we got here. Not even to the boys."

"You noticed that, too, eh?" She could tell he was shutting down, but she'd hoped having Erica and the boys here would help.

"You know how he thinks he should be able to save everyone. And when he can't, he can't deal."

I can relate.

"Someone very wise recently told me that there is no one way to grieve. Everyone goes about it in their own way.*"*

Truth was, none of them were doing great. And they probably weren't grieving in what was considered a healthier fashion. But they hadn't faced a loss of this magnitude since Carla's mother passed some thirty-five years before. Taking that into consideration, along with the fact that they were all very sensitive people who loved big and loved deeply, she thought they were doing pretty good to be functioning at all.

"And don't think I haven't noticed your behavior too, Carla."

"Me?"

"You've been despondent, and you're damn near skeletal."

"Oh, come on, Erica." She waved her off.

Erica rolled her eyes. "I ain't the only one worried, Carla. Maurine—"

"Maurine's not one to talk."

"No, she's not. But she's noticed. And so has Janice. She talked to me about it at the funeral."

"Janice?" She wondered if that was before or after their private conversation under the tree.

"She said you looked exhausted."

"I'm fine," she said, still thinking about Janice and her concern for her. Was she wrong or did she seem to be more concerned about her now than she ever had before? Was that simply because of her loss, or was there something more? "Would I be out here with you and the boys if I was as despondent as you say?"

"Yes."

She shot her a look.

"You would, Carla. Because you wouldn't want me to worry and you wouldn't want to disappoint the boys."

Carla sighed, defeated by Erica's accurate insight.

"Janice is right. You are exhausted," Erica said. "That's very obvious."

"I won't argue with you on that."

Val turned around with a big grin, oblivious to their conversation. "I think I got me one!"

"Really?" Carla went to him, glad to be distracted. "Okay, pull your line from the water real slow." She helped him lift it carefully from the creek. And all three boys guffawed when they saw the dark brown crawdad dangling on the end, one claw gripping the bread.

"Whoo, doggie!" Val said. "I got me a big one!"

"Set him down," she said gently, leading them away from the water. "Once he feels the ground he might let go."

They gathered around as Val lowered his line to the ground. The crawdad released the bait and Carla pinched it behind the head and held it up.

"Okay, you want to be gentle when you hold them so they don't get hurt. Anyone wanna give it a try?"

They backed away. "Nuh-uh."

She laughed. "Okay, then get some creek water in your bucket and bring it here."

The boys did as instructed, and she set the crawdad inside.

"Wow," Victor said as they peered down. "He is a big feller."

"This is so dang cool," Denny said. "I wish Daddy woulda showed us this a long time ago. We coulda been catching crawdads our whole lives."

Carla tousled his hair. "Why don't you give him that ball of bread he was after?"

Denny perked up and Val and Victor fought over who got to remove the bait from the hook.

"Boys, you can all feed him," Erica said, already pinching off small pieces of bread from the bag. They rushed to her, forgetting the bread on the pole, and Carla pulled off the wet bait and gave it to Denny.

"Go ahead, Bub. Toss it in there."

He knelt and dropped it inside. The crawdad went after it, once again attacking it with his claw.

Denny beamed up at her. "He's hungry, ain't he?"

"Seems so."

"What are we gonna do with him when Mama makes us quit?"

"We put him back in the water."

"You mean let him go?"

"Uh-huh."

"But I wanna keep him."

"You can't, Bubba. He wouldn't live very long and we wouldn't want that."

"My papaw says we're supposed to eat 'em."

"Do you want to eat him?"

Denny looked at the crawdad and shook his head. "Nuh-uh. No way."

"I never did either. So, I always just caught them for fun and then put them back. I thought it was only fair, seeing as how I got to go home at the end of day. They should be able to as well."

The twins hurried to the bucket and knelt alongside Denny.

"Be careful, now," Carla said. "Don't get too close or you'll get pinched. And let me tell ya, it hurts."

The boys fed the crawdad and she stretched and looked back up the hill toward the house. A small group of women were headed their way.

"Looks like we've been found," she said, already feeling exhausted at the thought of dealing with more well-meaning people offering their condolences.

She felt like she hadn't had a single moment's peace since she'd stepped off the plane. Someone was always interrupting or stopping by or needing her for something.

She should be getting used to it at this point.

But for whatever reason, she wasn't.

Maybe that's because there's no end in sight.

Chapter Seven

E rica turned to see who was approaching.
She shaded her brow. "Who is that? Is that...who is that?"

"Looks like Darlene and her two daughters and...I think that's Tonya."

"Tonya? Isn't that Mitch's girlfriend?"

"Uh-huh."

"What's she like?"

Carla shrugged. "She's all right." She watched as Tonya and the other women, her distant cousins, approached.

"I think I've only met her once. Mitch don't come around much anymore since he moved to Gastonia." Mitch was Cole's best friend from childhood, and though he wasn't family, they all considered him as such.

"Ya'll catch anything good for supper?" Darlene asked as they walked up and embraced Carla and Erica in hugs.

Denny straightened. "No way! You ain't eating my crawdad."

Darlene chuckled and held up her hands. "Okay, little man. I won't even think about it."

"What are ya'll up to?" Erica asked.

Darlene started in on how she was aiming to get into Maurine's to clean, so Maurine wouldn't have to worry about doing it at the present time, which was her way of offering love and support rather than bringing food. But Carla's focus went to Tonya who had come to stand next to her.

"Can I talk to you for a minute?" Tonya asked.

Carla was surprised by the request, but she sank her hands into the back pockets of her cutoff shorts and said, "Sure."

They walked farther away than Carla expected, leading her to believe that whatever Tonya was about to say, she didn't want it to be overheard.

"What's up?" Carla asked when they finally came to a stop.

But Tonya, who was slightly older than Carla and a whole head shorter, wouldn't look at her.

Uh-oh. This is not good.

"Is something wrong?"

She blew out a breath.

"Tonya?"

"God, I don't know how to say this."

Carla saw the distress on her face, and suddenly she had a feeling she knew exactly what was about to be said. She had experienced something similar with someone else on her last visit home, after she'd come out. Only that person had been an actual family member, someone who was blood related. Tonya, who she didn't know well at all, was Mitch's girlfriend. Even so, this felt strangely familiar and hauntingly awkward.

"I'm guessing this is something you haven't told anyone else?"

She reddened, confirming Carla's suspicion.

"No, I haven't told a soul."

"But you're going to tell me because you're hoping I'll understand."

She looked at her quickly, as if surprised at her correct assessment.

"I'm hoping, yeah."

Carla glanced off into the distance, suddenly so very tired, like the wind had just left her sails. Dealing with her own emotion as well as trying to comfort everyone else with theirs, had really taken its toll. And now…this. Did she have enough strength left?

"Okay, so shoot."

Tonya laughed, incredulous. "It ain't exactly that easy."

"It's not going to get any easier by standing here either. It will only make your suffering and anxiety last longer."

She still didn't speak.

"Here, I'll help," Carla said, growing impatient. "You're having these feelings…"

Tonya blinked and then appeared confused, like she didn't know how she knew that.

"I'm…well, yes."

"For anyone specific or just in general?"

Her discomfort seemed to intensify.

"Someone specific."

"And I'm guessing we're not talking about Mitch here, are we?"

"No."

"I just wanted to be sure."

Tonya was quiet again, which got under Carla's skin, and she realized her irritability was most likely due to fatigue. But her foul mood continued, regardless of her self-awareness.

She went in for the kill.

"So, who is she?"

Tonya's mouth fell open and she turned away. "How did you—"

"Know it was a woman?" Carla scoffed. "Come on, Tonya. Why else would you seek me out when there are plenty of others, who you're a whole lot closer to that you can confess to? I mean, come on. You're just so obvious."

And I'm being a bitch.

I am.

But I'm just so fed up.

I just want this to be over so I can go find somewhere quiet to collapse. Where? I don't know. I guess a damn closet would suffice at this point.

"I'm obvious?"

"Yes."

She looked panicked. "You think people know?"

Carla closed her eyes and tried like hell to control her rising frustration. "No, that's not what I'm saying. I just meant you're obvious to me." She pinched the bridge of her nose, hoping for some control, thinking about how she'd need to bring some Advil with her into that closet for a preemptive strike on an impending headache.

"So, who is she, Tonya? And how is it you need me to help?"

"I—she's. She's my massage therapist."

"Oh, okay."

Wow, that could be hot.

She imagined a beautiful woman knocking on her door at home, wanting to come inside to rub her down with hot oil. She palmed her forehead.

I'm delirious. I'm overly exhausted and I haven't been laid in a very, very long time.

"I don't know what to do," Tonya said. "With Mitch and everything."

Carla laughed, unable to hold it in, and clutched her T-shirt at her chest. All the feelings of betrayal she'd endured when she'd learned of her ex, Megan's affair, came marching back in.

"You're cheating on a guy who is like family to me and you think you're gay and you want *me* to tell you what to do?"

"Well, I—I was hoping you would know what to do."

"Oh, good God."

"If you don't want to, then say so. You don't have to be mean about it."

"Mean? Tonya, last time I was home, you and Mitch were talking marriage. And now you're coming to me, someone you hardly know, telling me you're sleeping with a woman and doing so behind Mitch's back and somehow, you're expecting me to tell you what to do? Do you know how crazy that is?"

Tonya started to walk away. "Just forget it."

Ah, fuck. Just fuck. Fuck my life.

And fuck me because I can't let her go like this.

"Wait," Carla said. She had to at least try to understand where she was coming from. Even if it did strike a very sensitive nerve in her. Even if Tonya was being ridiculous in expecting someone else to tell her what to do. "Come back."

Tonya did but she crossed her arms over her chest, obviously pissed off.

"Is this your first time being with a woman?" Carla asked, having removed the attitude from her voice. Being with a woman for the first time was something she could understand. That much was common ground.

"Yes."

Carla thought back to her first experience. She softened some more as she recalled how she'd felt. How unbelievably powerful and emotional it had been.

"Are you in love with her?"

She seemed shocked at the question and her tough girl gaze shifted.

"Tell the truth," Carla encouraged. "Otherwise your asking me for advice will have been a big waste of time."

She pushed out another big breath. "Yes."

"Okay. So, you want to be with her? Like in a relationship type deal?"

"Yes."

"Do you love Mitch?"

She reared back a little at that question, like she'd been verbally slapped.

"Yes." She shook her head, her face twisted. She was obviously very distraught. "That's why I'm so—"

"Are you in love with him?" Carla asked softly, trying to get her to focus.

She clamped her mouth. Bowed her head. "No, not anymore. Not for a while."

"Is he in love with you?"

She kicked at the grass. "I think so. He says he loves me."

"Then, it's probably safe to say that what you're doing to him is unfair, right? You're not in love with him, but he doesn't know that. All he knows is that he still comes home to the girlfriend he loves every night, thinking she loves him. So to him everything probably seems fine. But it's not. Because not only are you deceiving him with your feelings, you're doing so with your body. You're having an affair." She swallowed, the words feeling as if they'd come directly from her own broken heart.

"But she's a woman not a man, so it's not the same—"

"That doesn't matter, Tonya. Even though I know that the feelings you're having in being with a woman are very different from the ones you've had with a man, it's still wrong. It's still an affair. You're cheating on him. End of story."

"But it does matter. It *is* different. You just said so."

"I know this isn't what you wanted to hear, especially in coming to me, but I'm not going to sugarcoat what you're doing just because you're doing it with a woman."

"I thought you would understand."

"I do understand what it is you're feeling for her, Tonya. I do. And there's nothing wrong with those feelings. But you need to go explore that on your own and do right by Mitch. He's human, you know. And he's a good guy. He deserves someone who wants to be with him just as much as he wants to be with them. Don't you agree?"

"That's why this has been hard. I feel bad because I care about him and his feelings."

"No, you feel bad because you're cheating on him and you know it's wrong. That's why you feel bad. It has nothing to do with his feelings at all." She had very little sympathy for her in this regard. She'd never understood why people didn't suck it up and end their relationship before they got involved with someone else. To her, it was beyond selfish.

"I do care. I don't want to hurt him."

"If that were true, you would've done right by him and ended things the second your fantasies about doing anything with her crossed the line into intentions."

She turned her back to her and Carla heard her crying.

"I'm not a bad person, Carla. I'm not."

"No, you're not, Tonya. I think you got very caught up in your newfound desire for a woman and made some bad choices. Choices that you've tried to justify and excuse. But that doesn't mean you're a bad person. You're human. Just like everyone else. Everybody fucks up. It's how you handle things afterward that really shows who you are as a person."

She cried some more, and Carla gently rested her hand on her shoulder.

"Your woman," she said. "Does she love you as you do her?"

"Yes."

"Then I'm sure she probably wants to have you all to herself."

"She does. She's never been okay with me continuing my relationship with him."

"Then I don't think you need me, Tonya. I think you know what it is you need to do."

"I have to face this, don't I? And end things with him. Face-to-face. No matter how bad it may hurt."

She turned and wiped her tears. "When I do it, you know, break up with him, should I tell him about her?"

"That's a tough one, Tonya. And something only you can best decide. Because if you tell him, your sexuality will be exposed. That kind of news doesn't stay secret for long around these parts."

"No, it doesn't."

"If you're not ready for people to know, then you might just want to tell him it's not working. That you feel differently than he does."

"That makes sense."

"But I do think he will eventually find out. You don't exactly live in a metropolis where you and your new lover can just disappear into the crowd."

Darlene called for them.

"You should probably go," Carla said. "Suddenly having secret conversations with me, the well-known gay, won't help your discretion any." She smiled.

Tonya returned it. "Probably not."

Carla patted her on the shoulder, hoping she did at least help her a little.

They all said their good-byes and Tonya whispered a thank you to her when they embraced. Carla gave her an extra squeeze and she and Erica watched them head back up the hill.

"What was that all about?"

"You wouldn't believe it if I told you."

"She looked upset."

"She'll be okay." Carla glanced at the boys who were fishing again.

"You, on the other hand, don't look like you will be."

"I'm so drained I'm about to pass out. You might have to leave me here for the crawdads to consume."

"Then for heaven's sake, go to bed."

"Where? Darlene's hell-bent on cleaning the house. And people will still be coming in and out all day." Most of the relatives from out of town had gone home, but there were still a dozen or so local folks who would continue to drop by for the next few days at least to ensure they were adequately supplied with food and support. That was just how things went when someone passed away.

"There must be somewhere you can go to get some rest. I'd suggest staying with us at Grandma's, but we've got a full house now with my family and Daddy and Uncle Rick. But you know, Carla, there are a lot of people in this town who would gladly take you in. All you'd have to do is ask."

"I know. But I'd hate to ask. And everyone around here are pretty much in the same situation we are. Small house, big family. I probably wouldn't get any more peace there than I have been here."

And peace and quiet is what I'm after.

Erica suddenly brightened. "What about Janice?"

Carla startled.

"She said she offered you a place to stay. She was worried about your back, I think. Because you told her you were sleeping on Maurine's couch."

Carla allowed Janice's words to replay in her mind.

You're always welcome.

But would she really be okay with her staying?

She was so brain dead she couldn't continue to contemplate. She was so tired she even cast aside her long-held worry that Maurine might get upset if she left.

She looked back up the hill at the gravel driveway next to her grandmother's house. Two more vehicles had pulled in since she'd last checked and others would soon arrive as well. They'd want her time and attention, especially since she lived so far away and didn't get to see everyone very often.

She felt awful that she dreaded interacting with them when they only meant well.

Maybe once I get some rest, I'll feel better. I'll feel up to it.

"It would be good for you," Erica said, touching her arm. "You should take her up on her offer."

"I think I might just do that," she said as yet another car pulled into the drive.

I think I might just do that.

Chapter Eight

The house was quiet, save for the soothing sound of Eartha Kitt singing about love. Janice hummed along as she sat painting in her study. She was perched on a stool at her drafting table which wasn't inclined, like its design was intended for, but flat and covered in newspaper. Various bisque ceramic chess pieces stood like little soldiers, waiting for their turn.

She turned the piece she held in her fingers carefully and continued painting the details of the knight with her liner brush. So far, she was satisfied with the deep, royal color scheme she'd chosen for this particular medieval style set. The completed pieces had turned out great and the knight was looking fantastic. She couldn't wait to work on the more detailed pieces like the king and queen. She could already imagine how magnificent they were all going to look once finished and glossed. Only, she wasn't quite sure yet what she was going to do with this set when she did finish. Sometimes she sold them, sometimes she kept them. And a choice few, she gave away. But currently, she was running low on space and she was beginning to doubt if she could let this one go to a stranger.

"I may have to find someone special to give you to," she said, adjusting the arm on the light for a better look. "But who?"

The doorbell rang and she stared through the doorway into the dim hall, unsure she'd actually heard it. She checked the clock next to her framed vintage Twilight Zone poster. It was ten fifteen, late into the evening. She had friends that sometimes came by unannounced for a bite to eat and a casual chat, but that was usually in the early afternoon or around supper time. A visit this late from one of them would be unusual.

It rang again and she put down the knight and brush and stood. She rubbed her hands on her old blue jeans as she headed for the door, trying to remove any wet paint from her fingertips. She hurried into the living room and slid the cover of the peephole aside. She went to her tiptoes to peer through.

"Oh, my Lord." She stepped back and covered her mouth in complete astonishment. "Oh, my Lord."

She held her throat, worried her voice would fail her. Then she took a deep breath and opened the door. Carla Sims stood just beyond the worn screen.

"Hey," Carla said with a soft smile. Her face was partially shaded under the brim of what she recognized as an Arizona State ball cap. The shadow from the hat and the trickery from the porch light somehow sharpened her features. And those gorgeous features, along with the sinewy look to her bare arms in the white tank top she had on, made it difficult for Janice to process and make sense of her presence.

"Hey," was the result of that difficulty.

"I tried to call," she said. "A few times, actually."

"Oh, I turn off my cell and my home phone when I—need to relax."

Carla slid her hand in the pocket of her cutoff jeans and Janice tried very hard not to openly gawk at her, but her legs, like her arms, were long and sinewy, and she looked so southern tomboy in that outfit, right down to the white canvas sneakers she wore with no socks. And it became clear to Janice that she'd never see another woman who moved her more than Carla Sims did at that very moment. She knew there would never be anyone else who could totally and completely overwhelm and arouse her just by standing on her front porch on a hot summer night in cutoffs and a tank top. No one. And though she knew it, she had trouble allowing herself to accept it. That was something she was still struggling with. But even if she did accept all the thoughts and feelings her recent discoveries had evoked in her, she didn't have a clue what she would do about it.

While Janice's sluggish mind was suddenly reawakened and running wild, Carla seemed to be either sensing her inner chaos or she was experiencing some of her own, because she looked uneasy and began rubbing the back of her neck like she'd done under that tree at the funeral. Now, however, Janice worried that the gesture signified more than physical discomfort.

"Are you—"

"I thought—"

"Please, go ahead," Janice said, feeling a fool.

"At the funeral—" Carla glanced away and laughed as if she, too, felt a fool. "God, I feel stupid." She shifted her stance and Janice saw her luggage.

Oh, my Lord.

She pushed open the screen door and stepped onto the front porch.

"You came to stay," she said, trying to sound calm. "I'm so sorry. I didn't realize—"

"I know," Carla said, interrupting. "This is unexpected." She reached for her luggage. "I shouldn't have assumed you'd still be okay with this. I apologize." She tried to walk away, but Janice stopped her by covering one of her hands with her own.

"Where are you going?" She just got here. She couldn't leave. She couldn't get her all excited like that and then just walk away. No. She wanted her there. With her. In her home.

"You weren't expecting me, and I understand."

"I don't expect to see anyone on my porch at this hour." She smiled, a little surprised at how quickly the usually confident Carla Sims had panicked and tried to leave. "You have to remember where you are. Showing up this late in this small town usually means someone's coming with bad news or someone's coming for…" she trailed off, embarrassed at what she was about to say.

"Coming for what?"

Janice laughed. "Nothing."

Carla caught on. "Ohhh."

She reddened and Janice just about died at seeing her react to the idea of her showing up on her porch for a romantic encounter.

Could she possibly…feel like I do?

Ha. That had only and would only ever happen in my dreams.

"Come on, let's get you inside." She tried to take the bags from her, but Carla resisted.

"I got it."

"I insist."

"There's no need. I got it."

"But you're my guest. I should take them for you."

"I know that's been engrained in you since conception, Janice, but really, I can carry my own bags."

Janice put her hands on her hips. "I realize that, *Carla*. I'm just trying to be polite and show a little hospitality. I'm not trying to insult your ability to carry luggage. Now, let me help."

"No, you're too—"

"Too what?"

"Small."

"Small?"

"These are heavy."

"Oh, so it's you who's insulting me."

Carla shook her head and laughed. "I'm just trying to be polite," she said with a grin.

Janice yanked a bag from her and then stumbled a little from being off balance.

"See?" Carla said.

"Oh, hush. I just lost my balance. I'm not some delicate little lady." She opened the screen door and motioned for Carla to enter before her. Janice followed her in and closed and locked the door behind them.

"You are little," Carla said as she took in the living room.

"You're already testing your welcome, Sims. You might want to stop while you're still ahead." She lugged her bag in farther and turned left toward the bedrooms.

"You're shorter than me," Carla continued, teasing her. "That's all I meant."

"I think a lot of women are shorter than you, Carla. We can't all be Amazons." She bypassed her study on the right, which was still illuminated and filled with the sounds of another love song, and entered the guest bedroom beside it. She flicked on the light and set Carla's bag in front of the closet.

Carla followed, dropping her other bag to the floor.

"Amazon?" She raised an eyebrow. "I may be above average in height, but I am so not an Amazon. I can only wish I had strength like that."

"You look...pretty strong to me." Janice heated at her own words, and when Carla looked at her quickly with obvious surprise, she glanced away and cleared her throat.

"So, is this going to be okay?" She busied herself smoothing down the homemade quilt on the bed. "You've got a nice queen-size mattress, an empty closet." She crossed to the dresser. "Plenty of drawers. And," she picked up a remote control, "your own remote for the ceiling fan and light. If that doesn't absolutely blow your mind and sell you on the place, I don't know what will."

Carla laughed. "It's pretty impressive, I must say."

"I aim to please."

"Yes, it seems you do."

They fell silent and Janice swore she could literally feel the temperature in the room rise.

"You have your own bathroom," she said, breezing past her. "It's here." She turned on the light in the bathroom which was next to her own bedroom and across from the study. "There are towels and washcloths and all kinds of toiletries in the drawers and under the sink. I even have new toothbrushes should you need one."

"Wow, okay." She leaned against the doorjamb to the study. "This is great, Janice, thank you."

Janice shrugged, hoping she came off as casual and relaxed when she was anything but. "I have the room and you need a quiet place, so it works out. It's no trouble."

"Still, it's very kind of you to have me."

There was another pause and this time Carla glanced away. "What's in here?" She stood in front of the study.

"Oh, that's my study."

"Can I…go in?"

"Sure."

Carla walked in and Janice trailed behind.

"This music." She grinned. "I like it."

"Really?"

"That surprises you?"

She shrugged. "A little."

"I can appreciate vocal jazz," she said, looking around. "Especially the classic stuff. Only, I like to take mine all alone, in the dark, and sometimes with a nice glass of wine."

"Alone," Janice said softly. Maurine had mentioned her breakup some months ago, but Janice had assumed she'd been dating since then. Was she? She felt a twisting tightness in her gut at the possibility.

"Here lately, yes," Carla said.

"You're—not seeing anyone?"

She let out a short laugh. "Uh, no." Then she quickly changed topics. "Great posters," she said, taking in all the vintage movie posters Janice had collected and framed. "You're a classic sci-fi movie buff. How did I ever forget that?" She moved to the framed *Frankenstein* movie poster. "And, yes. I remember now. It all started with Mary Shelley's *Frankenstein*. Your all-time favorite book. You read that and thus began your lifelong obsession with Gothic literature. And from there you got into the classic Frankenstein films and fell in love with the old horror and sci-fi flicks." She sank her hands into her back pockets as she studied the *Bride of Frankenstein* poster. The movement caused her muscles to flex beneath her tanned skin. Janice felt her pulse beat in her neck, and for a second what she was seeing before her seemed surreal. Carla was in her study, scantily clad, deeply tanned and slightly moist with sweat, which set off the cologne she always wore. But tonight, it smelled a little different, and Janice knew it was probably because it had mingled with her perspiration as well as her pheromones for hours, all day long, in the heat and in the sun. Now her skin was coated with their heavenly mixture and Janice wanted to know what that mixture would taste like if she put her mouth there, in the crook of Carla's neck, where the essence of her collided.

Would it taste like heaven? Or would it be more primal and taste more like a nectar she desperately needed to survive?

"Janice?"

Carla was looking at her, obviously having said something.

"Hm?"

"You okay?"

"I was just amazed that you remembered all that."

"I always found your interests a bit fascinating," she said. "You were so different from Maurine. You were...deeper. More introspective. And you thought about things a lot. Big things. Like why we exist and what does it all mean. I remember one time, we were lying out under the stars back behind Grandma Betty's house, and Maurine had gone in for something, and you told me the universe was infinite. That it went on forever." She smiled and moved her gaze from the poster back to her. "I didn't sleep peacefully for weeks after that."

"What?" Janice laughed. "Why?"

"Because knowing that scared me to death. How could something just go on and on and never end without anything beyond it or outside of it? Meaning that there is nothing else. Nothing. Just fucking space. The concept of that, of realizing that there probably isn't a God, not as we perceive or understand God to be, scared me. It still does."

Janice just stared at her, awed by the way her mind worked.

"You had thoughts like that then?"

"Uh-huh."

"I didn't know," she said. "I wish I had." A brief flash of memory came, and she saw Carla lying next to her on a blanket out under the stars. She was smiling and pointing at the sky. "I remember now," she said. "We used to lie out under the sky a lot during the summer months. You loved it. And you would beg Maurine and me to go out with you. I even started calling you Stargazer."

Carla seemed touched. "Yes."

"Why did we stop doing that?"

"You guys grew up. Moved on to bigger and better things."

She crossed to the drafting table and once again changed topics. "What's this? You paint, too? Now, that I didn't know."

"Just ceramics mostly. It relaxes me."

She knelt to examine the knight she'd been working on.

"There's a lot of detail. Looks pretty tedious."

"It is."

"That relaxes you?" She straightened.

"Believe it or not."

"Must be the focus," she said, moving on to the books on her bookshelves. "Probably takes a lot of that to paint so intricately. But I'm sure that's what keeps your mind off other things."

She was still so observant. Insightful. "It does."

She turned to face her. "Do you have anything finished you can show me?"

"Sure." She led her back into the living room and into the adjoining dining room. She used it as a den and furnished it with two large leather chairs flanked by end tables, a coffee table, and numerous shelves where she had a lot of her work displayed. She switched on the lamps and Carla went straight for the shelves and examined her completed chess sets.

"These are incredible," she said. "Can I pick them up?"

"Sure."

She held up piece after piece, examining the details of the hand carved ceramics.

"What a difference," she said. "From the white to this. You must get such a rush when you finish one. To see all that color and shine and the absolute perfection in detail. I can see why you like doing this so much. You're very good."

"Thanks." She was a little overwhelmed at her admiration. She was a little overwhelmed at everything.

Carla smiled at her. "There's so much more to you than I ever realized. Where have you been hiding all these years? And more importantly, *why* have you been hiding?"

"I—"

"It doesn't matter. I know now and I plan on exploring all of your layers." Her eyes danced and Janice swooned. "If that's okay with you, that is."

Her mind once again failed her, overloaded with both panic and excitement. She said what she'd already said a few times before. The only word she could think of and possibly mutter coherently.

"Sure."

Chapter Nine

Carla ran the towel through her hair one last time before she finger-combed it in front of the bathroom mirror. The shower had felt wonderful after the long, hot day, most of which she'd spent in the sun with Erica and her boys. It was late, and though she'd arrived at Janice's exhausted, she now felt refreshed and for some reason seemed to have the elusive energy that had been evading her, and she knew she wouldn't be able to settle down to sleep anytime soon.

She finished with her hair and rolled her two favorite colognes on her wrists and neck. Their scents were both unisex and meant to be worn alone. But she'd found, by accidentally applying one over the other one crazy morning getting ready for work, that she liked them best combined.

Why am I putting them on now when I'll be going to bed soon?

She studied her reflection, curious at both the newly present energy and her choice to put on the cologne. Any answers, however, were quickly ignored as she focused on her gray cotton shorts and matching soft gray bra. They were a sleep set she'd bought at a popular lingerie store, and she wore them every night. But given her circumstances at Maurine's, where anyone could walk in at any moment, she'd thought it best to wear a T-shirt over the bra. Now, with Janice, she did the same, but she wasn't happy with the way it looked. She picked at it, then fingered her hair again and then caught herself and sighed.

Why am I so worried about how I look?

And, for that matter, how good I smell when I've just stepped out of the shower?

The reason, she was reluctant to admit, was probably still sitting in the living room where she'd left her and probably still looking girl-next-door gorgeous in a worn, paint-stained pair of blue jeans and a body-hugging T-shirt.

Yes, she'd noticed. She'd always thought Janice beautiful, so that wasn't anything new. But that had been before, when she'd seen Janice through a filter, like a thick screen on a window. A screen that long-time family friendship had erected, a screen she'd never been aware was even there. That screen had kept her from seeing the details, the layers, and the depth of this woman.

Now that filter was dissipating, and with every blink of her eyes, she was seeing more and more. And what she was seeing was leaving her mesmerized.

Her jaded attitude toward love and relationships didn't seem to be stopping her. Nor did the very real possibility that Janice was straight, like she'd always known her to be, thereby dampening any notions that she was somehow suddenly feeling otherwise for Carla.

All she could think about was the way Janice had looked at her in the church. Under the tree. And tonight, on the porch. There was something there. Something different. Something more.

Maybe Janice was seeing her differently now too.

Oh God, what a thought.

She killed the light, needing to move, to walk, to go. She padded into the living room intending to tell Janice good night so she could go to bed and feign an attempt to read until her eyes could no longer remain open. But that idea went right out the window when she entered from the hallway.

Janice was curled up on the end of the couch in the dim lamplight, holding a glass of red wine. Another full glass sat on the coffee table next to a plate of cheese and crackers.

"I thought you might be hungry," she said. Her thick auburn hair was down around her shoulders, rather than in the ponytail she'd sported earlier, and her eyes, which were a crisp blue-green, reflected in the light. Despite their cool, crisp color, however, they seemed to be giving off waves of heat, like the waves of heat she often saw as a distant blur on a long stretch of road in the Arizona summer.

"It's probably been ages since you've last eaten." She gave her a soft smile, and though Carla recognized her gentle, genuine concern, she was too caught up in looking at her through the new filterless window to pay attention to anything else.

Her features were fine and delicate-looking, making Carla want to lightly touch her face, to run her fingertips along her beautiful brow and high cheekbones, and then down to her lovely rose-colored lips. How would she react to her touch? Would she close her eyes? Would she sigh, completely overcome? Would she open her eyes and part her lips, longing for her kiss?

"Or maybe just some wine?" She stood and held up the other glass from the coffee table.

Carla nearly backstepped, so slammed with sudden desire she couldn't respond to her.

Janice, too, had also changed into sleepwear, most notably a tight-fitting, virtually see-through tank top. And somewhere below that, were a patterned pair of sleep pants.

She forced herself to stare at her forehead, for nowhere else was safe. Not her fiery eyes or her beautiful face. She just focused on her forehead and tried not to think about the visible weight and fullness of her breasts or the hint of pink from their circular centers.

It has been way too long since I've seen a nude woman.

She let that excuse bounce around her mind for a few moments, hoping it would suffice and explain why she'd just about been knocked off her feet. It really had been a long while since she'd been with a woman. But was that really the only reason why she was reacting so strongly? Or was there something more? Like maybe Janice herself?

"Carla?"

She snapped back to reality and tried to recover with a quick smile as she took the offered glass. She sat on the love seat perpendicular to the couch and took a few swallows.

"Mm, thank you," she said. She helped herself to a cracker with cheese. Janice sat on the end of the couch closest to her and watched her eat.

Carla avoided eye contact, wondering why Janice would wear something so provocative. Surely, she wouldn't have worn something like that to tantalize her, would she? She'd told Janice she wasn't dating, so she knew she was probably lonely, and more than likely sex-starved, right? But even if Janice was attracted to her, her wearing something as revealing as that seemed a little forward and risqué for her. She knew Janice to be quiet, more reserved, more of a romantic. Maurine was always the wild one.

"So, you like my sets?" Janice asked.

Oh, hell yes.

Wait.

What?

Carla coughed, having swallowed her wine wrong as she realized Janice was asking about something other than her breasts.

"Sorry?"

"The chess sets."

"Oh, yes. Very much." She gulped her wine like she was dying of thirst. She nearly finished the glass.

"I'll go get us some more." Janice headed into the kitchen.

Calm down. You aren't exactly sure what's happening or why she's wearing what she's wearing. It's not a good time to assume anything.

Janice smiled when she returned and poured Carla another glassful. She left the bottle open to breathe and sat and crossed her legs. She sipped her wine and Carla took several more swallows from her own glass and took in the quaint and cozy living room. The colors were deep red and gold, and they were shown off nicely with throw pillows, artwork, and various other items throughout the room. It was tasteful and both warm and welcoming.

A lot like Janice herself was.

Warm. Janice is warm. I'm warm. Yes, I'm feeling warm.

She didn't drink often, and she'd forgotten what a lightweight she was. Nevertheless, the warmth was leading to relaxation and that felt good. Especially after the week she'd had.

"I like this house better," Carla said, recalling the one Janice had shared with her ex-husband, Chuck. It had been larger and more modern, but this one had Janice's influence. Janice's touch. "It's more you."

"Thanks, I like it, too."

"I can tell," Carla said. "It's nice, seeing you so content."

"Thank you," she said, obviously touched. "I am quite happy now."

Why is that, I wonder.

She drank more wine. "You know, a lot of women would probably be depressed after what you went through with the divorce and then being on your own and everything. But you don't seem to have gone that route."

"No, I didn't. And you don't seem as though you have either."

Carla felt the sting at the reference to her relationship and Janice must've seen it.

"I'm sorry, I didn't mean to upset you," she said.

"No, it's fine. It's just…I was never depressed because I was too hurt and too angry. And once those feelings passed, I think I was just so relieved that they were gone and so relieved that she was gone and that the whole thing was over that I just moved right on. I just focused on my life and on my future."

"She…cheated?"

Carla looked at her. "I thought you knew."

"Maurine said your relationship had ended. She didn't say more, and I didn't press."

"She probably didn't know yet herself. I didn't tell her the entire story until everything was over and Megan was gone for good. That, unfortunately, took some time. We were tied together in some financial aspects and with our home. And, she, for a time, tried to convince me to give her another chance. But I wasn't interested, even if she really did regret her affair and was willing to change. I decided then that I'm done with love."

"Done with love?" She shifted as if uncomfortable. "That sounds a little extreme."

"It's where I am. To think about falling that deeply again for someone scares me."

"It could happen though," Janice said. "You've considered that, right? That your feelings may change. If you met someone… who…someone special."

Carla stared into her wine as her mind tried to explore the reasons Janice might have in asking her these questions. But her need to shield herself overshadowed her curiosity into Janice's possible motives.

"I'm not saying it can't happen, I just—I'm not sure how I would handle it if it did. Love and relationships… Let's just say I'm not holding out any hope where those two things are concerned." She sighed.

"I understand. You've been through a lot. It must've been really hard."

Carla laughed a little, feeling the wine full on now. "Not any harder than it was for you, I'm sure. We both got the shit end of that stick it seems."

"I wasn't hurt, though. Not like you."

"But he…had an affair, didn't he?"

She turned her glass on the armrest and seemed to be lost in the way the wine moved inside it.

"Yes, but I wasn't in love with him like I should've been. I didn't…yearn for him in that way."

It took Carla a second to understand what she was trying to say. "You two always seemed so happy. So good together. You were so easy around each other."

"We were. I think that was only because we were such good friends," she said. "Best friends. And I miss him. I miss his friendship and the comfort of knowing he's there. He's a wonderful man, as you know. Very kind and good-natured and all, but there just wasn't that…"

"Desire."

"Yes."

"Was there ever?"

Janice met her gaze. "No. But I didn't know that then, didn't understand that what I felt for him wasn't enough. I loved him and he loved me. I thought it was that simple. I thought that's how it was."

"But you knew what desire was. What lust was. Didn't you?"

"I knew about those things, sure. I just didn't feel them. So, I thought that stuff must be for the romantics and the poets." She seemed reflective as she turned her glass. "Maybe that's why I love literature so much. For the romance of it all. That's what I really want, but for some reason haven't ever had."

"Why do you think that is?" Carla asked softly.

She half shrugged.

"I was different."

Janice drank, taking two large sips. Was she nervous about the conversation?

Carla could sense her anxiousness, but she couldn't let it go. She now wanted, more than anything, to know everything. Who was this woman who'd been hiding right underneath her all these years?

"How are you different, Janice?"

"I was different because I didn't feel those things."

"Have you ever?"

She visibly swallowed. "Not then, no."

"But you do now?" The question came out on a whisper and she was so desperate for her response, she thought she might fall off the edge of her seat from the anticipation.

"I—am aware of those feelings now. I know they are possible."

"How do you know?" Carla finished her wine.

"Because something happened. Something that caused me to take a look at myself."

Carla could feel her blood pounding in her ears. "What was it?"

She looked into Carla with a heat that pressed into her skin, teasing and caressing it, like the hot hand of a lover.

"What does it matter?"

"It matters," Carla said. "You matter."

"More wine?" she asked, suddenly rising from the couch. Her glass was nearly empty, and she was offering to take Carla's.

Carla hesitated, completely startled but wanting to do anything to keep her talking. She handed her her glass.

"Please."

Janice started to walk away toward the kitchen.

"Janice?"

"Yes?"

"The wine is…here, remember?" She motioned toward the bottle on the table.

"Oh." She laughed and returned to her seat. "Maybe I've had more than I thought."

Or maybe it was our topic of discussion.

Janice refilled their glasses and they both sat back and drank.

Carla drank a little more and tried to come up with a way to get her to answer her question, but she was growing more and more tired. The wine was working wonders on her mind and her muscles and she worried she might melt into the couch. She also worried that Janice would be able to tell what she was thinking because she was unabashedly taking her in now, studying every part of her body, openly admiring the lingering athleticism of her physique. For a woman who'd given up gymnastics decades ago, she still looked firm and toned, especially in her arms and shoulders. Carla had always told her how much she admired her throughout the years, even encouraging her to build her body and compete in fitness. But Janice hadn't been interested, and most of the time she'd tried to downplay her looks. As Carla thought back, she recalled how she'd even blushed at her compliments. Had it been because she really was incredibly modest, or had it been because it had been her who was saying it?

Looking at her in that tank top, it was very obvious that she was embracing her looks now. She looked even more defined than she had been the last time she'd seen her. Maybe she was putting some time in on the weights after all. Whatever the case may be, she looked good. Better than good. She looked ravishing. Carla couldn't tear her eyes away from her and, thanks to the wine, which had drowned almost all of her inhibitions, she realized she'd never wanted to be a tank top so badly in her life.

Janice was about to take another sip of her wine when she caught Carla looking at her.

"I'm staring," Carla said suddenly. She hadn't meant to speak aloud, but she was so hypnotized by her mouth and those tempting lips, she couldn't help but want to witness the wine staining them red as she drank. "Forgive me," she said, knowing she sounded crazy. "I need to sleep." Fatigue flooded her, and all she could think about were the dangerous flash floods that wreaked havoc in Arizona during monsoon season. She felt helpless, like a person who'd been caught in one by surprise. She was being overtaken, soon to be swept away.

Her eyes rolled as she fought to stay awake. "I'm so tired."

Janice was speaking to her, but she sounded so far away. She tried to reach for her, but her arm felt too heavy to move. Still, she could see her. Each time she was able to focus, she could see her and could even when she eventually closed her eyes for good.

"I see you, Janice," she said. "I see you."

Chapter Ten

Janice sat holding her wine, stunned into stillness.
"Carla? Can you hear me?"
She was out, switched off just like a light.

She set her glass on the coffee table and rested her hand on Carla's leg. The firm warmth of it struck her, like she'd been bitten. She could feel the hot venom rushing through her veins, causing her heart to pound. She shook Carla quickly and called her name again. But there was nothing.

She removed her hand, hoping the heat coursing through her would ease.

It did not.

Too much had transpired. She was reacting to far more than the touch. Carla had been looking at her, staring at her. And it hadn't been just any kind of look. She'd looked at her like she wanted her. She was sure of it.

It had started with her open admiration of her body, which Janice had noticed but quickly disregarded, convinced she was reading into something innocent because of her own attraction. And because she honestly couldn't believe that Carla could ever feel that way about her. The idea was too farfetched, and she was content keeping it where it belonged. In her dreams.

But that last look, when Carla was intently watching her drink… as if she yearned to be the wine. That had been unmistakable.

That was desire.

Carla had wanted her, if only for a moment and she'd failed to respond or say anything at all. She'd froze. Like a deer in headlights. She had seen the headlights aimed right for her, but she hadn't been able to bring herself to move.

Unbelievable.

Now Carla had passed out on her. Any second chance she'd had at talking to her or sharing any of her feelings, were gone. This was turning out to be one of the most profound and yet unusual nights of her life.

Carla took in a deep breath, almost like she was aware of Janice's thoughts. She moved a little, pressing herself back into the cushions of the love seat. Her hands were limp in her lap, empty glass leaning along with her to the left, her head now hanging slack in the same direction. She'd come to her for some decent rest in an actual bed. Janice couldn't leave her conked out in an awkward position on her love seat. There was no way she was going to let her sleep like that.

"Carla? Carla. Carla, it's time to go to bed. You don't want to sleep out here do you? Not when you have a nice, comfy bed waiting for you."

Nothing. She was totally gone.

Janice now had her very own Sleeping Beauty passed out cold in her living room.

"Not exactly romantic for our first evening together, is it?"

She stood and stepped over Carla's feet and settled in carefully next to her. She took the glass from her hand and set it on the table.

"Carla?" She squeezed her hand and studied her. The angles of her face were aglow in the lamplight and she looked peaceful and almost angelic. Her blond lashes added to that look, their color contrasting with the tanned skin they rested against. A lone lash sat below her eye, and Janice smoothed it away with her thumb. The touch didn't seem to bother her, and Janice couldn't resist doing it again. She held her breath and traced her fingers along her forehead, brushing back her short hair. Then she ran her fingers down the outside of her temple to her jawline.

"Dear Lord," she said as she shuddered at the impossibly soft feel of her. She continued down to the graceful column of her neck and settled in the small dip near her collarbone, the place she'd wanted desperately to taste. Mind and body spinning out of control, she leaned into her, unable to help herself. She brought her lips a mere inch away from her and stopped. She closed her eyes and breathed deeply, aware that she was losing control. But in doing so she inhaled her scent, the very one that had been driving her absolutely crazy since she'd first smelled it on her last visit home, the very one that had sent a shockwave of pressure directly between her legs when she'd walked in from her shower.

An audible cry of sorts came from her, and she squeezed her hand again, desperate for her to wake.

"Carla?" She released her hand and cupped her jaw. "Wake up, Carla." Being so close to her, and holding her like that, like a lover would, tempted her even more. She wanted to throw caution to the wind and crawl atop her, take hold of her face, and wake her with her mouth, kissing and devouring her neck and her lips, tasting her and consuming her until Carla completely came to and responded by kissing her back.

"Carla? Oh, God, please wake up." She groaned and rested her forehead in the crook of her neck. "What am I going to do? I've finally got you. Here in my home, on my couch and right now in my arms. And yet, I can't have you." She laughed, incredulous.

I have to stop this. I'm driving myself mad.

She tugged on her, desperation turning to aggression. It was what she had to do if she was going to be able to move her. "Carla, come on. We're going to bed."

"Wha?" she slurred. "We're going to bed? Sounds good to me." She grinned. Janice pulled her up and slung her arm over her shoulders.

"Can you walk? I need you to walk."

"'K. I will walk."

Janice walked with her as best she could, anxious to get her to bed where she could get some rest and sleep this off, and most importantly, allow her to retreat to her own room for some much-needed distance between them.

"Almost there." They made it down the hallway and entered the guest bedroom where Carla had thankfully left the lamp on.

Janice walked her to the bed and pulled back the covers just before Carla fell onto the mattress.

"My shirt," she said, eyes half open slits. She fumbled with the hem, trying to remove the T-shirt. Janice wanted to help her, but she was hesitant. Was she wearing something underneath it? What if she wasn't?

Carla continued to struggle, and Janice gave in and helped her. She was wearing something beneath the shirt, but the thin cotton bra didn't cover much, and her eyes quickly traveled over the tight, etched muscles of her abdomen and back up to her small, firm breasts where her hardened nipples pressed against the thin material of the bra.

"Sleep. We both need sleep." Janice refocused and touched Carla gently on the shoulder and helped her to recline. Then she lifted her feet and positioned her for the night and hurriedly covered her before she tortured herself anymore.

Carla was already fast asleep again, oblivious to everything.

She has absolutely no idea how she affects me.

She watched her breathe, took in the quiet beauty of her.

How can she be so alluring even while asleep?

She kissed her softly on the cheek. "Good night, Stargazer," she said as she extinguished the light. She pulled the door closed behind her and crossed into her bedroom. She leaned back against her own door as it closed and took a deep breath. Her heart still raced, and her body was on fire. She entered her bathroom and turned on the shower. Then she turned and saw herself in the mirror.

"Oh, my God." She covered her breasts with her arms, alarmed that they were exposed. Carla had seen. She'd worn this in front of Carla. It was what she wore every night and she'd been so excited, wanting to hurry to set out some food and wine for Carla, she hadn't even given it a second thought when she'd changed into her sleepwear.

What she must think.

She lowered her arms and flushed profusely at what all Carla had been able to see. Did she think she'd worn this purposely? To seduce her?

She was burning with embarrassment and she wanted to go wake her to apologize and explain, but then she recalled the way she'd stared at her and the hungry look she'd given her. She'd obviously liked what she'd seen.

"Oh, my dear God."

She stripped and stepped inside the shower. The cold water was a shock to her system, and it stole her breath. She prayed it would douse the flames of her desire, hoping, for her own sanity, that that old familiar saying about taking a cold shower was true.

Janice peppered the eggs she was scrambling, adjusted the heat, and then peppered the diced potatoes that were frying in an adjacent pan. She hummed along to the Stereo MC's song "Connected" that played on her iPhone, and so far, the music was helping to put a little spring in her step and distract her from her memories of the night before. Carla's confession to staring at her, along with the hungry look on her face, had not left her with any peace. And when she'd thought about herself and what she'd done in response... well, needless to say she hadn't slept a wink. Carla might have been a little forward with her desire, but at least she had the excuse of alcohol and exhaustion. It was possible she hadn't even been totally aware of her behavior. But as for her own, it was as real as the heat coming off the frying pans. And it had sprouted from the roots of utter desire. Not the buzz from too much wine or the fatigue of grief and lack of sleep. As authentic as it was, however, she hadn't been courageous enough to express it while Carla was conscious. Instead she'd just about ravished her as she'd slept and then poured her heart out to her knowing she couldn't hear her, couldn't react or respond. Couldn't, if she were being totally honest, crush her with rejection or, even more nerve-racking, tell her she felt just as strongly for her. And then there was the see-through tank top she'd been wearing. As if everything else she'd done hadn't been shameful enough.

She shook her head, the embarrassment still too much. The only calm in sight so far was the distraction of music and the growing drowsiness from hours of overthinking and tossing and turning. She'd finally just got out of bed and dressed, giving up on any possibility of sleep.

Thankfully, though, she'd been alert enough to make sure she'd slipped on an adequately threaded T-shirt with her shorts. She'd still been worried about what all Carla would remember when she emerged from her bedroom and found Carla's door open and her room empty. She'd immediately checked for her luggage, her guilt automatically leaping to Carla having packed up and left. But to her relief, her luggage remained by the closet. She'd still stared at her perfectly made bed in confusion and disappointment, though. Here she'd been worrying so much about what to do and what to say, she'd felt off-kilter suddenly realizing she didn't have to. Not until later when Carla returned that is.

She just hoped she wasn't upset. She didn't want for either of them to feel uneasy or awkward. That would only make for a long, uncomfortable stay.

"Lord." She rubbed her temple, her worries jumping to whether or not she could keep her feelings under control. But wait a minute. If Carla really was attracted to her, why would she have to?

Because I'm scared. I'm scared of these feelings, even if they have made me feel more alive than I've ever felt before. And I'm scared of who I'm having these feelings for. Carla is Maurine's niece. Her niece. And Maurine has no idea that I'm having these feelings at all, whether they're for Carla or any other woman. She has no idea. She thinks I just need to find myself a new man.

There were just too many roadblocks on that path for it to lead anywhere other than dreamland.

She sighed and her body slouched, like she'd just exhaled the strength from her bones.

"Haven't heard this song in a long time."

Janice jerked, hand to her chest. Carla was standing in the doorway, coated in sweat, wearing nothing but a black sports bra and matching running shorts.

Dear, sweet baby Jesus.

"Sorry, didn't mean to sneak up on you."

Say something.

She forced a laugh and inwardly cringed at how fake it sounded. "It's okay."

Say something else.

"I love a little jolt of sheer terror first thing in the morning."

Carla leaned against the doorjamb and laughed, apparently amused.

Janice tore her eyes away from her and stared down at the eggs. She'd gotten a quick glimpse of her and that had been more than enough to weaken her knees and bring her to the realization that her previous use of the word sinewy had not been the adequate one in describing her. Her body was defined and her muscles very well-developed. She did indeed appear to be much stronger than she'd given herself credit for. That skinny little tomboy who had run around in her bare feet trying to catch lightning bugs in a Mason jar had grown up.

Had she ever.

"Your eggs," Carla said.

"Huh?" She blinked. They were burning right before her eyes. "Oh, damn." She moved the pan from the burner and stirred, but they were ruined. "Damn it, I don't have any more." She'd wanted, even more so now that Carla was there, to have a good breakfast. Carla especially needed one. She switched off the range and tended to the potatoes.

"Don't worry about it," Carla said, leaning down toward the pan with the potatoes. "Those smell really good. I love them all fried up with onions and peppers like that."

Janice perked up a little. "Do you feel like eating some?"

"I am tempted, I must say."

"I made plenty."

Why had she made enough for two? Was she somehow secretly hoping that Carla would return for breakfast?

"Is it all right if I grab a water?" Carla asked.

"You're welcome to everything in this house, Carla."

Including me.

She flushed. *No, I can't go there.*

"You don't have to ask."

Carla grabbed a water from the fridge and returned to lean against the doorframe. She drank heartily, and a thin stream of water ran down her chin to her chest.

Janice again had to tear her gaze away.

I can't even watch her drink.

"Sorry about last night," Carla said, suddenly bringing Janice to rapt attention.

"Wha—?"

"I was pretty out of it."

Janice waited for her to say more, to see if she'd let on to how much she remembered, if anything, but she didn't.

"Oh, no biggie. You were really tired."

"I don't even know how I ended up in the bed. I'm assuming you had something to do with that."

She doesn't remember.

She doesn't know what I said or what I did.

But I do.

And she knew she'd never be able to forget what it felt like to touch her skin for the first time, to run her fingers deftly across her face, to lean in and inhale the soul stirring scent of her.

"A little."

"I hope I wasn't too much trouble."

She spooned the potatoes onto two plates.

"Don't be silly." She smiled at her, doing her best to seem unaffected, but Carla was staring at her intently. She fumbled with the spoon.

Then again, maybe she does remember some things.

"I had a little too much wine. I don't drink often so it doesn't take very much to affect me. And I tend to get rather honest when I drink and sometimes, a little…forward. Or so I've been told."

Are you trying to tell me that anything you may have said or did was solely the result of too much alcohol?

Maybe I've been right all along.

She was simply drunk.

"Ready to eat?" She carried the plates to the table and retrieved the silverware. She was wound tighter than a top and she fumbled with the utensils and dropped them onto the table. She recovered quickly though and forced another smile.

Carla hitched her thumb back toward the hallway. "Sure, I'm just going to go jump in the shower real quick."

Janice laughed, her nerves right on the edge of hysteria. She couldn't sit there and wait and suffer through this craziness. And she for sure couldn't sit there and eat with her after her shower, when she'd smell so good it would make her toes curl.

"Um, no."

"No?"

She was just as surprised as Carla was at her assertiveness, but she was doing so to protect herself, to somehow try to contain the wild current that was just waiting to burst through the damn and surge through her veins.

"You're going to eat while it's hot." She sat.

"But—"

She needed for this moment to be over so she could escape without spontaneously combusting all over her carefully decorated country kitchen.

"Carla Sims, I know you have manners. So, you need to use them and sit and eat this food while it's good and hot." She eyed the chair next to her. "Go on, sit your pretty little hind end down."

"Yes, ma'am." Carla pulled out the chair and sat, smiling like the devil himself.

"I ain't playin' around, Carla," she said, but her stern attitude was already fading.

"Oh, I know. You're as serious as sin."

"That's right."

They both ate in silence for a while until Janice decided to give up her stringent facade.

"I had forgotten that you run." She took a bite and watched as Carla did the same. "I thought you'd left for the day."

"Without saying good-bye?"

Janice shrugged.

"I would've at least left you a note. After all, I do have manners, remember? Which is why I didn't want to sit down and eat with you all sweaty and gross."

"You're not gross." *More like yummy.* She quickly sipped her juice.

"What are your plans for the day?" Carla asked, finishing off her water.

Janice rose and began filling a glass of juice for her. "I'm glad you asked." She put the juice away and returned to the table, handing Carla her drink. "I need to go grocery shopping, so you need to tell me what you like to eat."

Carla held the glass as if it were foreign. "You don't have to serve me, Janice."

Janice rolled her eyes. "Don't fight me on these little things, Carla. You'll lose. Badly."

She shook her head. "I always forget how impossible everyone is here when it comes to having guests."

"Like I said last night, it's southern hospitality and I know you'd do the same for me in your home."

"Not to this extent. I'd let you get your own juice and carry your own luggage."

"You would not. You would treat me just like I'm treating you. Doing things for people, especially guests, is how we show love around here. It's been that way for generations, and whether you want to admit it or not it runs through your blood just like that red mud outside does."

"I know where I come from, Janice. I don't need reminding of my roots."

"You can't deny what's in your blood. No matter how far away you go."

"I'm not. Nor will I ever. But that doesn't mean I can't evolve and believe and behave differently than the way I was raised. I thought at the very least that you would be one to understand that."

"You think I don't understand that?"

"I don't know. Do you? You're sitting there arguing with me about how I would treat you in my home. Or how you think I should treat you, if I was true to my blood or my roots."

"I'm only saying that you can't forget where you come from."

"I haven't, Janice. This is where I was born. Where I was raised. That will never change. But it isn't home."

Janice looked at her, shocked at the statement.

"Phoenix is my home now," Carla said. "It has been for many years."

"But this is—"

"Where I'm from. It's not where my heart is."

Janice turned away, her words affecting her in ways she didn't expect and didn't necessarily like.

"Why does that upset you?"

"It doesn't."

"You've never been very good at lying, Janice."

"I'm not lying. I'm—glad you're happy. That you've found where your heart belongs."

"You know, your happiness matters too. Have you ever considered that your heart might also belong somewhere else?"

Janice straightened and began gathering her dishes.

"I need to know what you'd like from the grocery store."

Carla was quiet and Janice could feel her eyes on her.

"I'll make you a list," she said. "And leave you some money."

"Carla, don't. You know darn well I won't take your money, so don't make me fight you on it. I'm too tired and I'm cranky about ruining breakfast."

She set the dishes on the counter and returned to the table for Carla's.

"Okay," Carla said. She offered her a soft smile. "I may be hardheaded sometimes, but I know when to back down from a beautiful woman."

She called me beautiful.

Carla took in the last spoonful of her potatoes and handed her plate to Janice. She finished chewing before she spoke.

"Thank you. It was really good." Her eyes were deep and seeking, like they had been beneath that tree the day of the funeral.

What is it that she's searching for?

"You're really good to us, Janice. Really good to me."

"I—supper's at six," she said, turning to head back to the sink. How could she tell her how much she cared without giving away just how deeply that care really went? The way Carla looked at her sometimes, she'd see right into her. "I'll keep it warm for you if you're late."

She heard Carla stand from her chair. "I should be here on time."

Janice waited, expecting to hear her move. But there was only silence.

"Maybe someday," Carla said, "when you make it out to my home, I'll be able to repay you for your kindness."

She closed her eyes, Carla unknowingly bringing up the very thing that had gotten to her at breakfast. It was another dream of hers that had paralleled her fantasies of Carla until the two eventually had intertwined.

Me. In Arizona. With her.

It sounded so good coming from her. Her voice bringing a long held dream to life.

But it was still just a dream. She couldn't allow herself to get overly excited in thinking it might actually be a possibility.

She opened her eyes and was careful to steady her voice.

"You wouldn't have to do that, Carla."

There was another brief silence until Carla spoke again.

"Maybe not. But I'd like more than anything to get the chance to try."

Janice heard her walk away then, and for a few long seconds, Janice felt like she'd taken her heart away with her.

Chapter Eleven

The screen door groaned as Carla pulled it open and rested her hand on the front doorknob. Janice had told her, a few times this past week, that she didn't have to knock before she entered. That as her house guest, she should feel welcome to come and go as she pleased. Still, Carla hesitated. Not because she didn't feel welcome or comfortable, but because she worried about walking in on Janice at an inopportune moment, the vision of her in the threadbare tank, haunting her. Janice hadn't worn it since, and Carla wondered if it was something that haunted Janice too. The way she'd avoided eye contact when she'd emerged from her bedroom the following evening in her pajama pants and a much darker, thicker T-shirt, had led Carla to believe that maybe it did.

She knocked on the front door and Janice hollered. Carla stepped inside, and two things hit her senses at once. The warm, welcoming smell of supper, which she'd come to look forward to upon her return every evening, and the sound of old, crackling jazz. She followed the music to the den, loving the authenticity of the sound, like she'd stepped back in time when recorded music was raw and simplistic.

She saw the record player first and got lost for a few seconds in the way the lamplight reflected off the album's glossy surface. Then she saw Janice, who was sitting next to it in one of her leather armchairs, reading a hardbound book.

"Etta James," Carla said. "Her voice can soothe the sharpest of inner turmoils."

"You know Etta James?" Janice asked as she adjusted the volume.

"Of course."

"I didn't know."

"You seem surprised again at my interest in music."

"I didn't think someone like you would be aware of artists like her."

"Someone like me?"

"I mean—" She seemed to struggle for the right words, frantic-like, something Carla had noticed her doing a lot of recently. She seemed terrified of saying the wrong thing. Was it because of her? If so, why? Janice had never been hesitant to speak her mind before. It was one of the things Carla had always admired her for. "I meant, someone younger."

Carla couldn't help but smirk. "I'm only seven years younger than you. And besides, everyone, regardless of age, has varied tastes in music. I play Etta sometimes in my classroom when the kids are first arriving in the morning and they love her."

Janice shook her head, as if she needed to hurry and explain, like she'd quite literally said the wrong thing. She opened her mouth to speak, but then stopped. And then, something came over her with the flash of her eyes. She visibly relaxed and the sense of worry that was always quick to surface, seemed to have vanished.

"But they weren't *aware* of her before that, were they?"

The impish grin Carla had seen so much of growing up spread across her face. She hadn't seen it in so long, she'd forgotten how much it affected her. But now the effect it was having surpassed anything she'd felt before. Maybe it was her sudden change in demeanor. The way she was sitting, all calm and confident, or the way she was looking at her, like she was the one who was now amused by Carla. Whatever the reason, it was sexy.

Janice was sexy.

And she was watching her with that damn grin still on her face. Waiting. Waiting for Carla to respond. She seemed prepared to wait a lifetime if need be. As if to prove it, she slowly crossed her legs. But it seemed to Carla to be a move made for more than just comfort. Carla could've sworn she'd done it for her, knowing she'd look, wanting her to look. Was this the tank top all over again? No, she'd seemed oblivious in the tank top. This was calculated. Intentional. It worked. Carla couldn't resist trailing her eyes down the shapely form of her legs, helplessly lingering on the noticeable curves of muscle until she came to the painted red toenails on her elegant looking feet.

"That wasn't my point," Carla said, her body temperature rising.

"No, but you inadvertently proved mine."

She scratched her cheek with fingernails that were red like her toes, and unexpectedly, Carla had an intruding thought as to what they would feel like grazing down her back in the throes of passion.

She could almost feel the fiery trails they'd create running down her skin.

"They liked her and looked her up," she said, despite the direction her mind had turned. "Asked me to play more of her. Some downloaded her songs. That happens a lot when I play something they haven't been exposed to. So, my point is, that regardless of age or anyone's differences, people can have an array of tastes in music. All it takes sometimes is a little curiosity."

There was a subtle wildness in her eyes now, an uninhibited energy, that seemed to brighten their color, which was further accentuated by the matching blue-green of her blouse.

"You're saying I shouldn't make assumptions."

She closed the book in her lap and set it on the end table next to the record player. Carla saw the gilded letters along the spine.

The Poetical Works of Lord Byron.

"I was very surprised that you did. A woman of your intelligence."

She laughed. "So intelligent people can't make assumptions like that?"

"They can. And they sometimes do. But they know they shouldn't. And you...you're too open-minded for that. Too insightful. Or so I thought."

"Perhaps it's my small town mentality."

"Perhaps."

"Thank God for you then. You came to save me. You can crack open that mentality and fill it in with your big city insights."

"I don't know. You sound like you might be a lost cause."

"Doomed to spend eternity stuck in the confounds of my mind?"

"And here. In this town."

The impish grin faded, and she looked at her for a long while. Carla hadn't meant to be insulting, but she knew she had been. She didn't, however, understand why she'd pushed things with her.

Janice got up and turned off the lamp and came to stand before her. The lack of light didn't seem to bother her, nor did their close proximity. She dug in her pocket and took Carla's hand. She placed something cool in her palm.

"House key. So, you really can come and go as you please. And if you knock on that door again before you come in, I'm not going to reassure you with an answer. To me, your refusal to accept my well-stated welcome into my home is more insulting than your opinions about me and my mentality." She started to walk away.

"I didn't mean to insult you," she said, following her.

She was headed for the kitchen. "Don't worry, I didn't think that was your intention. Not initially anyway."

"I was half-kidding, honestly."

She laughed a little as she switched off the oven. "Half."

"I'm tired," Carla said. "I'm not thinking clearly. Dealing with everyone and being back here…"

"I know you're stressed." She slid on oven mitts and pulled a casserole dish out of the oven.

"Yes."

"And homesick."

Carla sank her hands into her pockets. "A little, yes."

Janice retrieved two plates and removed the tin foil from the top of the dish to spoon out the steaming contents. It was chicken casserole. One of Carla's favorites from childhood. Janice had somehow remembered and made it for her.

She's so generous and kind.

And I'm an ass.

"I've never been to Phoenix," Janice said. "Or spent much time in any big city really, but I can understand, somehow, even with my limited mentality, how going from a place like that to here could be a big jolt. I guess it doesn't matter if you're from here and know what to expect or not."

"You have no idea," Carla said softly, getting the silverware from the drawer. "It's like two different worlds."

Janice carried the food to the table, then poured them both a glass of sweet tea. She joined Carla at the table.

Carla watched as she forked a bite of the casserole, blew on it, and then slid it into her mouth. A minute ago, she would've been captivated, stirred by the beauty in her every movement, no matter how subtle. A minute ago now felt like a lifetime ago.

"I heard your comment about your limited mentality," Carla said, forking herself bite after bite only to dump it again and again. She couldn't bring herself to eat. "I'm sorry. I shouldn't have said any of the things I said. I didn't mean to hurt you, and I definitely do not think of you as small-minded or anything like that."

Janice set down her fork. "You don't have to keep apologizing." She sighed. "You obviously believe some of what you said, or it wouldn't have even come to your mind. And that's fine. You shared your opinion."

"I really don't think that—" Carla stopped, knowing by the look on Janice's face that her insistence of total denial would not be believed. "I'm not sure why I said those things." She rubbed her temple, digging deep within herself to find the source for her comments. She owed Janice the truth and she needed to know and examine it as well.

Janice sat waiting quietly. She'd set down her fork, giving Carla her full attention. Seeing her sitting across from her at that table brought up many feelings. One of those feelings, though, was more prominent than some of the others.

"Do you remember our conversation the other morning? Over breakfast? The day you burnt the eggs?" Carla continued, not expecting a response. "Some of the things you said about my forgetting my roots bothered me. Not so much at the moment. Mostly I was just doing my best to try to make sense of what you were saying and then defending myself rather than thinking deeply about it. But later, after time had allowed for those things to seep in, I realized they did bother me. They actually upset me. So tonight, I think I took a shot back at you simply out of resentment and fear instead of coming to you and discussing it the right way."

"Fear?"

"A part of me feared you might really be small-minded and too set in your ways to understand where I was coming from. The thought of you possibly being like that…really scared me." Her voice cracked with a surprising rise of emotion. "But regardless, the way I handled the situation was wrong. I shouldn't have taken a cheap shot at you. I should've discussed it with you. I apologize. Again. Because I need to and because I mean it."

Janice propped her elbows on the table and folded her hands beneath her chin.

"It seems we've both made some assumptions we shouldn't have. I can't sit here and be upset with your assumptions and implications when I've done the same. I'm even thinking that way now, even though I know I shouldn't."

"What are you thinking?"

She appeared hesitant.

"Please, I'd like to know."

"I'm thinking, in response to your earlier comments tonight as well as your comment at the funeral about my possibly being homophobic, how surprised I am that a woman of your intelligence would make such implications about a person, whom you've been acquainted with for a very long time, yes, but whom you really don't know on a present, personal level. Which leads me to believe, ignorant as though it may be, that you doing so is due to your big city mentality, where everyone is enlightened and open-minded and far above small town folk like myself who are often considered to be backward. "

Carla stared, dumbfounded.

"Sorry you asked?"

"Little bit, yeah."

"We both screwed up. I'm incredibly sorry for my hurtful words. I wouldn't ever want to hurt you. You're sorry for yours. Let's just move on."

She grabbed her fork and pointed at Carla's plate.

"Your food's gonna get cold."

"I don't think I can eat."

"Don't let a good dinner go to waste because of something stupid."

"You saying that I think I'm somehow better than you is not something I can just forget, Janice."

"I said it was ignorant of me to think it. I don't believe it."

"I need to make sure that you don't. Because it is not in any way true."

Janice took a bite and chewed.

"Janice?"

She swallowed. "I don't, okay? I don't. Now quit behaving like a big city woman and mind your southern manners and eat. You know I made this just for you, so you refusing, regardless of reason, is just downright rude." She grinned. Impishly.

Carla laughed and buried her head in her heads. "I almost had a heart attack," she breathed. "It would seriously kill me if you thought that I felt that way."

"And vice versa."

Carla straightened and smiled back at her. She grabbed her fork and took her turn in pointing it across the table.

"That grin of yours," she said. "It's nice to see it again. Makes me forget all about being homesick."

Chapter Twelve

The soft jingling of bells sounded as Janice entered Dog Eared, a small used bookstore nestled in one of the original buildings in the center of town. She inhaled the scent of old, printed pages and welcomed the relaxation that washed over her. The past couple of days had been good, but noticeably different with Carla. They still talked and ate together when Carla was home, but there was a hesitation now to their demeanor, as if neither of them had the courage to lower the quick walls they'd both built after their heated conversation. Janice wished she were stronger, braver, so she could reach out to her, reconnect, see her laugh heartily and share her thoughts and emotions unapologetically as she'd done their first few days together. But Carla's distance, in her eyes and in her tone, kept Janice's wall intact. It was self-preservation, and admitting that was guilt-inducing. Especially in knowing how badly Carla needed to express her feelings with all she was dealing with. And Janice felt more guilt when she realized that as badly as she wanted Carla to share her feelings so she could process and heal, she wanted her to do so with her. Selfishly, she wanted to be the person she turned to and leaned on, when really, she should be wishing that Carla find someone, even if it wasn't her, to confide in.

But Carla had closed off, and Janice suspected she wasn't talking with anyone about her grief, not even Maurine. Janice could see it in the way she carried herself, like she'd noticed at the funeral, like she had the entire world upon her shoulders. She tried to hide it, replacing her usual report of the day's events with light conversations and friendly but shallow smiles that didn't come from her core.

Every time she flashed one, it stabbed Janice in the heart.

She was behaving like they were acquaintances.

Like we don't know each other. Like she's just a guest staying at my bed and breakfast.

"Janice, how are you, sweetheart? You doing all right?" Pearl Pine, the store's long-time owner, greeted her from behind the counter.

"I'm doing okay, Ms. Pine." She smiled at her, knowing she was putting on a face, just like Carla. It felt awful. She began to rethink her trip into town.

"Such a shame about Betty. Everyone's been so tore up over that. Her family looked so sad at the funeral. They doing okay?"

"They're doing as well as can be expected."

She shook her head. "They were so close, that family. So sad. And that Carla, Betty's granddaughter. I was worried she wasn't going to make it through the eulogy."

Janice stood at the new arrival table and picked up a paperback to peruse. She tried to concentrate on it, but Pearl continued with talk of Carla.

"I hear she's staying with you," Pearl said. "That's mighty kind of you."

Please change the subject.

Janice shrugged and again hid behind the mask of a smile. "Just doing what I can to help."

She chose another book, her nerves on edge. She'd gone out to run errands to try to clear her mind of Carla, and the bookstore, one of her favorite places, was the last place she'd expected to have trouble in doing so.

"How are you?" She decided to change the subject herself.

"Oh, I can't complain. My mind is sharp, and my body is functioning. That's a good day to me." She fingered the imitation pearl earrings Janice often saw her wear. They went well with her perfectly set, snowy white hair, as well as her name. Her blouse, a pale pink with shiny buttons and ruffled collar, was perfectly pressed.

"I'm glad to hear it," Janice said.

"You know, you are a good woman, Janice. Polite, kind, professional. Always willing to lend a hand. I can't say I'm surprised at you're letting Carla stay at your home, but in a way, I am."

Janice glanced up quickly.

"Why is that?"

She won't say it. She wouldn't. I've known this woman for years.

But Janice's face was already burning in anticipation.

Pearl dropped her gaze and began tidying the already neat countertop. "Because she's, well, you know, a homosexual."

She said it. She actually said it.

Janice squeezed the book in her hand so tight she could feel it marking her skin. She'd heard people in her community state their opinions about the subject throughout the years, some of them even her own relatives. She'd disagreed and spoken up a few times only to be verbally attacked and ganged up on. So, she was aware of how people felt, and she'd chosen to no longer confront anyone on the matter. The last time she had, she recalled, had been years ago. Right after college.

The recent discoveries she'd made about herself had, of course, brought people's disapproval to mind. It caused her a lot of worry when she thought about it. So much so that she'd eventually just refused to deal with it. The second it crossed her mind, she forced it away. And she'd justified that with the excuse that she wasn't out. No one knew of her attraction to women. So, she'd told herself it wasn't an issue.

Pearl began reorganizing the display of bookmarks. She must've taken Janice's silence as an invitation to continue.

"I just don't know if I'd be comfortable with that if I was you. A single woman living alone and all."

"Why, you think she might hit on me or something?" The words were out before she could stop them. An instant fury began to brew inside. It seemed to grow stronger by the second and she wondered if she'd be able to contain it.

Pearl glanced at her. "Well, yes. That would be something I'd be worried about."

"I think it's safe to say that Carla hitting on you wouldn't be something you needed to worry about."

"I don't know what people like her think. I'm single and I'm a woman. That may mean I'm a target. Or it may not." The subtle insult had gone over her head, which Janice found disappointing. She'd wanted it to sting. "But if I were you, I'd be concerned."

Janice lowered the book and inhaled deeply through her nose.

Is this what Carla deals with?

Is this what I would have to deal with?

Judged by a woman I've known for years? A woman who was good friends with my mother?

She considered, in a hasty, frenzied moment, to readily admit that she *wanted* Carla to hit on her. Just to see the look on her face.

"Well, I guess that's you then, Ms. Pine. I don't have a problem with Carla's sexuality. She's a wonderful person and I love her. Who she's attracted to and chooses to be in romantic relationships with isn't any concern of mine. Nor should it be yours. Especially since Carla doesn't concern herself with who you share your bed with."

Her face burned hotter. She absolutely concerned herself with Carla's romantic life. It was all she thought about. But it certainly wasn't because she disapproved. Pearl, however, didn't know, and though she wanted to stand tall and declare her feelings for Carla to her face, she kept control and remained poised.

"I'm a little surprised to hear this from you, Ms. Pine. Seeing as how long you've known Carla. I never would've pegged you for someone who judged people and held such prejudice. And I never would've imagined you unjustly snickering about someone to others, trying to spread fear and invoke judgment in them. But I guess I was wrong." She left the book at the table, her inner fury so close to exploding she was shaking. The bookstore was no longer her favorite place. It didn't matter how long she'd been going there or how good those worn pages smelled. To her, the bookstore had just fallen off the face of the earth.

She headed for the door.

"I do like Carla, Janice. I'm not saying—I—" Pearl couldn't seem to recover from her own statements. She'd boxed herself in.

Janice pushed open the door, causing the bells to clamor louder than before, announcing her dramatic exit. She turned back to Pearl, compelled to say one last thing.

"We're all human, Ms. Pine. And I know you're trying to defend yourself because you don't like being accused of being judgmental and prejudice and well, just an all-around shitty person. You're probably thinking how my thinking that about you is unfair. That I don't really know what's in your heart. Well, I want you to consider that Carla probably feels just like you do right now when people judge her. It's not a good feeling is it?"

She stepped out into the muggy air, leaving Pearl behind the counter with her mouth hanging open. She hurried down the sidewalk, feeling physically ill. Pearl had verbally slapped her in the face, insulting both her and Carla, and the anger it had provoked was to be expected. The fear that came along with it, was not. She fumbled in her purse for her keys. She cursed as she walked and continued to dig, wanting to get the hell out of this town. Her distraction caused her to slam into someone just as she pulled out her keys, sending them and nearly herself flying through the air.

"Oh, God I'm sorry," a deep voice said.

"No, it's—" Janice looked up, the voice registering. Her ex-husband, Chuck, stared down at her.

"Janice."

"Hi."

He knelt and quickly scooped up her keys. He placed them in her palm.

"I'm sorry. I didn't see you, and—" He fell silent. A merciful breeze played with his hair, which, she noted, needed to be trimmed. She studied his face, once so familiar, now seeming foreign. He still had the deep-set eyes, more of a milk chocolate color as opposed to the dark chocolate color of his hair. His nose was still long and straight, his jaw strong. His thin lips were creased with a kind smile. But none of it felt known. She'd had to reexamine it all to recall it.

He appeared to be taking her in as well, standing before her with his hands in his khaki shorts. His collared Polo shirt, which had always been his preference when it came to casual attire, was a light green in color and, along with his leather loafers, helped him achieve a relaxed but very presentable summer ensemble.

"You look amazing," he said.

Janice reacted with a quick inhalation, not at his unpredicted appraisal, or that her encounter with Pearl didn't seem to be evident, but at who she knew was the cause for her current appearance. Carla's effect had been very obvious to her, she felt it every second she was with her. And it had spawned a new sense of confidence in her and a motivation to look her best. She took the time to do her hair and makeup every morning and carefully chose her outfits, even going and buying a few new ones to accentuate her curves. She didn't normally take the time to do those things during her summers. But she really didn't think anyone else would notice.

Chuck, however, did. And next to Maurine, who hadn't said anything so far, he was, once upon a time, the only other person alive who would've noticed. It seemed he was still somewhat keen when it came to her.

"I mean it, you look…just lit up. Like you're glowing from the inside out."

She saw the sincerity in his eyes, and she knew he wasn't trying to overly flatter her or show a personal interest in her. She'd only ever seen that kind of interest and desire in him when he'd started his affair. She'd never been able to elicit such feelings in him and she didn't see them now either. He was simply being perceptive and honest.

"Thanks."

Please don't ask me why I look so good.

I'm too raw right now.

And I'm afraid you'll see it all.

He reached out, touched her arm.

"How are you, Jan?"

She almost sighed with relief. Instead she nodded and focused on being a little unnerved at the sentiment. It took her back to a time she'd left long ago, a place, like his face, she'd need to reexamine to totally recall. She had no desire to go there.

"I'm well."

"You sure look it."

As she stood there with him, with Carla rushing all throughout her, she felt a kinship with him. What he was seeing in her now was what she'd seen in him when he'd began his affair.

She'd done her best to understand him then, but now she knew she hadn't been anywhere close, despite her best efforts.

He'd looked so happy then, like he was walking on air. He, like she apparently did, had an inexplicable glow to him and a passion in him she'd never seen before. And though it had hurt to learn that she wasn't the cause of his sudden metamorphosis, she'd wanted him to have it, to keep it, to live it.

She'd let go, hoping someday she'd find that kind of happiness for herself.

She was experiencing it now, it was in her orbit, but she couldn't figure out how to reach out and grab hold of it or even if she should.

Could he see the dilemma that was surely clouding her eyes?

She shifted on her feet, worried he might. "How's Rochelle?"

"She's—fine." He seemed thrown by the question. "We're doing well."

He'd married her. His mistress. She'd wished him well and held no grudges, but she had declined his request to stay in touch. When they had seen each other in passing, which had been more than two years ago now, she'd been polite, glad to hear he was well, but she'd never asked after Rochelle. She had no ill feelings toward her, even though she'd slept with a married man, she just simply preferred to keep them and their life at a distance. Because in the end, she'd still lost her partner and friend.

Her lack of jealousy and anger over the whole thing, however, still caused her to wonder just how long she would've continued in their marriage existing in a numb-like state, convinced there was nothing more.

It was a frightening thing to ponder.

He nodded toward the bookstore behind her.

"I see you've been to Pearl's. Old habits die hard."

"They do, yes. But things change. It may be time for me to move on."

"Move on? I'm pretty sure you're the main reason why she's still in business." A curious look came over him when he saw her empty hands.

"Don't tell me you didn't find anything. You usually buy two bags full at a time in the summer."

"Not today." She heard the disdain in her voice, and he seemed to as well.

He gave her arm a squeeze. "You okay?"

"I'm fine."

He didn't look like he bought it. "How about a coffee?" He motioned again with his head, this time across the street to Lula's Cafe, a mom-and-pop coffee and muffin shop. It hadn't been around as long as Dog Eared, but long enough to garner a plethora of devoted customers.

He was being his kind, considerate self, and the temptation to give in and collapse in a chair across from him and spill her troubles over a mug of coffee and one of Lula Sinclair's homemade banana-nut muffins was there. But she knew she couldn't. Her run-in with Pearl had jaded her and she feared a similar experience with Chuck though she seriously doubted he would say anything of the sort.

Then again, she'd been wrong about Pearl.

"I can't. I need to run."

He seemed more worried than disappointed. A part of her was touched, but she reminded herself that he wasn't her partner anymore. Nor her best friend. He wasn't someone she could lean on.

"Rain check?" he asked.

"We'll see." She didn't commit, not even to that. "Pretty busy these days."

He dropped his hand, and the disappointment moved in and weakened his smile. "Well, whatever it is you're doing, keep it up. You're positively shining."

Carla came to her mind again, and she straightened, hoping the flames in her cheeks weren't noticeable.

He studied her and cocked his head. "Have you…met someone?"

She started to speak, to deny it, but she knew he'd see right through her.

"I really need to go." She moved around him.

"Whoever it is, he must be special."

"Good seeing you."

"He's a lucky man," he called out.

She crossed to her car.

"You deserve to be happy, Jan."

She unlocked her car and looked up to see him wave. She waved and climbed inside. She wanted more than anything to just sit and stew for a few minutes to process all that had just transpired. The thought of swinging by Floyd's Flowers to see Maurine instinctively crossed her mind, but even if Maurine should be there, Janice couldn't confide in her and she knew she wouldn't be able to hide her distress from her.

She started the car, backed up, and drove from the town square. When she thought of driving home, she felt a pit in her stomach. It didn't seem far enough away.

For the first time ever, she realized she felt all alone and lost in the very place she lived and loved. It was something she'd never felt before, and she thought about heading for the highway and speeding away to God knows where in order to feel free. But then, in a flash, she remembered that Carla would be there in her home, waiting for her, and the pit in her stomach vanished.

She drove toward home but knew the only reason why was because of Carla. Otherwise, she had no idea where it was that her heart would've taken her.

CHAPTER THIRTEEN

Carla pulled into Janice's gravel drive, threw the sixty-two Chevy truck in park, and killed the rumbling engine. She rubbed her eyes and sat looking at the sky through the windshield, comforted by the lingering smell of gasoline and worn vinyl of her grandmother's truck. Thunderclouds loomed in the near distance against the backdrop of the setting sun, threatening an evening storm. She rolled up the driver's side window and then exited the vehicle. The heavy door groaned in protest when she slammed it shut, but she needed to be sure it was fully closed.

The old truck was quite a chore to drive. It lacked power steering as well as fuel injection, which meant she had to prime the damn thing before trying to start it. That was something she'd always struggled to do just right, so flooding the engine had become almost expected. Now, thankfully, but for reasons unknown, she seemed to have it down to an art.

Only took me twenty-plus years.

But she supposed it was better late than never, especially since she'd just learned that the old truck was now hers. Yesterday, that kind of news would've truly touched her, bringing back bittersweet memories that she'd relive with both laughter and tears. That had been yesterday, though. When she and her aunt and uncles stood united and tight, woven together in love and grief. Today, all that had changed with news that went beyond her inheritance of the truck. News that had brought on heartache and anger.

She'd retreated to the truck then and driven around all day, trying to relive the past rather than think about her new reality. She'd thought about the truck and how she'd ridden in it as a child with her grandmother, eagerly bouncing on the bench seat, while an old song from an a.m. station crackled through the radio as she clicked and unclicked the buckle on the lap belt until her grandmother told her to stop.

If her grandmother were with her now and knew of her current anguish and relentless worrying about the day's events, she'd tell her stop, just like she had with the lap belt. But she wasn't there, and the weight of the day tried to engulf her again, as if it had been hovering in the air, like the storm clouds, waiting for her to emerge from the truck before it downpoured.

She gave the truck an affectionate pat and headed for the front porch. A handful of wandering lightning bugs lit up and floated across her path, a welcome to both her and the oncoming darkness. A welcome that was lost on her.

"You're home a little early today," Janice said when Carla entered the living room. She folded her arms across her chest as she leaned against the doorframe to the kitchen. She was barefoot wearing knee length brown shorts that were a shade darker than her crew neck shirt. The deep colors only seemed to enhance her auburn hair which hung in thick waves upon her shoulders.

Is there any color she doesn't look good in?

Carla sank her hands into the pockets of her trousers and felt her keys. She pulled them out and set them on the coffee table, the feel of the truck key too much all of a sudden. She glanced at some of the magazines sitting next to her keys.

"*Arizona Highways?*" She looked up. Janice shifted and she straightened from her lean. She appeared nervous. But why?

"The photos are really beautiful," she said. She took a step toward the table as Carla sifted through the magazines.

"*Desert Living?*"

She found more. There were close to a dozen different magazines with the same subject matter.

"You're interested in Arizona?" She was more than surprised, especially after all her talk about home and roots and red mud running through their veins.

Janice crossed to the table and gathered them together. She picked them up and disappeared into the den. She returned empty-handed and tried for that welcome home smile again. She didn't totally succeed.

"Why didn't you tell me?" Carla asked.

"It's just a recent thing. Guess having you here made me a little curious."

She was fibbing. Carla could see it in her uneasiness, and she'd seen the issue dates on the magazines as well as Janice's home address, so she knew she'd been getting them in the mail for some time. Question was, why was she so uncomfortable in telling her the truth?

Carla was too tired to try to find out. For whatever reason, Janice wasn't willing to share her reasons for her apparent long-held interest in Arizona.

She closed her eyes and felt her body go slack.

"You look beat," Janice said.

She sounded concerned.

Carla opened her eyes and saw an equal amount of concern in her gaze. She was once again voicing her perceptions, something that had been missing lately. There had been a noticeable difference between them that left Carla feeling confused. Though they'd made up at dinner that night after their disagreement, they'd both seemed to pull away after that. The guilt over the pain she'd caused Janice with her careless words had made her uncomfortable, and she'd been uncertain as to whether or not she should continue in burdening her with the daily stresses she was experiencing in dealing with family and friends. It didn't seem fair to do that to her when she was already going out of her way to have her in her home.

As to why Janice had pulled away, Carla could only speculate. She hoped that the pain she'd caused wasn't still affecting her.

With that in mind, along with the worry she was obviously causing, as evidenced by the look on Janice's face, Carla considered downplaying her fatigue. She wondered, however, if Janice would readily accept her attempt. An attempt, Carla knew, that would be half-hearted at best. She just didn't have the strength to try. She was simply too worn out for pretenses.

"Yeah," she finally said. It was becoming difficult to think. Difficult to even remain upright. She needed to sit. But where? Was supper ready? Should she hang out with Janice in the kitchen if she was still preparing it? She was lost for direction and frustrated in needing any.

Things were so strange now. She felt like an outsider in a stranger's home.

"I think I'm just going to go to bed." She started to turn, but Janice moved to her and took her hand.

"Come," she said.

She led her to the couch. Carla hesitated, still unsure.

"Sit," Janice said.

Carla did and she let out a sigh, the cushions feeling like clouds. Janice sat beside her, Carla's hand still in hers. She began to massage it with her thumb, a quiet gesture of soothing support. And with its continued repetition, a gesture that reassured she was willing to be there beside her for however long Carla needed.

She seemed to be back to the old Janice, and the familiarity of her loving kindness flooded Carla and caused a lump to rise in her throat.

"What do you say, Sims? Do you want to talk about it?" she asked after a long while. She touched Carla's brow, brushing her hair back with her fingertips. It was an affectionate move, like what a woman did to the one she loved. Carla warmed at both the light touch and the sentiment. It amazed her how her kind, melodic voice and soft skin-tingling touch seemed to be exactly what she needed at that moment.

How does she always know what to do and say?

How can she be so in tune to me?

Carla wanted to look into her eyes to complete their connection, but seeing the sincerity and caring she could already feel through her hand would surely cause her to either reach for her like a lover or completely break down.

It was safer to keep her eyes trained on her lap and talk.

"Hm?" She brushed her hair again. "I know something's wrong. But if you don't want to talk about it that's okay. We can just sit if you'd like."

Carla forced down the oncoming tears. She didn't speak.

"You can, of course, go to bed if you'd like, but—" Janice touched her cheek. "You just look so upset that I'm hesitant to leave you all alone. I feel like I should be here for you. With you. Even if it's just to sit by your side in silence."

Carla took in a shaky breath. "Are you sure? We haven't exactly been talking a lot here lately."

Janice moved her hand from Carla's cheek to her shoulder.

"No, we haven't. Is that what's bothering you?"

"It has been, yes. But no, that's not why I'm so upset."

"Okay. Is there anything I can do to help? Would you like a drink?"

"No," Carla said. "But thanks. I think I…" She took in another breath.

Janice waited, quiet.

"We met with Barry Freeman today, you know Grandma's attorney?"

"Yes, Maurine told me ya'll were going to go see him."

"So, you know then?" It would explain her intuitiveness and comforting support.

"Know?"

"About what happened with the will and everything."

Janice shook her head. "I haven't spoken to her since this morning."

She didn't know. Her kindness and affection were exactly what Carla had been assuming. She was just being her. And had she not been so upset over what had happened that morning, she would've taken a moment to really let her amazement of her saturate.

"She—" Carla tried to gather some strength. "Grandma left everything to me. Everything. Her savings, her house, her possessions, the land. All of it."

Janice squeezed her hand but didn't say anything. She didn't need to. She would know what her grandmother doing that meant. How it would've affected everybody, probably causing a great deal of upset and turmoil.

"I didn't know," Carla said, consumed with guilt. "I swear I didn't know."

"I know, darlin'." Janice released her hand and touched her shoulder.

"They're all so mad. So angry and confused."

"Ya'll didn't talk? Work things through?"

"No, not like we should've. Mr. Freeman read the will and it shocked the hell out of all of us. I mean I don't even think I'd totally made sense of what he'd said before Maurine got up and ran out crying and Rick stood up and accused Mr. Freeman of lying, acting like he was going to attack him. Cole managed to stop him, but then he glared at me and accused me of knowing all along. I tried to tell them I didn't and that I didn't know why she'd done this, but they wouldn't listen. They just gave me the most hurtful and heart-wrenching looks I've ever seen. Then they stormed out and I chased after them, but Cole climbed into Maurine's car with her and wouldn't even acknowledge me before they sped off. Rick stalked up to me and forced the key to Grandma's truck into my hand. He had tears in his eyes. He said, 'At least the truck will be easy for you to take to Arizona. Not so sure about the house and the land. But I'm sure you'll find a way. She always said you were the smart one.'"

Her chest ached as sobs tried to break free.

Janice sighed and wrapped her arm around her.

"He's just upset. He didn't mean it. That man doesn't have a mean bone in his body, you know that."

"That's what hurts me the most. Knowing he would never say something like that. Not to me, or to anyone. That's how badly he's hurting and it's killing me."

Janice held her tight and wiped the tears from her face with the backs of her fingers.

"I don't know what to do," Carla said. "I'm so lost." She looked at Janice then and her breath caught as she found herself in her eyes.

She could see that Janice was holding her, not only there on the couch, but in her mind, wrapping her in her arms.

"You're not lost," she said. "You're right where you need to be, where you're safe and…loved. Where everything's going to work itself out and be okay again."

Janice pulled her into her arms fully, holding her to her chest in a warm, harboring embrace. Carla finally relented and fell completely into her, solaced by the cushion of her breasts and the rhythmic beat of her heart.

Loved.

She'd said loved.

And it's not scaring me.

It feels good.

She closed her eyes, sleep threatening to wash over her quickly. Just before she let it take her away, she heard Janice whisper one last thing.

"You're where you belong, right here, with me."

Carla absently picked at the warm grass as she sat staring at the rectangle of red dirt marking her grandmother's grave. She'd come to sit with her, hoping to feel her presence. She had so much to say and so many questions to ask, but all words had left her the second she'd seen the grave. The shock of her grandmother being six feet beneath that ground had left her with nothing but the substantial incumbrance that came with the reality of her death. She'd sat then, too heartbroken to speak, too heartbroken to go. The summer sun had seeped into her skin, causing a burning that she registered but did nothing about. She was there, next to her grandmother, sitting in the grass and soaking up the sun, yet she was so far away that her surroundings and, life itself, seemed to blur. When her cell phone had rung, she didn't alert or even contemplate who might be calling. She just casually pulled it from her pocket, glanced at the screen, and answered.

Now, after a poor attempt at trying to persuade Nadine to tell her to come home, she had the phone to her ear, only half-listening, because just the opposite was happening. Nadine was trying to convince her to stay in North Carolina.

"I'm telling you everything is fine here," Nadine said. "How many times do I have to say it?"

Carla threw the grass in her hand aside, frustrated. She'd missed the end of school and it wasn't yet sitting right with her. She'd known that might happen, but it bothered her, nonetheless. There were, of course, other reasons causing her sudden desire to return home. She'd touched on the will and her family problems with Nadine, but she'd remained close lipped about the other, quickly evolving issue.

"I should've finished out the year with my students," she said. "Like everyone else."

"Carla, please. You know as well as I do that the last few days are lazy ones. Your substitute did a great job at keeping the kids in line, and you'd already packed up most of your room. And Roseanne was fine with everything. I know you've spoken to her."

Carla wiped the sweat from her brow and squinted into the sunlight despite having on her aviator shades. Roseanne, who was principal of the school, had been nothing but nice and understanding.

"Yes."

"And?"

"She told me not to worry about anything."

"See? It would be pointless to rush back at this point. Everything has already been taken care of."

"I just—need to."

Nadine was quiet for a few seconds. Then she spoke softly. "I know you're upset over the problems with the will, Carla, but, hon, you can't run from it and think you're going to somehow leave it behind. You're going to have to take care of it. And trust me, it will be a lot easier doing that there than here. Trying to deal with family and tie up loose ends like that from a different state is difficult, I speak from experience. And, Carla, you know you need to work things out with your family. There. In person. You guys are so close and there is so much love between you, you don't want to leave things like they are right now."

"You don't understand how upset they are."

"Well, of course they are. They're hurt and confused, just like you. You're all in pain and still grieving, for God's sake. So, give yourself a break. Give them a break. They'll come around, you know they will."

"No, I don't, Nadine. I just don't know anything right now." She stood and angrily brushed the grass from her behind. Though Nadine was right about what needed to be done, as she often was, she wasn't saying what Carla wanted to hear, and she'd obviously heard her irritation in that last statement.

"Okay, what's going on? You only get this stubborn and pessimistic when you're facing something you can't predict the outcome of. Don't tell me it's just your family issue, either. We both know that will work itself out at some point, even though it doesn't feel that way that right now. So, there has to be something more. Otherwise you would've bucked up, ready to go forward with a little hope and perseverance, just like you always do after we talk things through."

Carla took a long look at her grandmother's grave. She put her hand to her heart, told her she loved her, and turned to head back toward the church. Sweat stung her eyes and soaked through her clothes, causing her T-shirt to stick to her back. But that mild discomfort wasn't the reason why she hadn't yet answered Nadine.

"Carla? Will you please talk to me and tell me what's bothering you?"

She palmed her forehead and laughed at herself, knowing what she was about to say sounded bizarre.

How had this happened?

Why was it happening?

And how could it be with someone I've known forever?

"Carla?"

"It's...a woman."

Silence.

"A woman?"

"Yes."

"A woman."

"Yeah."

"In the middle of all this? Of all you got going on? Carla, what the fuck? What are you doing messing around with a woman? I mean I guess I can *sort* of understand maybe a need for comfort in all your grief, but to just up and sleep with someone, and at a time like this, doesn't sound like you." She paused, obviously exasperated, and took a breath. "I mean what the *fuck?* You don't even like casual sex. You always say you could never have sex with someone you don't know. Carla, my God—"

"Nadine." But she kept going. Carla raised her voice. "Nadine."

She finally stopped her verbal tirade as Carla stopped beneath the tree she'd stood under with Janice the day of the funeral. Its cool shade was a nice break from the sun, and she recalled how calm she'd felt when Janice had come to stand by her, not saying a word, just letting her know she was there with her, with nothing but love and support, should she need her.

Just like last night.

"I know her," she said, recalling how she'd woken early that morning to find herself lying in her arms on the couch. They had been entangled, wrapped up in each other and pressed together like their forms had been melded together. They had to have fallen asleep quickly, because Carla's shoes were still on and they both were still dressed in yesterday's clothes. But that didn't seem to have stopped them from finding comfort.

Carla hadn't moved for a long while, relishing her warmth and the soft contours of her body while she continued to sleep, breathing softly, her hair cascading around her shoulders, framing her peaceful face with the color that reminded her of a glowing ember.

"She's a family friend," Carla said, coming back to Nadine. "I've known her my whole life."

More silence.

"A family friend who's a lesbian? You've never mentioned her—"

"I don't think she's—I'm not sure she's gay." She leaned against the broad, rough trunk and picked at the bark, thinking about how absolutely beautiful Janice had looked when Carla had carefully roused her. Those piercing eyes of hers had opened slowly, and dozens of tiny crystals seemed to be shining from their depths.

"Um, I'd say sleeping with you kind of pushes her more toward that end of the spectrum don't you think?"

Carla laughed. "I haven't—we haven't." They *had* technically slept together. "Been intimate."

She heard Nadine sigh in her classic, *you're driving me batshit crazy, Carla*, fashion. Carla tried to explain.

"I'm pretty sure she's having feelings," Carla said.

"And you obviously are as well."

Carla once again palmed her forehead, knowing any denial would be futile.

"Yes."

Another long silence.

"Now?"

"Uh-huh."

"Amidst all this? The death, the drama, the—"

"Yes." Carla could almost hear the cogs of her mind working. She knew what she was telling her sounded very unusual and totally out of character. The last Nadine had known, Carla wasn't planning on meeting anyone again, much less developing feelings for them. The failure of her relationship had completely vanquished her dream of a lifelong love, and Nadine's mere hints at possibly trying to meet someone new had been met with quick and firm rebuttals and an absolute insistence she didn't want to ever go there again. She was just too jaded, with wounds that had healed, but healed with scars that were still red, not yet having faded to match her surrounding flesh.

"This is—I mean—wow," Nadine finally said, sounding truly astounded.

Carla smiled, appreciating her friendship more than ever. She'd known she'd get it. The magnitude of what she'd just relayed was not going to be lost on Nadine. She knew Carla way too well.

"I've been staying with her," Carla said. "Sleeping on Maurine's couch was killing me and so was the constant onslaught of people. Janice offered me a quiet reprieve and I accepted."

"And now you're sensing a mutual attraction."

"I'm almost positive." She flashed back to the morning again, to when she'd just woken her, and recalled how she'd smiled shyly at her and greeted her with a raspy, sleep-laden and extremely sexy sounding, *"Morning."* They'd spent an awkward moment untangling and Janice had run her hand through her thick locks, as if she were worried about looking unruly.

Carla had quickly reassured her. "Do you know how many women would kill to wake up looking like you do right now?"

She had smiled again, but it was coy.

"You don't need to worry about your hair," Carla had said. "Or anything else for that matter."

Their eyes had locked, but Janice hadn't spoken. She'd said so much with her stare.

Carla had started to speak, but Janice had stopped her.

"Please, don't say thank you again."

Carla had cocked her head. "How did you—"

Janice had laughed.

She had a wonderful laugh, and the sound of it had pulled at the strings of Carla's heart, reminding her of times long ago.

Nadine's voice brought her back to the present.

"You're not sure what to do, are you?"

"No."

"You can't talk to her?"

"I can, but if I'm wrong, I'm afraid it will ruin everything. People here…it's not like Phoenix. This is the Bible Belt. Being gay…a lot of people still aren't accepting, and even if she's okay with it, and she's told me she is, that doesn't mean she's ready or willing to admit her own attraction. She might not even understand that what she's feeling is attraction."

"So, you're thinking about tucking tail and running home. From your family and from her."

"Do you have to put it like that?"

"That's what you'd be doing."

"I'm just so overwhelmed."

"That's completely understandable, and anyone in your position would be. Your heart is being tugged in all kinds of directions. The only way to stop that is to deal with one thing at a time. And if I were you, I'd start with my family. You're smarter than the average bear, Carla. I know you can find a solution, one that everyone agrees with, and you guys can patch things up and move on. I'd make that my first priority and leave things be with the woman for now. You fear talking to her about your attraction, so just continue on as is. I know it's been a while for you, but I'm pretty sure you can control yourself, right?"

Carla laughed softly. "I'm going to have to. I can't risk making that first move without being one hundred percent sure it's what she wants. She's too good of a friend and I'm a guest in her home."

"So, if anything happens, it will be her doing?"

Carla's mind whirled with excitement as she imagined what that would be like.

"At this point, yes. I have to let her take the lead."

"What would you do if she did make a move? You might want to think about that in case it does happen."

"I don't know, faint? I haven't been with a woman in so long her touch just might completely overwhelm me and down I'd go."

Nadine laughed. "You might be right."

"No, but seriously," Carla said. "I'm not sure how I would react. I just know that I'm seeing her in a whole new light now, and I'm discovering so much about her. She's incredible and I don't know how I've missed seeing that."

"Maybe you didn't. Maybe you've always felt for her, but you didn't think you would ever be able to do anything about it, so you put it in its place. Tucked it away somewhere deep and dark where it wouldn't drive you crazy and constantly tempt you to confess your feelings for her. She might have done the same thing with her attraction to you. A lot of people have to do that at some point in their lives, for numerous reasons."

"It would explain the déjà vu I experience with her sometimes. But that could just be me remembering our past." She sighed, the conversation stirring up more than she'd bargained for but glad that it had. She'd needed a new perspective and a point in the right direction. "I'd better go. I've got a lot to think about."

A lot.

"You'll be okay. Just remember our motto."

"If you don't know, you better FITFO."

Carla laughed at the meaning of the acronym.

Figure it the fuck out.

"God, I miss you so much right now."

"I'm there with ya, hon, so you hang tough, okay?"

"I will. I'll talk to you soon."

"Kisses and hugs and all my love," Nadine said in their traditional good-bye.

Carla didn't respond right away. She stared out beyond the front of the church, where the green disappeared at the edge of the hill. She had a lot to face and a lot to deal with, and it all lay ahead at the bottom of that hill where the old Chevy sat waiting for her in the parking lot. Now, however, she felt like she could handle it, thanks to Nadine and the one other person who had shown her continuous support and understanding, literally holding her in her protective embrace the night before. She thought about her as she said good-bye to Nadine, using the word that meant the most to her in this world, a word Janice had used the night before as she held her in her arms. A word she never imagined would be paired with Janice Carpenter.

"Love," Carla said, lowering the phone slowly from her ear, still lost in her stare beyond, still lost in her thoughts about the mysteriously beautiful woman who had always been there, but had now suddenly become front and center.

She closed her eyes and once again paired her image with that all-encompassing word.

Love.

CHAPTER FOURTEEN

Janice slowed her pace as she walked down the grassy incline back behind her great-aunt's house. Storm clouds, thick and heavy looking, had just slid in front of the sun, casting a dark shadow over the surrounding modest brick homes, a silent warning of their intent. She was grateful for the temporary reprieve from the sun, but the air still felt stifling and smothering, with a humidity level just as high as the temperature.

She smoothed her hands over her tightly bound hair, glad that she'd put it up in a ponytail. Her choice to wear a lightweight tank top and cotton shorts also seemed to have been wise, especially now that she found herself out in the heat, approaching her great-aunt's garden.

"Hey, Mamie," she said, glad to see she was just as active as ever, hunched over the black soil in a bright, flower-pattered muumuu and oversized straw hat.

Though her real name was Millie, she had always preferred to go by Mamie, and Janice, along with Mamie's grandchildren and great-grandchildren, had always referred to her as such. She turned, appearing startled, and then grinned with recognition after pushing up on her horn-rimmed eyeglasses.

"Well, I'll be." She stood with hands stained from the earth for a gentle hug and kiss. "It's good to see you, sugar. Let me tidy up here and we'll go on in the house before that thunder a-gets us."

"I'm surprised you aren't already inside," Janice said, knowing how much storms bothered her. Thunder had yet to grumble, but the storm was right on top of them, and usually Mamie took more precaution, taking cover inside away from the windows with the lights shut off.

"It kindly snuck up on me. Shoulda been payin' more attention." She glanced up at the cloud cover. "We better hurry. It's a-coming."

Janice helped her tuck away her gardening tools under the overhead porch and then carried the bucket she'd packed full of freshly plucked vegetables.

"Garden's looking good," Janice said. Mamie brushed her hands together and then opened the basement door. They stepped inside the dim space that always had a smell that made Janice think of the word murky, even as a child. The washing machine was going on the other side of the room, and Janice was awed that Mamie could still carry baskets of laundry up and down the basement stairs, a feat other women her age might find difficult. Mamie was a force to be reckoned with at eighty-six years old, and Janice figured all the physical work she still did was what kept her so spry. She could only hope to be that vigorous at her age.

"The tomatoes come in nicely, and I got some cucumber, and some corn and green beans. But there ain't been much else. I reckon that rain will help everything along."

Janice followed her slowly up the stairs and into the kitchen. She set the bucket next to the sink as Mamie removed her hat and washed her hands. Her white hair was tied back into a bun, her wrinkled face a little scarlet from exertion. She had the fine features that most of the Carpenter women had, which many folks had often pointed out and complimented them on, making them easily identifiable as family. Janice liked to think that had an artist created their faces, he would've insisted on using a very fine tipped drawing pencil in order to get the sharp details and distinctness of their facial structure just right.

Mamie wet a paper towel and wiped herself off.

Thunder growled loudly and Mamie looked up as if she'd be able to see it.

"Lord, it's a-coming."

Her brow creased with what Janice knew was anxiousness. Some people teased Mamie over her fear of storms, but in Janice's opinion, she had good reason to be scared. She'd been flooded out of her home when she was five and her family had lost everything, barely escaping with their lives. The water had come in the middle of the night and they'd had no warning or time to prepare. But the memory that bothered Mamie the most about that night, according to her, was the fear and torment she'd heard as people cried and shouted and sometimes, screamed, as the fast-moving water took a loved one away.

"Why don't you go sit down and I'll get us some tea?" Janice asked, retrieving two glasses from the cabinet. She poured the tea as Mamie switched off all the lights, convinced it would prevent a lightning strike, and disappeared into the living room. Janice found her in her favorite recliner, which she'd had so long it was molded to her form.

She gave her the tea and sat on the ancient vinyl couch across from her and waited for her eyes to adjust to the dimness. The only light came through the window, and it was weak and gray and unable to fully permeate their space. Janice could see Mamie, however, and she could take in the layout of the room, so her view was sufficient enough.

Mamie's house was tidy and what some would call sparse, with nothing but the absolute essentials. There was a mid-century coffee table holding a single, solitary book. It was a book about the history of their town and therefore, special enough to display. A smaller table was on Mamie's right side where she kept her telephone and drinks. A standing light, one that Mamie could reach from where she sat, was just behind that table. On Mamie's left, which Janice could not currently see, was a good-sized magazine holder where all of Mamie's beloved crossword puzzle and word search books were kept alongside her magazines.

They sipped their tea, and Janice's gaze went directly ahead to the remaining piece of furniture. It was an old dresser that was being used as a television stand. Janice didn't want to even try to guess how long Mamie had had that particular television set, but it had knobs to change the very few channels Mamie could pick up with the antennas.

"What brings you by today, sugar?" Mamie leaned back and adjusted her glasses.

Janice sat back too and crossed her legs. "It's been a while since I've seen you and I've been thinking about you a lot lately. And you always told me when someone crosses your mind, you should go and cross their path."

"This wouldn't have anything to do with Betty Sim's a-dying would it?"

Janice shifted, supposing it could be. She didn't want to tell her that, though.

"Lord, child, I know I'm old, you don't have to sit there looking like the cat that swallowed the mouse." She set her glass on the table next to her. "You ain't got to worry yourself. I'm a-doing just fine and dandy."

"I was sure you would be."

"But you was worried."

Janice shrugged. "Maybe a little."

Mamie chuckled, and then stared out the front window in what looked like sad contemplation.

"It's a shame, Betty getting sick and going so fast. I wish I woulda called her. It woulda been nice to talk to her one last time."

"She knows you cared, Mamie." Mamie and Betty hadn't been outrageously close, but they had known each other for a very long time. Janice felt for her, knowing that Mamie would've wanted to attend the funeral, had she not been in Wilmington, visiting her grandson, just as she did at this time every summer. "Your heart was with her and that's all that matters."

She didn't appear to be comforted. "Her kin, they doing all right?"

"They're having a bit of a hard time adjusting, her passing away so suddenly and all. But they'll pull through. They're strong people."

"I remember you and that Maurine was attached at the hip when you was little. The Lord almighty couldn't a torn you two apart."

Janice smiled wistfully. She had seen Maurine earlier that morning. She'd been quiet and distant with her recently, and Janice had assumed it was in response to Carla coming to stay with her. But, as she'd discovered that morning, her mildly cold distance had since hardened into ice. Her disdain had shifted from Carla's residency with her to the will. She was downright pissed at Carla, and it seemed that feeling had extended to Janice as well. She was convinced that she had sided with Carla, and her paranoia had probably all but been confirmed when Janice tried to get her to understand that Carla hadn't known about Betty's final wishes.

Maurine had bit into her then with harsh words.

"Since when have you and Carla been so tight?"

"Was having one Sims girl as a best friend not enough for you? You got to have two now?"

Her hurt and jealousy were palpable, and Janice had tried her best to get her to see reason. But when it had come to trying to explain her and Carla's sudden closeness, she'd faltered and stumbled over her words, which made their relationship sound shady, like maybe they were shutting Maurine out or keeping something from her.

Truth was, she was hiding something.

She was hiding her feelings for Carla.

And she was becoming more and more certain that Carla was doing the same.

"We were pretty tight, weren't we?" she said, the guilt over Maurine's hurt turning her stomach.

"Poor child must be heartbroken as close as she was to her mama."

"She is. They all are."

"What about that little old granddaughter of Betty's? She come home for the funeral?"

"Carla." She sipped her tea, her mouth suddenly dry. "Yes, she did."

"Good. That'll help Maurine a little. They was always more like sisters than they was aunt and niece."

The guilt expanded, and she felt it trying to climb her throat. She hesitated in telling Mamie about Carla's current living arrangement, but she knew she'd find out sooner or later. In this town, the only boundaries that were respected regarded land. Personal boundaries and privacy? You had to drive into the city for those.

"Actually, Carla's been staying with me."

Mamie turned from the window and fixed her eyes on her. The surprise she'd felt at that information had only shown itself for a second before she regained control. A second was a lifetime when it came to hiding emotion, though and more than enough time for Janice to see it.

"Wasn't she the one who was always running around trying to catch lightning by the tail?"

The corner of Janice's mouth lifted as her own attempt at hiding what she felt failed. Mamie's description of Carla was spot-on. Even now when she was besieged with stress and grief and sadness. That lightning chaser was still there, and Janice could see it in her eyes sometimes. Like when she returned from a run or showed off her sharp wit. It was like watching Carla being brought back to life, back to her true form, if only for a few seconds.

"Yep, that's her. You couldn't have described her any better." She tried to lower the upturned corner of mouth, but she had a hard time, too amused and excited as she pictured Carla in that state.

"You're quite fond of her," Mamie said, causing Janice to quickly refocus on her. She was wearing a grin, similar to what Janice felt was on her own face. But Mamie's seemed to be almost mischievous.

"Yes, I suppose I am."

"There ain't no supposing about it. I can see it in you."

Janice felt her cheeks burn and her gaze abandoned Mamie's before she could stop it, and she knew that would only feed into whatever it was Mamie was after. She had her suspicions as to what she was digging for based on her comments and the grin, but she had a hard time believing that a woman Mamie's age, with such a conservative background, would ever think that she might feel something more for Carla than friendship.

"I didn't realize ya'll were so close."

Oh, Lord.

Maybe I'm the one who's naive here.

"We—I—" She pressed her fingertips to her forehead, desperate to get a hold of her nerves. "Our...closeness is more of a recent thing." She cleared her throat and could feel the scrutiny of Mamie's lively eyes.

"Mm." She nodded once, like she understood. "She still got all that tomboy in her?"

Janice shifted again, her discomfort growing.

How in the world do I answer that?

Yes, Mamie. She's a stunningly beautiful, almost graceful looking grown woman who still has a little bit of that tomboy in her...

And it's sexy as hell.

"I—she's grown up a lot, Mamie. She's a teacher as a matter of fact. High school."

"I'll take that as a yes, then."

Janice blinked at her. *Oh, heaven above.* "Sorry?"

She waved her off. "Did I ever tell you about your great-aunt Gale? My younger sister?"

Janice shook her head in confusion. Of course, she knew who her great-aunt Gale was, but she had no idea what Mamie was referring to about her.

Rain began to fall before Mamie could answer, seemingly a quick foreshadowing of how Mamie's probing would soon cause the world to fall down on Janice. They both looked out the front window at the heavy downpour. The rain was coming down so hard the drops looked connected, like hundreds of silver streaming lines.

Mamie's old rotary phone rang, and its shrill was shocking, causing Janice to startle and spill some tea.

She shook it off her hand and made sure it didn't get on her tank top.

Mamie answered the phone and greeted Ethel, her long-time neighbor, and in hearing Mamie's invitation for Ethel to come over to wait out the storm, Janice knew she should go. She returned to the sink to wash her glass. She was drying it with a dishtowel when Mamie hung up.

"Ethel's coming by," she said. "She don't much like thunderstorms either."

"I'm going to go ahead and go then so you two can visit. I have some errands to run anyway."

She put away the glass and walked back into the living room to stand at her chair.

"It's good you and Ethel have each other," she said, smiling down at her.

"I reckon so." She took Janice's hands. "We all need somebody in this life. Some of us find someone, and if we're lucky it lasts a good spell. And there are some of us that don't. Your great-aunt Gale, well, she was never married, never found a fellow she cared for, but that didn't stop her." She laughed softly. "I reckon that's why the good Lord puts all kinds of people in our lives. So's we always have someone if we need them. Gale, she had one of those people. A good close friend to walk by her side." She pumped her hands up and down, letting her know what she was about to say was important. "I know you wasn't ever happy being married, sugar. But you ain't got to be alone. You can have yourself someone and it don't have to be a husband. It can be someone else who's special to you."

She paused, looking up at her with a loving warmth Janice could feel seeping into her skin.

Was she referring to Carla?

Could she really be?

A light rapping came from the carport door. Mamie smiled at her with regret, the end to their conversation as obvious as her quiet disappointment.

"You ain't got to say nothing," she said. "You heard me out and that's all I wanted." She sighed. "You know I don't like you driving in a storm, but I ain't gonna argue with you. You're as stubborn as your daddy was, and arguing with him plum wore me out."

There was another short series of raps.

"Promise me you'll drive careful."

Janice nodded. "I will." She knelt and kissed her. "I love you."
"I love you, sugar."

They parted and Janice hurried to the door. Ethel greeted her with a bubbliness that was usually infectious, but Janice was as oblivious to that as she was at what she was saying. She excused herself politely and said good-bye and stepped into the muggy air, not even focused enough on reality to ready herself for the cold onslaught of rain she had to endure to get into her car.

Nothing, it seemed, could bring her back from where her conversation with Mamie had taken her.

Nothing could bring her back from her fantasy of a future with Carla.

CHAPTER FIFTEEN

The home phone at Janice's house beeped rudely in Carla's hand.

"Figures." She turned it off and thought about using her cell phone, but the battery was low on it too, so she decided to call it quits for the day. She gathered her files and the spiral notebook she'd been jotting notes and thoughts in. It was after four and she'd been sitting at the kitchen table for hours in dire contemplation about the will. She'd spoken briefly with the attorney, picking his brain for ideas, but he'd told her he thought Betty had made the right decision in leaving everything to her. She'd pondered that for a while and then tried to call him back with more questions. But the dead phone signaled the much-needed stop to her day. The headache that had started as a tiny seed earlier was now a full-blown menace, reinforcing that signal to stop. Maybe now that she had quit, the two Tylenol she'd swallowed ten minutes before would finally kick in.

She picked up her things, along with the phone, and headed for her room.

The thunder from the rainstorm spoke to her overhead, letting her know it was still present and it meant business. Janice was still out running errands and probably caught in the middle of it. Carla hoped things weren't too bad out there. Janice had been gone since late morning, and a small tinge of worry came to life in her mind. She hadn't worried about the safety of a woman in a long time, and she almost allowed herself to overanalyze why she was doing so now. But instead, she told herself that Janice was someone she cared about and being a little concerned about her in a bad storm was perfectly acceptable.

She entered her room and put away her files. Then she crossed into Janice's room in search of the charging base for the cordless phone. It was sitting on her nightstand along with a couple of books and a lamp. She rounded the bed, noticing the red, velvet-looking duvet cover and well-matched throw pillows. Larger pillows were positioned at the headboard, and Carla couldn't help but want to touch them. They looked so thick and soft and a few had different textures. She placed the phone in the cradle and sat on the bed. She ran her hands along the alluring fabrics and felt the cool satin of her sheets as her hand sank between pillows.

Her body tightened, a sudden thrill coming over her as she thought of Janice purposely choosing these sensual things for her bed, her most sacred, intimate place. The romantic appeal of it was calling to Carla, and she began to imagine Janice wrapped up in the silky sheets, her beautiful body gliding against them as she writhed in ecstasy, her head tilted back, splaying her fire-like hair, releasing a throaty cry.

Carla had to force herself to remove her hand, her excitement rising to a dangerous level. She stood quickly, needing to put some distance between herself and this room and she bumped the nightstand causing a book to fall. She picked it up and did a double take as she returned it to its place. A ball of disbelief wedged in her throat.

"No," she said. "No way." She touched the book cover and reexamined the title, convinced she was imagining things. But recognition of the title registered, and her body burned so fiercely she thought she'd leave burn marks on the carpet.

"Hi."

Carla turned, the burning colliding with embarrassment. She swallowed and it actually made a sound.

"Hi." It came out on a weak breath. So many thoughts and feelings were rushing through her, one slamming into another, imploding, exploding, multiplying, she was sure nothing else could move her so profoundly.

She was wrong.

Janice stepped fully into the room and Carla saw, first her wet, dripping hair, then her glistening face and then…her tank top.

God bless America.

It was the only thing that came to mind, everything else, including her grip on sanity, fled.

She blinked, ensuring the reality of what she was seeing. What she'd seen a few nights before had been a mere tease. What she was seeing now, which was *everything*, with absolutely nothing left to the imagination, was downright flabbergasting.

"What's going on?"

It was Janice. She was talking. She'd said something. But Carla was transfixed by the puckered circles of her dark pink areolas on her full, rounded breasts.

"Hm?"

Her eyes followed Carla's. She looked down at her chest.

"Oh, no." She attacked her shirt with hurried hands, first trying to pluck it from its press against her body and then grabbing at the hem. She had it up and over her head before Carla could even blink again.

Then she stood there, with her limp shirt at her side, wearing nothing above her waist but a white bra. Or what was normally a white bra. When it was dry.

And it was *so* not dry. And her breasts were so beyond beautiful. They might as well have been completely exposed at that point with the very wet, very thin fabric of the bra doing very little to cover anything. In fact, Carla reasoned, if she were to put her mouth on her breasts at that moment, with the bra still on, there was no doubt in her mind that Janice would feel it. She'd probably even cry out like she'd just imagined her doing in her bed. And the goddamned thought of that had her so worked up she was about to come out of her skull.

She clenched her fists, determined to control the pounding rush of blood in her ears. But she knew she wasn't hiding her arousal well. Her breathing was too shallow, too loud. She made a noise, completely involuntarily, short but high in pitch. It caused both of them to jerk and Janice glanced down at herself again and reddened like a ripe plum.

She turned and Carla heard her mumbling. She was scrambling to get out of the bra and Carla rounded the bed, intent on giving her some privacy. But Janice turned on her, catching her near the door. Her arms were folded across her chest, pressing into her breasts, bra dangling from one hand.

"Sorry," she said, as if she'd done something horribly wrong.

"No, I'm—"

"Could you give me a moment, please?"

Carla retreated, feeling a fool. "Of course. I'll just go—I'll be in the living room."

She left her quickly and just about ran down the hall. She reached the couch but was too worked up to sit. She paced, hand to forehead, fingers massaging with worry. Rational thought was slow to arrive, and when Janice entered the room, dressed in knit capris and a T-shirt with the name of her college on it, Carla was still just as excited as she'd been when she'd seen her in the wet shirt. Seeing her covered in fresh clothes didn't do a damn thing to douse her desire.

"I—" Carla tried again.

"You were…in my room," she said softly. Her rained-soaked hair was combed back, and the skin on her neck and arms still glistened with moisture. Her eyes were like daggers, their blue-green intensity piercing Carla's body and her psyche. The tiny sharp pinpricks were as relentless as her gaze.

"I'm sorry," she said, sounding weak and hesitant. "I was returning the phone."

And caressing the very sensual sheets and pillows your goddamned glorious body lies upon and touches every night.

"Is that all?"

No.

I also saw what you're reading.

And up until you walked in the room, I thought nothing could hit me as hard as that did.

"Mm-hm."

She studied her a moment longer and the rainfall increased, hammering the roof. Thunder cracked loudly, shaking the house with flashes of lightning hot on its tail. The house lights flickered, mimicking the thunderbolts, and then died in an instant, leaving them in near darkness.

It was yet another element added to the scenario, giving even more power to Carla's tumultuous feelings. First there had been the allure of the bed, then the surprise of the book and then, heaven help her, the sight of her beautiful body in the wet tank top.

And now, they were not only totally alone, with that thick, visceral charge of electricity between them.

They were also in the dark.

Chapter Sixteen

White flashes from lightning illuminated Janice's face as she stared out the window at the storm. She'd broken eye contact a few seconds after the power failure and moved to the window. They hadn't spoken for several agonizing minutes and Carla wasn't sure if she should. She kept a close watch on Janice, searching for signs that would suggest she was upset. But looking at her so intently had left Carla entranced by the elegant features of her face each and every time the storm lit her up.

"It wasn't my intention to invade your privacy," Carla said, unable to take the silence or guilt she felt over the ordeal any longer.

Janice's gaze shifted slightly, but not toward Carla. She hugged herself as if she were cold.

"I better get the candles," she said, finally tearing her gaze away from the storm. She crossed to the kitchen and Carla followed, unprepared for her sudden movement and disregard to her apology.

"Anything I can do to help?"

Janice halted just as quickly as she'd moved and turned and crashed into Carla. They both jumped a little and offered hurried apologies that sounded high strung with nerves.

"I just—need to get into that drawer," Janice stammered, as they both kept moving in the same direction, unintentionally mirroring each other, trying to get by.

Carla relented and held up her hands in defeat. "How about I just stand still? Would that help?" She smiled and Janice seemed to relax some.

"I think so." She walked around Carla and slid open a deep drawer close to the sink. She pulled out several wide candles and closed the drawer with her hip. When she tried to carry them, however, some fell. "Shit."

"Here, let me," Carla said, hurrying to her. They knelt at the same time, reaching for the same candle, and bumped heads and hands.

"Ow, shit," Janice said, grabbing her head.

Carla winced and rubbed at her own. "Are you okay?"

"Yes." She looked at Carla. "Are you?"

"I'll live."

They reached for the same candle again and hands collided. They both inhaled, reacting to the contact. Their eyes met once again, and Janice brushed her fingers along the back of Carla's hand. Lightly, deftly. Almost as if it were imagined. Carla glanced down and lifted a single finger, wanting mutual contact. And just as her finger touched hers, Janice pulled away.

She gathered the candles, scooping them up against her chest. She hurried back into the living room and Carla watched from the kitchen doorway as she deposited them on the coffee table. Her movements were quick and deliberate. She was obviously flustered.

"It sometimes takes them forever to get the power back on, so I get the candles going right away, just in case." She stood looking down at the candles with her hands on her hips. It seemed to take her a while to realize something was missing, her mind probably still back in the bedroom, replaying the scene between them.

"Where do you keep your lighter?" Carla asked.

She looked up. "Right. We definitely need that don't we?" She ran her hand through her hair like she was still battling her nerves. "It's in the kitchen. I'll get it."

"No, let me. I'm right here. Where is it?"

She looked uncomfortable, like she didn't want to tell her.

"It's in the big drawer by the sink."

"The same drawer as the candles?"

She looked away. "Uh-huh."

She'd overlooked the lighter that been right there in front of her. And it seemed she didn't want Carla to know.

Maybe her mind really was back in the bedroom.

Could she not tell that Carla's was too?

"Got it," Carla said, turning to retrieve the stick lighter. She carried it into the living room and handed it to Janice, who took it quietly and lit two candles. Carla picked up the rest before she could fend her off.

"Where to?" She was trying to sound lighthearted to help ease the tension, but it didn't seem to have any effect on Janice.

"Uh, the kitchen." Her embarrassment showed with the flush of her cheeks as she confessed another visit to the kitchen was needed.

"Okay." Carla set a candle on the counter and Janice followed. They lit one candle there and then walked down the hall to place one in the bathroom and one in each of their rooms. When they stood at the dresser in Janice's room there was a noticeable silence, the aura of their encounter still palpable.

Carla felt it. It was almost like it was alive and had a heartbeat. And the bed behind her fed that pulse. It was calling out, beckoning with its heavenly linens, making Carla want to feel them all over again, a temptation much like she had every time she held an open rose. She could never resist touching the impossible softness of the alluring display of petals. She wanted to take Janice in her arms and lay her down on that open rose of a bed and make love to her amidst those soft petals, knowing that they were kissing and stroking Janice's nude body in unison with her.

"What? What is it?" Janice asked, glancing over at her. She sounded apprehensive and must've felt Carla's eyes on her. She clicked the lighter repeatedly with no success.

You.

You are everything.

"Nothing." Carla placed her hand over hers, stilling her. She felt Janice react, even though it was subtle. She gently took the lighter from her and slid the small lever to the other fuel chamber. She pulled the ignition trigger and lit the awaiting wick.

"Lord, I am so absentminded today." Janice attempted a laugh, but her apparent nervousness stifled it, especially when Carla didn't laugh with her. The candlelight was teasing, illuminating and shadowing Janice's face, mesmerizing Carla with the ever-changing contours and angles. Laughter was the furthest thing from her mind.

Carla wasn't sure what she wanted more. To take her in her arms to the bed, or to continue to stare at her, lost forever in the undertow of her beauty. Janice pulled her from her inner dilemma by taking the lighter back. She was once again watching Carla curiously.

"I'm a renowned expert on lighter usage," Carla said, hoping to explain her own obvious staring. "I get a lot of practice back home during monsoon season."

"Monsoon season?"

"You haven't read about it in all those magazines?"

She reddened further and looked away.

Why do those magazines make her so uncomfortable?

Carla smiled softly, confused by her discomfort but wanting more than anything to lesson it.

"Let's go relax and I'll tell you all about it."

Carla led the way to the couches in the living room. She sat at the end of the love seat closest to Janice who sat at the end of the sofa. It reminded Carla of their first night together and how welcome and relaxed she'd felt. And then she recalled the night she'd sat directly next to her and how Janice had held her, comforting her, until they'd fallen asleep in each other's arms.

Her longing to feel her again almost took precedence, but she couldn't go there at the present, even if just in her mind.

"We get storms in the summer," she said. "Monsoons."

"In Phoenix? In the desert?" She met her eyes briefly, showing an attempt to move beyond her current state of unease.

"Uh-huh. Every summer."

"And I'm guessing, since they're called monsoons, they aren't like this storm."

"They're usually more powerful than your average thunderstorm. A lot of strong winds and blowing dust along with the heavy rain. Haven't you ever seen those giant walls of dust on the news?"

"Yes," she said, sounding more alive. "That's what ya'll get?"

"Sometimes."

"They look so impossible, like they can't be real."

"They're real all right. Pretty cool to look at too. But you do not want to get caught in one. Especially if you're driving."

"I would think not. Has that ever happened to you?"

"I've been caught in a couple of dust storms, but thankfully nothing that endangered my driving."

"Are they ever dangerous? These storms?"

"They can be. The strong winds can cause damage and the heavy downpours cause flash flooding."

"And power outages," she said. "Hence your expertise on lighter usage."

Carla saw a hint of a grin.

"Yes, ma'am. I've had to light a lot of candles in my day."

"You don't sound like you enjoy that."

"I don't, no. Why would I? Losing power in Phoenix in the middle of July is awful. It's way too hot to be without air conditioning. And for days at a time? Nightmare."

"I didn't even think about the heat. What do you do?"

"Me? I leave. I get the hell out. If I hear it's going to take more than a day to fix the power, I drive a couple of hours north and stay up there until things are taken care of. But that's worse-case scenario. The power is usually up and running again within a few hours. That's been my experience anyway."

"Sound like something you might want to see?"

"Me?" Her eyes were wide. "I don't know. I haven't really tho—"

Carla waited for her to finish. She didn't.

"Did I scare you?"

She looked at her with alarm. "Scare me? No, of course not. Why would I be scared to come to Arizona?"

"I don't know," Carla said softly. "I was referring to my description of the storms."

"Oh. No. Storms don't frighten me. I kind of like them." She ran her hand through her hair and then propped her elbow on the armrest and leaned her cheek into her palm.

Is she trying to appear unaffected? If so, for whom? Her or me?

"You should come. I think you would really like Arizona."

Janice was quiet.

"Janice?"

"Mm, yes, maybe I would like it."

"Have you thought about coming?"

Thunder rolled above them and the rainfall increased, assaulting the roof with machine-gun sounding clatter.

"I don't know. Not a whole lot I guess."

"Really? I thought with all your reading about it, you would want to see it for yourself."

She drew her feet up to rest at her side.

"You said it was beautiful, right?" Carla knew she was pressing her. But she felt driven to discover why she was so reluctant in discussing her obvious interest. "Don't you want to see it in person?"

She smoothed her pants. More so than was necessary.

"Janice?"

She whipped her head up. "I said I don't know, okay? I haven't given it a lot thought."

Carla blinked, surprised at her reaction but still confused by her answer.

"Why not?"

Janice looked right into her and spoke quickly. "Because it wasn't possible. Because it wasn't reality. It was a dream." She closed her mouth and turned away as if she'd said too much.

Wasn't possible? Wasn't reality? How long has she been thinking about this?

"A dream," Carla said. "There's nothing wrong with having dreams."

She didn't respond.

"You know, if you want to come, you can. You'd have a place to stay. I'd love to have you."

She remained silent.

"That makes the dream a little more possible, doesn't it? Dreams sometimes can come true."

She breathed deeply and Carla thought she saw her shudder.

"Janice."

Carla leaned forward, trying to catch her gaze.

"Yes, Carla," she said.

"I feel like I've upset you again and I don't understand why. And I want to understand."

"There's nothing to understand."

"How do you know?"

"Because I don't even understand," she said. "So, how could you?"

"Try me. It's worth a shot, right?"

She shook her head. "No, I don't think in this case it is."

"What do you have going on in that beautiful mind of yours, Janice? What could possibly be so upsetting? And what could it possibly have to do with Arizona?"

Lightning flashed, intruding upon the candlelight. Thunder cracked a second later, and when Janice looked at her again, she had a storm of her own brewing in her eyes.

For a moment, Carla was struck breathless, speechless. She searched that storm thoroughly for answers to her questions but found nothing she could hold on to. Every time she was sure she had something, and she reached for it, it slipped from her hands. There was one thing that kept bobbing to the surface, however, always just out of reach but very clear in sight.

"Is it me, Janice?"

She blinked. Once. Then a few times rapidly. Her lips parted. Carla could sense that she wanted to move but she didn't. She kept very still and even held her gaze. Then she pressed her lips firmly together as if remaining so stoic was of great difficulty to her.

"I don't have a problem with you being gay, Carla. I've told you that several times now."

"I wasn't referring to my sexuality. And you didn't answer my question."

"I did."

"I asked if I was the reason why you're upset. You saying you have no issue with my sexuality, doesn't really answer the question. So, I'll ask you again. Am I the reason you're upset?"

"No."

She was firm, both in tone and in posture.

Carla sighed and rubbed her forehead.

"I'm not sure I believe you."

"I don't know how to convince you."

"You could tell me why you're so upset and why you close off when I bring up the magazines or anything having to do with Arizona."

She finally shifted, bringing her feet back to the floor. She had her palms on her thighs and looked as though she were about to stand. Carla feared she was about to run.

"Just, please. I—Are you really okay with my being here? Because if something has changed and you would feel more comfortable if I wasn't here, then I would understand." She wasn't getting anywhere with her other attempts. Janice wasn't letting her in. So, at the very least, she needed to be sure her presence was something Janice wanted.

"I don't want you to feel obligated."

"I don't," she said, but her voice didn't have the strength it had before. "And I don't want you to leave."

The rain stopped and the rumbling thunder sounded like it was moving on.

"I would ask you if you're sure, but judging by the look on your face right now, I'm thinking that wouldn't be a good idea."

"I prefer you taking me at my word. The first time."

Carla nodded. "Yeah, I'm finally getting that."

"I will say this though. If you ever need to talk, about anything, you can talk to me. I mean that most sincerely."

"Okay."

"I care about you. A great deal. More than you probably realize."

Carla was now the one who could no longer hold eye contact. She was confessing more than her words were construing and there was a part of her that didn't want Janice to see that.

She swallowed and turned to Janice with a newfound smile, intent on releasing them both from the tension.

Janice, however, seemed to be ahead of her. She quickly stood, a smile of her own beaming down at Carla.

"How about a walk? Storm seems to have passed. Might be nice to get some fresh air. Albeit muggy, humid air."

She's not going to tell me.

She's going to keep putting on a front.

Whatever it is she's hiding, she's just not ready to share it.

Carla was crestfallen, but she kept her smile. She had to continue to think of Janice and her position as her friend.

"Sounds good."

"I'll get our shoes." Janice hurried down the hallway.

Carla rubbed her forehead again and sighed, wondering if she should ever try again.

Wondering if Janice would ever be ready to open up.

CHAPTER SEVENTEEN

The morning was bright and vibrant with color. Janice stood at the kitchen sink washing last night's dishes, thinking about how she would've never put off cleaning up after dinner when alone. But she and Carla had been deep in conversation and Janice had been so enraptured, she'd easily agreed to leave the dishes for another time, choosing instead to join Carla on the front porch with a bottle of homemade muscadine wine she'd brought home from a family friend. They'd sat in the gliding chair for hours, talking, drinking, and staring off into the darkness until the tiny glowing bulbs of the lightning bugs dissipated.

Janice couldn't ever remember feeling so warm and content, and she was sure that had way more to do with Carla than the wine.

She stared out the window at a cardinal hopping from limb to limb, basking in the pale yellow of the early morning light. His red plume was stark against the green leaves, keeping her attention. She was riveted by the colors, amused by his movements. He couldn't seem to remain still and yet he didn't seem sure as to where to go next. He just kept hopping from limb to limb.

His unsettlement struck her.

Somehow, to this cardinal, she could relate.

For she too, felt like she was hopping aimlessly from limb to limb. The more time she spent with Carla, the more demanding her attraction became. She was incredibly intelligent, which Janice had known, but visiting with her one-on-one for an extended amount of time had opened her eyes even more. Carla was well educated and well-read and she still had that insatiable thirst for knowledge she'd had as a kid.

Their conversations, some deep and intellectual, some funny and lighthearted, left her stimulated and intrigued and far from satisfied.

The physical appeal of her had been indomitable, along with what she had initially known about her, but they had nothing on the desire she felt now.

She wanted her.

Oh, yes, she did.

Mind, body, and soul.

She'd taken her to bed in her mind every night, as she often did, and grazed her fingertips along her own body while dreaming into the darkness. Knowing she was there, across the hall, a few steps away, was torturously arousing, and she'd slipped her hand between her legs on more than one occasion, bringing herself to climax quickly and powerfully, which helped to keep her in her own bed and away from Carla's.

And though she was trying to continue to hide her attraction, she knew Carla was picking up on it. She'd nailed her to the couch with her gentle but well-targeted questions and Janice had managed to squeeze through the walls of Carla's force field on that occasion, but she was certain Carla would pin her down again at some point.

For some reason, Carla wanted to know what she was thinking, what she was feeling. But Janice couldn't see what could come in telling her her deepest truth. If Carla was offering to lend an ear as a caring friend and only a caring friend, then she couldn't tell her. That might jeopardize their friendship. If she was offering to lend an ear as someone more than a friend, as someone who sensed and shared in Janice's feelings of attraction, she couldn't tell her then either. Carla had said she wasn't looking for love. She wasn't interested in another relationship.

Janice's suspicions of Carla's mutual attraction didn't matter. If Carla wasn't interested in love or relationships, then her interest in Janice was probably strictly physical. Merely sexual. And Janice wasn't sure she could have a casual affair with her, as wildly passionate as she presumed it would be, and then be perfectly fine when she left. She was highly doubtful she could, and she didn't know what that kind of heart break would do to her.

Carla wanting her like that though, looking at her the way she sometimes did, did things to Janice that kept her up most nights. Carla desiring her had seemed so farfetched not that long ago and to think it might be happening seemed absolutely surreal.

Was Carla really the type who could engage in casual affairs?

Janice had no way of knowing, no experience in any sort of relationship outside of her marriage. But there was a tiny twinge in the back of her mind that told her that wasn't who Carla was.

If that were true, then what would that imply about Carla's attraction to her?

She glanced back up at the cardinal, curious to see if had finally settled.

He was gone.

"Good morning," Carla said smoothly as she slid in next to her at the sink scooting her over. She, like Janice, was fresh from the shower and she smelled so good Janice's legs weakened.

"Morning."

Carla took the washed coffee mug from her and rinsed it. She smiled over at her with eyes that looked like liquid sunshine.

"You're not going to try to shoo me away from the sink, are you? Because I'll fight. Tooth and nail. I ain't scared of you no more. Well, not as scared as I was anyway."

"That's disappointing."

"Is it now? You prefer me fearing you?"

Janice laughed. "It has its advantages."

"Such as?"

"It keeps you in line. And you do as I say."

"Oh, I see. You like bossing me around. Making me do what you want."

Oh, dear Lord, the thoughts I'm having.

Janice dropped a plate, splashing soap bubbles onto her forearms and shirt. She could feel Carla watching her as she continued to wash, trying to appear unaffected.

"Did I ever thank you for dinner last night?" Carla teased her, changing the subject. "Because it was spectacular."

"Numerous times."

"Well, tack on another."

"I guess you weren't kidding about your love for Mexican food."

"More like my need. Love has been bypassed." She grinned. "Anyway, thank you. I was having withdrawals."

"It was no trouble. I'm glad you liked it."

"You went out of your way to make those enchiladas for me. Don't think I didn't notice."

"I may have felt a little bad for you," Janice said, passing her another dish. "So, I thought I'd give it a try to see if that would make you feel less homesick."

"You succeeded. And someday, when you come to Phoenix…" she paused and seemed to search for words. "If you ever come, I'll do the same for you." She cleared her throat and Janice was relieved she'd put the topic to rest. Reliving that conversation was not something she wished to do at the moment, and she'd been grateful when Carla hadn't broached the subject again.

Janice fumbled with a saucer.

"You're a really good cook," Carla said. "I love that. I love a lot of things about you." Her voice once again trailed off. She stared out the window and Janice wondered if she'd meant to say what she had. She spoke again and sounded playful.

"You're probably the most interesting person I've ever met." She nudged her.

Janice laughed. "You're laying it on thick now, Sims."

"No, I'm serious. I can talk to you about anything and everything and you somehow understand. If you don't, you're still empathetic and willing to listen. You're just so open-minded and you're willing and able to look at all sides to things and to try and understand from different viewpoints. That's brilliant, Janice. And I love it. Why do you think I sit and talk your ear off and ask you a million questions? I want to know what you know. I want to know your mind. I want to know you." She smiled. "I don't feel that way about many people."

Janice's heart pounded. She was so moved she could do nothing but stare down at her soapy hands.

"Did I upset you?" Carla asked.

"No," Janice said softly. "You didn't—"

"I always seem to upset you."

Janice could see the regret come over her face.

She struggled to explain. "You don't upset me, Carla. You…"

"What?"

"Move me. You make me…feel."

Carla slowly took the dish from her hand and rinsed it.

"Is that so bad?"

Janice dipped the last of the dinner dishes from the night before in the water and began to wash.

"No. It's…just different. No one has ever had that much interest in me, much less made me feel."

"Well, fuck them then." She nudged her again. Softly. "Isn't that what you said to me at the funeral?"

"I believe I did, yes."

"Did you mean it?"

"Yes."

"So, do I. Because as far as I'm concerned, Janice, anyone who's passed you by or let you get away is a fucking fool."

Janice dropped the bowl, this time while passing it to Carla, and it hit the center divider of the sink before it splashed into the water, causing a loud raucous.

"Shit, sorry." She went to retrieve it, but Carla stopped her by gently taking hold of her wrist. Neither of them moved and Janice's pulse became a hard, thudding one that caused her to tremble. Carla had to have felt it.

Oh, God. Will she pull away?

Would they continue on with this palpable unspoken attraction?

Carla answered her by slowly sliding her hand downward where her wet fingers glided into her palm. The move was so deliberate and profound, its eroticism was almost lost. *Almost.* But Janice definitely felt the tingle of her fingers along her sensitive palm. Every nerve ending in her hand stirred to life in the wake of her touch, and Janice couldn't help but gasp. Carla's delicate stroke feeling as if it were occurring some place far more intimate.

Carla had to know. She had to know exactly what she was doing. This touching, this careful sliding of her hand in hers? This was not the touch of a novice. And it was not a mishap or an accidental collision. This was the touch of a woman who knew women. It was being done with thought and purpose.

Carla wanted her.

There was no mistaking it now.

Oh, God, yes, Carla.

Take me.

Fucking take me.

"Carla," Janice whispered, desperate to say those words aloud. She looked at her, hoping she could see her need in her face.

But Carla's eyes were closed, and Janice watched her body shake as she exhaled.

Oh, dear God, she's as turned on as I am. She's feeling it too. Both of us wanting it so badly we're shaking.

"Carla."

"Just…give me a second. Just, please."

She slid her fingers up into Janice's where they weaved and caressed the sensitive inner edges, teasing and arousing. Janice clenched her eyes as a ravenous desire began to beat between her legs.

She couldn't take anymore. Her legs were failing her, and it was taking everything she had not to throw herself at Carla and beg for the mercy of her touch.

She tried to tell her. "Carla—"

"Forgive me," she said, stilling her hand.

Janice waited, listening to them both breathe, convinced she could hear both their heartbeats in the air between them until Carla spoke again.

"I—just wanted to know what your hand would feel like in mine."

Her words reached in and caressed her heart just like she'd managed to do with her hand. Romantics, poets, artists...nothing any of them had ever spoken or created compared to what she'd just heard from this woman.

"Carla," she said, trying to squeeze her hand.

"I better get going," she said, easing her hand from Janice and opening her eyes. The gold in her eyes was ablaze now. Glowing and burning. "I'll be—" Her words fell as she dropped her gaze to Janice's mouth, and allowed it to linger for a split second more. "Back this evening."

Janice wanted to reach out for her, take her in her arms and kiss her passionately. But Carla would resist her right now, she knew it. She could see it. As much as she obviously wanted Janice, there was something holding her back. Something that felt an awful lot like heartbreak and perhaps the fear of another one.

I'm not the only one who's scared.

That somehow made Janice less afraid.

Carla was vulnerable, unsure of acting on her feelings.

They were one and the same.

Carla turned to walk away just as Janice reached for her.

"Wait, don't go." *Not now. We should talk. Share. Confess. Love.*

Carla paused. "I need to, Janice. I can't stay here with you right now. I know you won't be able to understand why. Maybe someday you'll be able to." She headed for the doorway. "I'll see you tonight."

She disappeared and Janice heard the front door open and close. She dropped her hand and leaned back against the sink. She pressed the heel of her hand to her forehead, once again feeling like that crazy little cardinal.

She didn't know what to do.

Should she put her feelings on the back burner and just focus on keeping Carla comfortable and supporting her as best she could until she left?

Or should she carry on as is with her emotions and desires going up and down and all over the place with each and every encounter, with no promise of stability or rational end in sight?

To an outsider looking in, the choice would seem obvious. But she wasn't an observer in this situation, she was the one living it, feeling it.

And while putting her feelings for Carla on the back burner sounded like the wise thing to do, she knew, with what had just transpired, it would be absolutely impossible.

Because she felt more alive and aroused now, standing barefoot in the middle of her kitchen on an everyday average morning, than she ever had in her entire life.

Chapter Eighteen

Carla stood on Maurine's front porch balancing tomatoes in her arms while debating whether to knock or open the door and call out as she'd done for years. She never would've predicted she'd have to consider such a silly thing, but it was her new reality and at the moment, it felt like a vital choice.

She'd just come from Mr. Freeman's office and she'd been mulling over what he'd said.

Your grandmother didn't make this decision lightly, Carla. She trusted you implicitly and she had every faith that you would handle things properly and fairly. Your aunt and uncles, they've been through tough times, and she wasn't sure what the circumstances would be at the time of her death. She didn't do this to cause trouble, Carla, she did this to prevent it.

Those words were the reason why she'd decided to turn toward Maurine's for an impromptu visit. Her aunt and uncles hadn't had much to do with her recently and she wasn't sure if they'd even give her the time of day. But she had to try.

She took a deep breath, shifted the tomatoes, and knocked. Maurine's potted plants and flowers still outlined the porch, along with a ceramic dalmatian that had been passed down for decades and would no doubt continue to be. The bench swing she used to play on back when Great-uncle Lloyd lived in the house, squeaked as it swayed in the godsend of a breeze. She used to stand on it, hold the chains, and swing as hard and as high as she could, ignoring the warnings from her elders about the danger. She'd obeyed when they'd told her to stop, but as soon as they'd disappeared, she'd been right back at it, until one day she'd pushed a little too far and she and the swing had flipped, dumping her headfirst on the edge of the concrete porch and onto the grass a few feet below. She hadn't cried until she'd touched her head and saw all the blood. By the time Uncle Lloyd had reached her it was cascading down her forehead and face. That little escapade had resulted in seven stitches and several licks from a hickory switch. But she still liked to think that all the fun she'd had riding that swing had been worth it.

She smiled to herself as the breeze brought a hint of another afternoon thunderstorm. The thought of Janice and of being alone with her again in the dark during a storm, possibly even tonight, helped to keep her current anxieties at bay.

The door opened cautiously, and Maurine looked at her through the flimsy screen door. The door, like the swing, were things Maurine had yet to update on the old house and Carla was somewhat grateful. She liked coming back and finding things to be exactly like they were when she left. Like now, she wished things with Maurine were like they used to be. But in taking just a quick glance at her, Carla could see that they weren't. Her eyes were distant beneath a faded Myrtle Beach ball cap. Carla surmised she'd been sunning on the red wood deck by the purple bikini top and cutoff jeans she wore. It didn't take long for the scent of suntan lotion to come through the screen.

"Hey," Carla said softly.

"Hey." She sounded tired, and her face was drawn and void of any emotion, like she had lost the energy to battle or to even feel for that matter. The fight and fire she'd always had seemed to be gone, leaving her soul vacant. It struck Carla hard.

She swallowed down tears.

"I, uh, picked your ripe tomatoes for you. Your plants were pretty weighed down."

Maurine pushed open the screen.

"Thanks." She took the tomatoes.

Carla hesitated with the hopes of being invited inside. When she wasn't, her nervousness grew and she had the urge to flee, the fear of facing another rejection all too reminiscent. But she'd come to talk, and Nadine was right, running wasn't going to solve anything.

"I see you've still got your green thumb," Carla said looking back at the thriving flower pots and numerous plants. It was a silly thing to say, but Carla was desperate to keep her engaged.

She shrugged. "I reckon."

Carla shifted, the wait for the invite driving her mad.

"Uh, would it be all right if I came in?" She slid her hands into the back pockets of her knee length denim shorts and rocked on her heels.

Maurine didn't hesitate very long before she shrugged again. "Yeah." She edged the door open farther and Carla entered and followed her through the house to Maurine's carefully decorated country kitchen. Gooseflesh erupted on her skin from the powerful cold of the windowed air conditioner wedged above the sink. Maurine didn't seem bothered by it as she rinsed the tomatoes and placed them on a paper towel to dry.

Carla's close assessment of her revealed a slack to her normally strong posture. The skin below her eyes appeared dark and sunken. She'd also lost weight. Her shorts hung lower on her already thin frame, and the shoulder straps to her bikini kept slipping down her arms, evidently irritating her. She cussed under her breath every time she had to push them back up. Her fair skin was pink from the sun, especially along her shoulders and cheeks, which was the only color to her pallor. Maurine didn't have the olive skin tone Carla and Betty had, so when she was depressed or down, she paled considerably. Maybe that was why she was risking sunburn to lounge in the sun. To give herself some color. That would be the only reason Carla could come up with as to why Maurine would forego protecting her creamy skin.

"Mind if I get a drink?" Carla asked as Maurine sliced into a juicy tomato.

"Help yourself."

Carla yanked open the old fridge and retrieved two cans of Pepsi. She shook her head and smiled. She could always count on Maurine to have two things in her kitchen. Pepsi and peanut butter.

The main staples of their childhood. A twelve-pack of Pepsi was chilling in the fridge and Carla figured a jar of Peter Pan peanut butter would surely be in the pantry. She had the urge to check and see, seeking some sort of nostalgic comfort to dull the nerves of the moment. She resisted and set a can of Pepsi down for Maurine, who eyed it but continued to cut the tomato. Carla slurped her soda and retrieved the Duke's mayonnaise and loaf of white bread and set them next to Maurine's drink. Maurine promptly dug out four pieces of bread, spread mayonnaise on all of them, and then carefully added the tomato slices. She salted the slices generously before finishing off the sandwiches with a press of her palm to the bread tops.

She handed Carla her sandwich on a paper plate and quickly cleaned up.

"Thank you." Carla knew she shouldn't be surprised at her silent generosity, but she was. The gesture stirred more tears, but she managed to hold them down.

Maurine took her plate and drink and walked to the back door. Carla followed and they stepped into the thick heat onto the deck. She sat across from Maurine in a flower-patterned lounge chair, slid down her shades from their position atop her head, and bit into her sandwich. Maurine did the same. They were under the cover of two oversized patio umbrellas that Maurine had most likely recently positioned for a refuge from the sun. An old radio with a wayward antenna was next to her chair, promising thirty minutes of uninterrupted hit songs from the eighties. The music, along with the coconut scent of the sun screen, brought back summers from long ago when Carla used to lie out on the deck with Maurine and Janice. She'd felt so special, so grown up. They'd always included her when she'd asked and sometimes, she didn't even have to. She recalled Janice, stretched out on her chair in a black bikini, the Wayfarers she'd saved her money for looking stylish on her face, while Maurine read fashion magazines under the cover of the umbrella, her own hot pink designer shades on her face. Carla could remember feeling a little excited at seeing Janice in her bikini, but she hadn't understood why. She'd just known she liked looking at her. Liked looking at every last bit of her.

She missed those days.

When the three of them were happy and enjoyed each other.

Now everything was so messed up. Maurine wasn't even spending a lot of time with Janice.

"I miss you," Carla said, sipping her soda.

Maurine chewed on a bite from her sandwich, staring straight ahead through the oversized lenses of her trendy sunglasses.

"Don't you miss me?" Her silence was maddening.

Maurine sipped her own drink. "I don't feel much of anything these days."

Carla's heart sank and she wasn't sure what to say. She let the silence seep in between them. After a short while, she heard the clamoring of claws on the deck steps. Magpie, the neighborhood Labrador who seemed to belong to no one and everyone, emerged with his black and pink tongue hanging low and his sizable butt wiggling. His short curve of a tail swatted the air rapidly and seemed to be the power supply to his dancing hind end.

"Hey, boy." Carla held out her hand and he sauntered to her. She rubbed his thick head which was warm from the sun. He had the smell of free-roaming hound on him along with a wet and mud coated underside. Both gave away his recent and favorite activities of chasing wild animals, rubbing and rolling himself on dead ones, and trouncing aimlessly through the creek. She was surprised but grateful he hadn't brought one of his treasures along with him. He was known to collect and hoard his goods, hence his name. She pulled apart her sandwich and fed it to him, unsure as to when he last ate. When he finished, he collapsed in a shaded corner and cleaned his paws.

Carla turned her attention back to Maurine and followed her line of sight through the deck railing to the hilly fields beyond. She could just barely see the sparkles from the twinkling of the creek water at the far end. She was always so moved by the beauty of the Sims land.

"I'm sorry to hear that," she finally said to Maurine. "I'm sorry for a lot of things." She paused, waiting for a response from Maurine but got nothing. "I've been doing a lot of thinking lately though, about all this stuff and I want to run some things by you. I came by today to see if you would hear me out."

Maurine swallowed another bite. "I don't know. I don't want to get upset again. I…I just can't cry anymore. I don't have any cry left in me. Do you know what happens when you don't have any cry left? The pain still tries to get out, only it can't, not with tears anyway. And you find yourself wishing for tears of all things. For the ability to cry. But nothing happens. Nothing changes. You come close to crying sometimes. But, well, we all know close don't count in nothing but horseshoes and hand grenades."

More silence ensued and Carla felt like she'd just been gutted, and Maurine appeared just as morose, having tossed her plate and what was left of her sandwich aside. She sat with her arms crossed over her chest but didn't quite pull off angry and defiant. Her body was too weighted down with sadness for that, her face too drawn.

"I'm so sorry you're hurting so badly, Maurine." It killed her to think of Maurine crying at all. She was always so strong, so formidable. Hearing she'd cried so much that she no longer could continue, hurt her beyond measure. "I can't make what's happened go away. I can't bring Grandma back and I can't take away your pain. I can do one thing, though. Which is what I want to talk about. But first, there's something else I need to tell you. Something I don't think you're aware of."

Maurine glanced over at her, but she didn't show any interest.

"It's about the will." Carla went on. "Grandma didn't write that will recently. She wrote it ten years ago."

Maurine shrugged. "What does that matter?"

"Maurine, think about where everyone was at in their lives ten years ago. You were going through a nightmare of a divorce, your house was at the constant threat of foreclosure because Clint wouldn't pay his half of the mortgage payment on time, you were scared of both him and your future, and you weren't sure where you were going to live."

"Cole was in a deep depression because his wife had left him, and Erica had just been in that awful car wreck and was recovering. He was also having trouble with his job which he eventually lost and was unemployed for two months. He had to live with Grandma for close to a year before he got back on his feet."

"And Rick, Jesus," Carla said.

"That's when he hurt his back at the sawmill."

Carla nodded and kept talking.

"He was laid up for six months. In horrible pain. His girlfriend took pretty good care of him until she said she couldn't do it anymore and left. You ended up moving in with him. Helped you both out I guess."

"But do you remember the worst part of it all?"

Carla continued.

"Rick got mad at Cole. He blamed him when his girlfriend left him because she then went after Cole. Cole didn't do anything wrong, but Rick didn't believe it."

"They didn't speak for months." Carla studied her, hoping she was reaching her. "Remember?"

Maurine swung her legs over the side of the lounge chair to face Carla and threaded her hands together on top of her head.

"Our lives were a disaster," she said, removing her sunglasses. Her eyes were serious and sad and finally absent of resentment. "I didn't even think about any of that." She looked at Carla for a long moment, then swallowed and glanced away. "You were the only stable one she had."

Carla responded softly, so relieved that she'd reached her. "At the time, yes."

She was quiet for another long moment. "I'm so sad for her now. She must've been worried sick about what to do. So, she did the only thing that made sense. The safest thing."

"She knew I would do my best to do right by everyone. And I'm going to. I don't know how ya'll could've ever thought anything different of me."

Maurine studied her and seemed to be moved by the emotion she saw on Carla's face. She got up and took the few steps to embrace her where she sat. She pulled Carla to her waist and held her.

"I'm sorry, Carla. I'm sorry. I was—we were hurt and confused, but we should've never turned on you over it. We're—I'm just so stupid sometimes."

Carla teared up a little then. Her cheek pressed against both the warm, freckled skin of Maurine's abdomen and the rough denim of her shorts. When she pulled away, she wiped at what was left of the moisture from her tears and Maurine's suntan lotion.

"Families tend to get that way in these sorts of matters," Carla said, swinging her legs over the side of her chair to make room for Maurine.

Maurine sat next to her and helped Carla remove her sunglasses. She looked into her eyes.

"Can you ever forgive me?"

Carla nodded. "Silly, I already have."

Maurine smiled and her eyes welled with tears.

"Hey, look, you've got tears," Carla said.

"I do, don't I?" She took a finger and swept some away. "I don't think I've ever been so happy to cry."

"Me neither," Carla said. "Somehow these tears feel good."

They both laughed softly, and Maurine shook her head. "Lord, I wonder what Mama's looking down and thinking about all this."

"Oh, she's pissed. There's no doubt about that."

"She'd give us all an earful, wouldn't she?"

"Would? She's already doing it. Can't you hear her? She's telling us all to stop this shit and get on with our lives."

Maurine looked up at the approaching storm clouds. "She's the only one I know who could go to heaven and still raise hell."

Carla laughed and wrapped an arm around her neck. "You got that right." She looked up at the sky with her. "Now it's time to make everything else right." Tiny icy drops of rain pricked her face. She grinned.

"We hear you, Grandma. We hear you."

Chapter Nineteen

"Oh, no," Janice said as large raindrops splattered onto the pavement around them. "It's coming down again." She looked to Carla to see if she was concerned. She wasn't. She appeared to be just as happy as she had been when she'd walked in the front door an hour ago, greeted her with a loud, and boisterous hello and hurried off to shower and change.

"I know, and it's fantastic."

The rain fell a little harder. Janice instinctively cowered and searched for cover.

"We're going to have to run home." She pulled on Carla's hand, but Carla didn't budge. She merely smiled.

"Carla, come on." Thunder rolled through the dark gray clouds. They were still a good ways from the house. She'd been worried about getting caught in the lingering storm, but Carla had been so eager to go for a long walk, she hadn't been able to resist. Her cheerful mood was infectious, and as they'd trekked through the trail in the nearby woods, she'd filled her in on the catalyst for her newfound joy. She'd finally made amends with her family.

Carla resisted her and then tugged her in closer.

"Haven't you ever walked in the rain?" she asked, glancing up into the sky. She held out her palm and closed her eyes. The rain pelted her face and she laughed. "It's the best thing ever."

"But you just showered."

"I had sunscreen on me. It was greasy." She held out her palms, catching the drops. "Getting rained on is marvelous, not something I'd ever consider to be a nuisance, having just showered or not."

"It's cold," Janice said. She was only halfheartedly complaining. Carla was enjoying their predicament and seeing her so lighthearted and excited was wonderful and a long time coming.

"Cold?" Carla looked at her like she was crazy. "Come here." She pulled her closer and wrapped her arm around her shoulders. "Better?"

Janice nodded, instantly lost in her eyes and the firm warmth of her body. She could've taken her anywhere through any kind of force of nature and Janice would've let her. They hadn't spoken about what had happened at the sink and Janice thought about bringing it up now. Carla had acted like nothing at all had happened so she wasn't sure how to broach the topic and she had no idea what bringing it up would lead to.

For whatever reason, Carla was resisting her obvious attraction. Janice's guess was that it was due to the painful end of her most recent relationship. That was the likeliest of possibilities. The betrayal and hurt were probably still wreaking havoc on her heart, which was why she'd voiced her disdain for future relationships. Which, sadly, would include a relationship with Janice. But if perhaps those feelings of aversion were changing due to Carla's attraction to her, which could be the case, or Janice at least *wanted* that to be the case. Then Carla would be just as anxious about that happening than she was about love and relationships to begin with. The thought of trusting someone again was probably terrifying.

And I'm not exactly an out and experienced lesbian. Or any sort of lover with a lot of experience for that matter. Nor do I live close to her home. And let's not forget that I'm her aunt's best friend. God, is there anything else that can be piled on to this heap of deterrence?

They walked on through the rain with Carla smiling up into the sky from time to time. Thunder continued to grumble, keeping them company. The rain was constant but cooperative, holding back a heavy assault. The evening air had cooled, making for a pleasant stroll.

"It's going to take some more time for us to wrap up Grandma's affairs," Carla said, her eyes on the path ahead. "We have to decide how to divide everything and more paperwork will have to be drawn up."

She grew quiet and Janice wasn't sure if she was waiting for her to respond.

"I need to make sure you're okay with that."

"Why wouldn't I be?"

"Because it means I need to remain here in North Carolina a little longer."

She grew quiet again. Janice sensed her unease.

"If you're asking if you can continue to stay with me, then the answer is yes. Of course. For as long as you want. I'd hoped you would know that by now."

"It wouldn't be right for me not to make sure."

Janice enveloped her waist and pulled her closer, loving the feel of Carla's arm still resting along her shoulders.

"That was mighty polite of you, Ms. Sims. But not necessary."

They were approaching the edge of the woods. The house was in sight.

"And you don't need to thank me again, either."

Carla looked at her. "Oh, that I know, trust me. I wouldn't dare do that at this point."

"I'm glad to hear you've finally wised up. 'Bout time."

Carla squeezed her and the rain began to fall harder. Janice didn't panic or try to hurry them along. She stuck to her side, wanting their walk in the evening rain to last for all time.

They reached the house with wet heads and damp shoulders. Carla held open the screen while Janice stood hunched at the door, fumbling with the keys. Her fingers were slick, and she was too aware of Carla's close proximity. She couldn't seem to find the right key.

"Damn it."

Then she felt Carla's gentle hand on hers, and the keys nearly slid from her grip. She got caught up in her eyes, though, and Carla carefully took the keys and unlocked the door with ease. She motioned for Janice to enter first.

"Thanks." Janice was headed to the bedroom to change, feeling an absolute fool when Carla stopped her.

"No, don't," she said softly. "Don't go change."

Janice turned, confused.

"But we're wet," Janice said.

"I like it," she said. "Don't you? It feels good. Like I'm brand new." She tousled her hair. Her face fell when Janice didn't agree.

"Oh, I forgot you're cold. Never mind then."

"You're not?"

Carla shook her head. "Nah."

"Because I can get you a towel at least."

"I'm good." She turned toward the kitchen and Janice hurried to her bedroom to quickly change and comb her hair. When she returned to the living room the wine and glasses were on the table and Carla was lighting the candles.

"Just in case," she said with a wink. She handed Janice a full glass and smiled at her as she sank into her usual spot on the love seat.

They relaxed and began to talk as they drank. After the first glass the storm intensified with heavy rain and formidable thunder and lightning. As they finished a second glass the lights went out. Carla was busy pouring them a third when Janice noticed the effect the alcohol was having on her.

"You look so different now. So happy," Janice said. "I can't believe the change from yesterday to today."

A smile spread across her face and it looked so loose and easy Janice wondered if it might actually slide off. She couldn't help but laugh.

"You look downright drunk," Janice added.

"That's because I *am* downright drunk. I'm allowing myself one last night of drink. Then, I'm done. I'm back to drinking upon rare occasion." She held her wine glass out for a toast. "But here's to tonight. To me for somehow making things right, to you for graciously seeing me through, and most especially, to fucked up families everywhere, may you sort out your problems simply because you're too tired to keep up the fight."

"Hear, hear." They clanked glasses and drank. Janice felt warm and content. She brushed her hair back from her cheek and became conscience of her appearance. Carla, of course, looked as sexy as ever in her Human Being T-shirt, which was damp and clinging to her body, black athletic shorts, and androgynous hand-tousled hair. Janice, however, worried she didn't look as appealing.

That worry was soon doused by Carla intently staring at her as she sipped her wine. Though she'd caught her doing that several times during her stay, tonight felt different. The heavy weight of her family drama had been lifted from her, and everything in her had come to life. It was like watching a flower garden grow on high speed. Happiness, relief, and joy had just sprouted. Seeing her this way was a sight to behold and Janice felt very lucky to be witnessing it.

Carla, however, appeared to be caught up in her. She seemed to be riveted.

Janice lowered her glass and saw Carla's eyes travel up and down her body. When her eyes finally returned to gaze back into her own, Janice could see and feel the fiery inferno of her desire. It was as if Carla had touched her skin with her eyes, running delicate fingers up and down her body.

"I'm staring again aren't I?" Carla asked.

The confession was familiar. It seemed Carla's inhibitions were easily drowned in wine, paving the way for forthright behavior and declarations.

Janice cleared her throat. "Yes." She was flattered by the attention and aroused at the hunger she could see in her. Carla was less stressed now and coming at her from a place of confidence and emotional clarity. It made Janice feel truly desired and she hadn't been afraid to answer her honestly and admit her acknowledgment.

"I have an excuse, however," Carla said, pointing at the bottles on the coffee table. "The wine, you see, has soaked into the pores of my exhausted sponge of a brain, leaving me somewhat vulnerable to behaving by the terms of my default setting."

"Your default setting?"

She grinned again and leaned in like she was about to share a secret.

"You know, acting on my very strong propensity for women. Beautiful, intelligent women."

Oh, that. Okay.

No big deal.

She's only blatantly flirting with me.

Janice rubbed the armrest with her fingertips, Carla's stare intense. But she held her ground, her courage having grown from all the time they'd spent together. She volleyed her serve, putting the ball back in her court.

"Are you always so articulate when you drink?"

She laughed. "According to my friend Nadine."

Carla continued to stare at her, and Janice continued to feel it whether she was focused on the armrest or not.

"You don't appear amused," Carla said.

Janice felt the corner of her mouth lift.

"Actually, I am. You're a well-spoken drunk. That's rather unusual I think."

"I bet you are as well. Come to think of it, you've had just as much to drink as I have and yet you don't even seem buzzed."

"I drink more often than you, Carla. I have wine almost every night."

"Alone?"

She looked up at her. "Yes."

"That's not right," she said.

"You mentioned you prefer being alone when taking in jazz with a glass of wine."

"I did, didn't I?"

"Is it not true?"

"It's true. It's just not really what I prefer. Well, not especially."

"What do you prefer?"

She looked at her for a long moment. "This."

"This?"

"Drinking wine with a beautiful woman next to me. Sharing the moment with her, engaging, connecting."

She continued to look at her and Janice had to glance away because she now wanted to react to the rampant need she was exuding even though Carla's motives were still unknown. She was about to get up, shove her back against the love seat, straddle her, and conquer her with a deep, searing kiss. It no longer mattered that she'd never been with a woman. She wanted Carla and she knew what she wanted to do to her.

It wasn't rocket science.

"Tell me, Janice. Is that what you really prefer also?"

Janice felt her skin heat.

"Which part?"

"All of it."

Janice sipped her wine, attempting to play it cool. But she doubted she was fooling anyone.

"It sounds nice."

"Like something you might like? Something you might want to experience?"

Janice finally met her gaze. "I am experiencing it. And I do like it. Very much."

Carla seemed taken aback by her honesty.

"Even though I'm a woman?"

"Yes, Carla."

"You wouldn't rather be doing this with a man? One you found attractive and interesting?"

Janice laughed a little. "No, I wouldn't. I would rather be here with you."

"Why?"

Janice laughed again, trying to hide her discomfort. "Geez, Carla."

"I want to know."

"Because I think you are interesting. And—"

Carla raised her eyebrows, waiting.

"Attractive."

She didn't respond. She just kept watching her.

"Satisfied?" Janice asked, taking another sip.

"No. Not even close."

"Why am I not surprised?"

"What do you mean by that?"

"That you never seem to be satisfied with my answers."

"That's because I'm not."

"Why?" Janice turned the tables.

Carla didn't even hesitate. "Because you don't tell me everything. And when it comes to you, I can't seem to settle for knowing anything less than everything."

Oh, I did not expect that.

"I wish you felt comfortable enough to truly confide in me like I do you."

Janice swirled the wine in her glass and thought about downing the remainder, wondering just how long it would take to calm her racing heart.

"You don't confide everything to me, Carla. You tell me a lot. But not everything."

"I'm more open than you are."

Janice took two large swallows of her drink. "I would have no way of knowing that, would I?"

"You know," Carla said softly. "You are way too perceptive and intuitive to claim ignorance." She drank more wine and then gave the glass a look of disdain. She set it on the table and ran her hands through her hair as she sat back and sighed. "I need to leave you alone. Stop with all the questions. I need to go to bed."

Please, don't. Not yet. I can't bear the thought of you walking away.

"You're fine, Carla."

"Yeah, right, I'm fine."

"You are."

"And you are—beautiful."

She burned a stare into Janice that was even more powerful than her sudden statement. Janice reacted with a pulse she was certain Carla could see and her skin was so hot and sensitive she was certain she'd come very close to dying at the slightest of touch. Carla had flipped a switch in her and everything she'd tried so hard to keep in check was crashing through and no longer was it possible to hide.

"That's why I can't ever seem to stop looking at you," Carla said. "That's why I didn't want you to change when we came in from the rain. I like the way you look when you're—wet. Like the way you looked that day when you found me in your bedroom. I like it a lot. But honestly, Janice, I like the way you look all the time."

Janice gripped the armrest. She stared right back into her. Nothing and no one could've made her stop. But the hunger in Carla dimmed slightly. Her eyes tried to close. She gripped her forehead.

"Fuck." She was trying to fight back against her fatigue, blinking and widening her eyes. "I'm not going to make it much longer. So, please, hear me now, okay? I need you to hear me."

Janice swallowed. "Okay."

"I've always been in awe of you, Janice. In awe of your beauty, your intelligence, your heart. I don't know why I never said so. I don't know why I didn't face that within myself. I don't even know why I'm telling you now when I know I probably shouldn't. I just suddenly feel compelled to tell you. I just suddenly feel like you should know. You should've always known."

Janice couldn't breathe and she touched her throat as she spoke. "Carla, I—"

"It shouldn't have mattered that you probably wouldn't ever have felt the same about me. It shouldn't have. I probably feared that. I probably feared that rejection and feared losing your friendship over my feelings because they made you uncomfortable. Hell, I fear those things now. But I can't let that fear stop me. You are incredible and you need to know that."

She glanced down at the coffee table.

"I'm not going to make a move on you or anything. I wouldn't— do that." She blinked again against the fall of her heavy eyelids. Her head tried to tilt back but she recovered. "Not unless…not unless… you don't have to worry." Her speech was fading along with the meaning of her last sentence.

Janice replied quickly, knowing she was slipping away.

"I would never ever worry about that, Carla. Actually, my feelings are quite the contrary."

Carla blinked at her and Janice waited, agonizing, wondering if she had enough clarity in her to make sense of what she'd just said.

"I don't—" She blinked some more, her eyes on the brink of closing for good. "Understand."

"Carla." Janice leaned toward her, knowing she was losing her. "I *want* you to make a move on me."

Carla's eyes closed and her head limped to the side. Janice tapped her arm. "Carla? Carla?"

No, no, no, no. Not now.

She stepped over her feet and sat next to her. She touched her face, gently turned her toward her.

"Carla?"

"Wha?" Her eyes opened halfway and fell shut again.

"Wonderful. I finally tell you the truth and you aren't even conscious." She sighed. "Another repeat of your first night here."

"Janice," she whispered. She opened her eyes again and tried to keep them that way. But it appeared to be a great struggle. "Janice." She took Janice's hand and placed it on her upper thigh. The firm feel of her lean muscle and hot skin caused Janice to close her own eyes.

Carla pressed down on her hand.

"I haven't been touched—so long," she said.

Janice shivered and looked at her. Honey colored slits of iris reflected the candlelight. Her hand controlled Janice's, attempting to move it up and down her thigh. Janice grazed her fingertips slowly up her leg and then back down.

Carla made a sound and bit her lower lip. Her delight was obvious and Janice nearly groaned, completely moved in knowing she was making her feel this way. But she couldn't continue.

Carla made another noise, this one of longing and disappointment. She tightened her grip on Janice's wrist.

"Please."

Janice spoke softly in her ear. "I can't."

Carla moaned and tried to open her eyes. She mumbled and then said two words again, very clearly.

"Touch me."

Janice fought for breath and some semblance of sanity. Her lust for Carla, to touch her, to make her feel good, was mere seconds away from drowning the sparse amount of rationality left in her mind.

Carla pressed on her hand as if she knew Janice was hesitating. "Janice. I want you—"

Oh, my fucking God. She was so tempted it literally hurt, her chest tightening like a vice. She pulled away, panicked by the temptation she had to give in to her.

Carla been through so much and she'd finally come through the other end. Now all that stress and heartache was leaving her, and she no longer had to carry it. Her mind and body were exhausted, but they were giving it one last hoorah in trying to get Janice for some needed touch and affection before finally shutting down. But she couldn't do it. If and when she ever got to touch Carla intimately, she wanted her fully awake and focused on her. She wanted to look into her eyes and watch her face as pleasure coursed through her. She wanted to talk to her, engage with her and listen to her cries. To have all that, she'd wait an eternity if she had to.

She stood and tugged on her arms. "Time to get you to bed, darlin.'"

Carla groaned in obvious defiance but managed to stumble to her feet.

They made it down the hall arm in arm and Carla collapsed onto her bed before Janice could ease her down. She clung to Janice, refusing to release her.

"Stay," she said. "Here with me."

She pulled on Janice's arm.

"I can't, Carla."

Not tonight. Not with you in this condition.

Carla curled up on her side and attempted to open her eyes. When she seemed to focus on Janice, she let out a laugh, surprising her.

"So stupid. I'm so stupid." She curled herself tighter. "Love hurts. Always gonna hurt. I can't..." Her eyes fell closed. "Hurt anymore."

Janice winced, her chest now tightening around her heart. The words came from pain, from within Carla, and now they were infiltrating her, causing more. She'd been right all along. Carla's feelings for her couldn't combat the lingering damage to her heart.

Despite the way they both felt about one another, it couldn't happen. To pursue anything further would ultimately only cause more pain.

To her.

And to Carla.

But it was devastating to finally concede it.

She covered Carla with a blanket. Then she knelt and kissed her just below her ear.

"Sweet dreams, Stargazer."

Chapter Twenty

"Can I get one of those?"

Janice's voice came to Carla from behind as she handed a lit sparkler to Erica's son, Victor. He grinned and bounded off after his brother, Denny, who was holding his sparkler high in the air. Carla smiled after them and straightened, turning her attention to her next customer, Janice.

"Sure." Carla pulled a sparkler from the box on the folding table. "But you have to promise to keep it away from your eyes and you can't put it close to your skin or anyone else's."

"Gosh, I don't know, then." She slid her hand into her white cotton shorts as the side of her mouth lifted in the playful grin that now made Carla's insides melt. Her eyes were already sparkling, making her request for one she could hold in her hand pointless. Their color was set off by her patriotic blue halter top covered in small white stars, appropriate wear for the Fourth of July festivities. Her face and shoulders were newly sun-kissed and slightly red. Her hair was in a ponytail which Carla understood due to the heavy heat, but she couldn't help but imagine reaching up to pull it free from the bind so the heavy waves could fall around her face.

It was a longing Carla had endured throughout the day as she'd spotted her off and on. She'd mostly seen her with Maurine, which Carla had been glad to see, considering how little time they'd spent together lately. Maurine, Carla knew all too well, had distanced herself from Janice for the majority of Carla's stay, even though the person she'd truly been upset with was Carla. But that was Maurine. She always reacted first and thought later. And though she was insecure at times and had a stubborn streak a mile long, when it came right down to it, she'd readily lay her life on the line for those she loved. Carla loved her for that. And she suspected Janice did too.

"Them's the rules, I'm afraid," Carla said. She held the sparkler up, waiting for her to decide.

Janice shook her head. "I better not, then." She motioned toward Val. "He might want one."

"Yeah," Carla said, eyeing him. "But he's a little busy right now." They watched Val as he sat feeding Magpie spoonfuls of soupy homemade ice cream. Magpie waited patiently, tail sweeping the ground, as Val concentrated on keeping the ice cream in the spoon as he aimed it toward his furry friend. He didn't seem to be doing it quickly enough for Magpie, though. The dog drooled and hurriedly attacked the spoon before Val even had it halfway to him. Val fussed at him, but Magpie paid him no mind, cleaning what was dropped on the ground and on Val's knee as he waited for another bite.

"Everyone seems to have liked your banana ice cream," Janice said. "Even the dog."

"Thanks, that makes me feel so good."

"Well, if it means anything, I liked it. I thought it was very good. Better than what I buy at the store."

Carla smirked. "It should be. It's got enough salt and sugar in it to kill an elephant."

Janice chuckled. "So, that's your secret."

"Not my secret. Great-uncle Lloyd's. Apparently, salt and sugar intake weren't things they concerned themselves with in his day."

Val shrieked with glee as Magpie knocked the empty bowl from his hand, cleaned it, and then started in on cleaning his bare chest and chin. Carla picked up the bowl, took the spoon from Val, and smacked his behind playfully as he took off to go wash up as she'd instructed. She tossed the bowl and spoon in the trash and got rid of the stickiness by rubbing her hands together. She smoothed down her white T-shirt with a faded American flag on the front and her khaki shorts, pleased they, too, were void of ice cream stains.

"They knew a good thing when they had it," Janice said. "They didn't worry about the rest. That's probably something we should all do a little more." She was looking out across the lawn where the grill Rick was manning still smoked with cooking burgers and hotdogs and kids ran and giggled while the adults lounged in chairs as they ate and chatted.

Carla removed her sunglasses, folded them closed and slid them into the collar of her shirt. The sun was finally turning in after a long, hot day of celebration and the nightly festivities were soon to begin. Rick and Cole already had the fireworks ready to go for everyone's immediate, personal entertainment, and the church just down the road would provide the larger, more professional fireworks for everyone when they began their show.

Janice, when it came to Carla, had been MIA, and Carla still wasn't positive, but she'd been wondering if she'd been purposely avoiding her.

She'd been unusually quiet the past few days despite their evening talks, which were still as thoughtful and lighthearted as they'd always been during Carla's stay. And when they weren't talking, they were sitting together on the couch, watching a movie, sharing a bowl of popcorn, their hands sometimes suspiciously colliding, causing quick laughs and quiet apologies. Of course for Carla, they caused so much more. Neither of them took it further, however. They just settled in closer, bodies pressed together as if neither wanted to ever separate.

That closeness had developed into a comforting familiarity. They had become intuitive, knowing what the other preferred, needed, or often times even felt, resulting in a competition of generosity. They did for each other, both happy and eager to give and help where the other was concerned. Carla couldn't ever remember feeling so well known and cared for and she was feeling so content, her longing to return home had lessened, almost to where she avoided thinking about having to return when the time came.

"Was there a deeper meaning to that statement?" Carla asked, once again pushing the thought of leaving from her mind.

Janice looked at her curiously but didn't answer.

"You sounded sad and then you got all quiet on me."

"Oh." She shrugged. "I haven't really thought about it."

Carla shook her head. "There's something about that answer that I still don't believe, regardless of how many times you say it. I know you pretty well now, Janice. You don't seem to say things that profound without having given it a lot of thought."

"Maybe you're reading into things that aren't there. Or maybe you don't know me as well as you think."

Carla sensed she'd taken offense. That, too, made her wonder. She knew something happened the night they'd walked in the rain, bits and pieces had come to her and the eroticism that had accompanied those pieces had made it difficult for her to believe they'd really occurred. But she hadn't dreamt them, and they felt way too real to have come from her imagination. Something had definitely happened, and those sporadic seconds of recall suggested that she'd finally voiced her feelings to Janice and Janice hadn't exactly run away. Carla wasn't certain, though she'd thought about that evening time and again, hoping to remember, but she had the feeling that Janice may have confessed something of her own.

Janice's behavior the two days following had fed Carla's suspicion. She had been quieter, more introspective. She hadn't been distant though. Just more...serious. Her smile seemed shy and she seemed to be very conscious of their proximity. When they were close or when they came into contact, she seemed nervous, and even a little jumpy. As if touching Carla were equivalent to touching a hot pan.

Now there was this...defiance. This challenge. Janice was facing off with her.

Could it be because her grandmother's affairs were finally settled? She'd informed her of that, relieved and grateful it was finally over. Janice had seemed happy for her, but now that Carla thought about it, her mood change had begun after that.

Carla considered shaking off her challenging comment, to just move on and enjoy the holiday. But something about the way Janice was looking at her, like she was *daring* her to engage with her on this, made her decide to do otherwise.

"Maybe you don't realize just how well I do know you. Or maybe you refuse to acknowledge it."

"What are you implying?" she asked, finally meeting her gaze.

"I'm not implying anything. I'm *telling* you I know you very well."

"And I'm telling you that you don't. You don't know my thoughts or my feelings."

Carla laughed. "Yes, regarding some things, I believe I do. Even if you haven't admitted them to yourself."

Janice's brow furrowed, and for the first time in years, Carla saw anger in her.

"What things? What thoughts and feelings of mine do you think you know about?"

"You really want to do this here? You do, don't you. It's why you're facing off with me like this. You want things said. You need them out in the open. Because this dance between us, these unspoken feelings and your hiding, you can't do it anymore. And frankly, neither can I. So, yes, Janice I'm pretty sure I know what you're thinking and feeling when it comes to some things."

"Such as?" She didn't even blink, but her cheeks were scarlet and her eyes too seeking to be hard with anger.

"Love," Carla let out.

Janice scoffed.

"Desire," Carla added.

She crossed her arms over her chest and tried to appear unaffected, but she was clearly shaken. Carla saw it all.

"You're full of shit, Carla Sims. You don't know how I feel about those things," she whispered looking away.

"Don't I?"

She wouldn't look at her.

"I do know what you're feeling, Janice. And I know exactly what it is you want."

"Yeah, and what's that?" She finally looked at her, eyes narrowed.

"Me."

The word seemed to hit her eyes first. The accusatory and disbelieving look she'd had just a split second before, was replaced with the shock of cognizance and exposure. She pressed her lips together, swallowed, and swayed ever so slightly. Carla braced her upper arm and she stiffened and forced back her shoulders.

She'd been unmasked, which was what she'd intended to have happen with her confrontation, even if she hadn't consciously been aware of it. But there it was. It was out now, and she was overwhelmed at the suddenness of it. Carla had to give her credit, though. She was doing her best to recover quickly.

"Do you have any idea how self-righteous and sanctimonious you sound right now? You don't know everything, Carla."

"So, you're saying I'm wrong?"

She started to reply but stammered.

"Why won't you just admit it? To me, to yourself. You hint at it at times. Throw me crumbs that I can see and sense, but then you backpedal. Why can't you accept your feelings, Janice? Why are you denying yourself the freedom to feel? Are you afraid to admit that you have feelings for a woman? Is that what it is? Because that's okay. Just be honest about it."

She stammered again, obviously flustered. The scarlet of her cheeks deepened, and her eyes flashed with what anyone else would see as anger. But Carla saw nothing of the sort. She saw fear.

"Please, talk to me," Carla said.

"Not everything is as easy for others as they obviously are for you. And you thinking you know everything…it's just asinine."

She turned on her heel, like she wanted to flee, but a young woman with short lavender colored hair and a nose ring stood in her way.

"Dr. Carpenter," the young woman said. "Happy Fourth." She smiled at Janice, but her attention was then solely on Carla.

"Dakota. Hi," Janice said. The adrenaline from their conversation was still evident, but she was obviously trying to adjust. She shifted her stance several times and she didn't seem to know what to do with her hands. The smile she gave Dakota was polite, but it wasn't full, and it didn't reach her eyes. And she made it a point to avoid looking at Carla, even though Dakota wasn't.

"What a surprise," Janice said, getting no reply from Dakota. When Janice finally noticed that Dakota's full attention was on Carla, her put-upon smile fell and a look Carla had never seen in her clouded her face, setting a truly pained expression in stone.

There was no mistaking what that look represented, no matter how hard Janice may try to deny it.

It was jealousy.

"I know, right?" Dakota brought her gaze back quickly to Janice. She pointed back over her shoulder. "I'm here with Trace. You know, Trace from class?"

"Yes," Janice said, seeming to only half-heartedly search the crowd.

"He's dating Wendy who I guess is related to someone here?"

"She is," Carla said. "She's a cousin. Somewhere along the line."

Dakota laughed and scanned Carla up and down before blazing a very noticeable "I'm extremely interested" look directly into Carla's eyes.

It didn't go unnoticed, by Carla or Janice, who appeared to be so intense and so wound up in response, Carla thought she rivaled the rattlesnakes back home in Arizona. In fact, if Carla were Dakota, she wouldn't dare step anywhere near her for fear of her strike. Dakota, unfortunately, didn't seem to be familiar with the ways of a rattlesnake.

"You're Carla Sims, right?" she asked, holding out her hand. "Dakota Reems."

"Oh, I'm sorry," Janice said. "Dakota, this is Carla. She's quite attractive and quite single. But don't let that fool you. Carla is no longer interested in love or relationships."

Carla laughed, stunned.

Dakota, however, seemed amused. She raised an eyebrow and gave a grin that bordered on smirk as she shook hands with Carla. "I hear you're a teacher, too. High school."

"She is," Janice said. "She's quite good, too, from what I heard from her late grandmother."

Carla said nothing, Janice's jealousy and hurt obvious, but her intent a mystery.

Dakota continued.

"I saw Dr. Carpenter over here talking to you and I asked Wendy who you were. So, I thought I'd come over and say hello." Again, the smirk. Again, at Carla.

Carla found the cockiness the raised eyebrow and smirk suggested unappealing. She would've felt the same if she'd met her alone, but meeting her this way, at the expense of Janice, aggravated her profusely.

She wasn't about to allow this young woman to use Janice to get close to her. It was rude and with the feelings Carla knew Janice had for her, seriously torturous.

"That's nice," Carla said, determined to make things right. "I've heard Dr. Carpenter is a wonderful teacher herself. Very popular with her students."

Carla saw Janice turn to look at her out of the corner of her eye. She was going to be taken aback and confused, but it would be worth it.

"She's great," Dakota said. "I didn't even like to read before I took her class. And she saved my friend Trace's ass by working with him one-on-one so he could pass."

"Really?" Carla touched Janice's shoulder and she flinched, her discomfort seemingly mounting. "That's so nice of you to say. I wish I'd had her for my lit professor in college. But God knows, I probably wouldn't have gotten anything done. I mean, look at her. I never had an English professor who looked like her."

She felt Janice tense, and at some point, she seemed to have stopped breathing.

Dakota appeared a little embarrassed and she laughed and scratched her brow as she spoke.

"Yeah, she's great. So, Wendy says you live in Phoenix?"

"Great?" Carla let out. "She's fucking fantastic. She's smart, she's witty, she's funny. I would've had a serious crush on her at your age. Hell, I have a serious crush on her now and I don't even have the benefit of having her as my teacher."

Dakota laughed again, this time her nerves evident and she glanced at them both. She finally seemed to be getting the message. Carla drove the last nail in the coffin just to be sure.

"It was so nice of you to come over here to say hello to her, to let her know how much you appreciate her and to thank her for all she did to help your friend. Really very nice."

"Yeah. Okay. Well, it was nice seeing you, Dr. Carpenter," she said. "I hope you have a nice summer."

"You, too, Dakota," Janice said with a smile that seemed to have had to break through concrete to fully expand.

"She seemed...nice," Carla said as Dakota walked away.

"I'm sure she did. She just about rode your leg." She shoved Carla's hand from her shoulder.

"I was being facetious, Janice. I didn't think she was nice at all," she said. "Why do you think I said the things I said?"

"I don't know. To embarrass her? To get her to fuck off? Well, it worked. She, however, doesn't know you didn't mean any of it. She thinks you meant every word you said. She doesn't know you weren't sincere."

"I was sincere." Carla touched her arm. "Janice. Look at me."

"I can't." Her eyes were welling. "Not right now." She shrugged away her touch.

"Are you worried she'll tell people there's something going on between us?"

"You think I'm worried about what people think?"

"Are you?"

"After all our discussions?"

"You made it clear you're okay with my being gay. But what about you? Are you okay with people thinking that about you?"

Janice visibly deflated, like a knife had just penetrated her full heart.

"You aren't, are you?" Carla said softly.

Janice straightened like she was trying to steel herself.

"This is...crazy. I'm not doing this."

"Janice, talk to me, please. For God's sake. Don't keep doing this to yourself."

"I have talked to you," she shot back. "I have…shared my feelings. I was scared to death to do so, but I still did it."

"I'm not following."

"You didn't then, either. And obviously you don't remember."

Carla searched her mind, trying to understand what she was saying, when it was that she'd shared her feelings with her.

"No, I don't." She shook her head, totally confused.

"There's a reason why you don't remember." She started to walk away. "You were drunk."

Carla watched Janice from a distance when Rick and Cole set off their fireworks. Janice held Erica's boys tight and shrieked with them in delight as the rockets flew and whined and the bombs exploded. She covered Victor's ears for him when things got too loud and hugged Denny close to console him when the fireworks he brought turned out to be a dud.

Carla was watching her stroke his hair and wipe his tears from his face when someone came to stand next to her.

"It's such a letdown when they don't work." Carla couldn't see all that well in the dim light, but from what she could tell, the woman next to her was about her height with short dark hair. Her profile was attractive and her build athletic. Carla didn't recognize her, but she could tell by her accent that she wasn't local. She was Southern, but definitely not from anywhere close to her town.

"I'll make it up to him," Carla said, referring to Denny, whom they were both looking at. "I told him if any of them turned out to be a dud, I'd replace them."

"Aren't you a good, what? Mother, aunt, friend?"

"Cousin," Carla said with a smile. "And he's a sensitive little guy. I hate seeing him disappointed."

The woman turned toward her and showed her round face and large, almond shaped eyes. She was attractive and Carla knew she would've remembered seeing her before. But she couldn't place her. She didn't seem to resemble anyone she knew.

"Protective as well," she said. "Sweet."

The whine of a launched firework caught their attention and it exploded in a huge ball of yellow stars, followed quickly by another and then another. The church had started its show, and though the woman next to her kept talking, Carla kept glancing at Janice, thoroughly enjoying the way the bursts of light lit up her face as she pointed and smiled with the boys.

"This is the closest I've ever been to big fireworks," the woman said. "It's amazing. These kids must be thrilled. Does this happen every year?"

"For the last few years or so," Carla said. "The church putting it on is relatively new. For around these parts anyhow."

"What a treat." She looked over at Carla. "I'm Andy," she said. She gave a wave.

"I'm Carla." She smiled at her but didn't offer to shake her hand. She was enjoying the fireworks and the way their beauty collided with Janice's, enhancing hers to a degree that left Carla breathless.

"I might have to make my way back here next year," she said. "You can't beat this."

"It's something," Carla said. "I'm usually not here for this myself. I always seem to forget how incredible it is until I return."

"You're not from here?"

"I am, I just no longer live here."

"I don't either."

"Yeah, I know."

She looked at her. "You do?"

"Your accent. It gives you away."

She laughed. "You aren't the first one to comment on my accent. I had a gas station clerk look right at me today and ask me where I'm from. And not in a friendly manner either. He said I talked funny."

Carla laughed. "I get that, and I was born and raised here."

"Do they look at you like you're from Mars, too? I told him I was from Georgia and he didn't seem to believe me."

"He probably didn't. To him, anyone not from here *is* from outer space."

Andy rested a hand on her shoulder as she bent over laughing. Carla couldn't help but join her.

"Where do you live?" Andy asked, gaining some control of herself.

"Phoenix."

"Oh, wow, so you're in a whole other galaxy."

"Yep."

They continued to laugh. "It's so nice to meet someone who shares my Martian status."

"Well, not totally," Carla said. "I do have blood relations here. A lot, actually. So, I can easily sneak back under the fence. You, I'm afraid, are hopeless."

"Oh, thanks. I feel so much better now." A huge firework boomed in the night sky, and Carla watched it in awe and then looked to Janice. To her surprise Janice was looking directly at her. Carla smiled and waved, but Janice did not return either. Her face was as stoned with pain as it had been earlier with Dakota. She turned away suddenly, as if she could no longer bear to look at Carla, but then glanced back at her as if she couldn't help it.

Carla felt her world spin as she realized what was happening. Andy was still talking and laughing softly right next to her, hand on her shoulder. Janice was watching with horror, assuming the worst. Carla had no doubt. She could sense it even from where she stood on the other side of the lawn.

And amidst the panic she now felt in seeing Janice's pain, three things came to her mind. Just as clear as day.

I would rather be here with you.

I find you interesting and...attractive.

I want you to make a move on me.

Carla closed her eyes as the memories she'd been so desperate to recall flooded her. Janice's voice repeating, declaring, confessing.

She did talk to me. She did tell me how she feels.

And I was too drunk to do anything about it.

"I gotta go," Carla said, pulling away. She should've chased her down and insisted they talk earlier when she'd walked away, but she hadn't wanted to ruin the rest of the holiday for her by causing any more stress. She hadn't seemed to be okay with anything Carla had said, so Carla had feared discussing it any further in their current surroundings wouldn't have been a good idea.

Carla crossed the lawn, weaving through pockets of people. Janice saw her coming and she said something to the boys and then hurried from the crowd. She disappeared in the darkness and Carla realized she'd been headed toward the parked vehicles. More fireworks exploded in the sky, and when Carla finally did locate her, her heart sank. Janice had made it to her car and Carla watched helplessly as she sped out of the driveway, kicking up gravel. Carla stared after her until her taillights were swallowed up in the dark.

And then, one final thing Janice had said floated through her mind.

Carla is no longer interested in love and relationships.

Carla knew then that she had to follow her. Knew for certain that she had to talk to her.

About everything. All of it.

She knew what doing so meant and knew what all that would entail.

She didn't, however, know what the outcome would be.

Nevertheless, it had to be done.

Janice was hurting, not just in jealousy, but in her hiding.

Carla couldn't let that continue, especially knowing it had everything to do with her.

Her own fears, which she had to admit, she'd been deferring to as well, needed to be put to rest once and for all.

She looked up at the sky as another huge rocket burst into a ball of red sparkles. The beauty of it was lost on her, though.

Because all she could think about was how she hoped that wouldn't soon be her heart.

CHAPTER TWENTY-ONE

Janice hurriedly retrieved an unopened bottle of wine from the rack next to the fridge and then struggled to uncork it. Her hands had begun to tremble on the frenzied drive home from Maurine's and they didn't appear to be calming anytime soon. She cursed loudly as she lost control of the bottle and nearly dropped it on the floor. She stilled, with a firm grip on the wine and forced herself to take a few deep breaths, in order to get control of herself. The breathing helped some, but her mind and heart kept racing just as they'd done when she'd peeled out of the drive back at Maurine's with those beautiful, booming fireworks shaking the earth and Carla Sims shaking her entire being.

The cork popped on the wine, startling her and causing her to lose her balance from having pulled so hard to free it. She quickly righted herself and filled a glass and took a few deep swallows, praying it would help to ease the aching and anguish currently torturing her. But her mind kept returning to Carla and the mystery woman she'd been laughing with. The woman who'd been touching her, behaving like they knew each other well, like they were familiar. Too familiar. Who was she? She'd never seen her before and neither had Maurine or Erica. And her looks hadn't exactly helped matters any. She was gorgeous and fit with a short, stylish haircut that Janice couldn't help but let lead her to wonder about her sexuality.

She drank as she thought about Carla possibly knowing the woman on an intimate level. Her stomach tightened and a painful churning began, just as it had when she'd watched Dakota all but drool over Carla right in front of her. Carla hadn't had any interest in Dakota and she'd quickly run her off, that much she knew. But Carla had appeared to be behaving differently with the mystery woman. She hadn't run her off. And she wasn't acting disinterested or standoffish. It had been quite the opposite from her viewpoint.

She fought bending to quell the ache in her gut, knowing full well what was happening but still battling like hell to admit it. She was way too old to feel something as ridiculous and silly as jealousy. Especially since she'd never been jealous before. Over anyone. So, it couldn't suddenly be hitting her now. Why would it? No, it didn't make sense.

She swallowed down the reason and truth with more wine, doing her best to drown them, to drown out even the slightest thought that her feelings for Carla were stronger than any she'd ever had for anybody else and that was why she was suddenly experiencing things like jealousy. She finished the glass, flooding that relentless and pesky truth with alcohol until it was saturated enough to ease a bit and allow a soothing warmth to spread through her. There. That was a little better. The world wasn't ending. Even if Carla had interest in another woman. Life would go on.

It would.

Right?

She grabbed both the glass and the bottle and crossed into the living room to head for her bedroom, intent on going to bed to submerge any and all doubts in the wine until she was drunk enough to fall asleep. Hopefully, she would be deep in a peaceful dreamland well before Carla came home. If she came home. The pain came again as she considered that Carla may go home to spend the night with the woman.

She lowered her head and hurried through the living room before the churning overcame her. But a smooth, familiar voice stopped her dead in her tracks.

"Hi." Carla was standing near the couch, apparently having entered the house silently, keys still in her hand. The look on her face showed a hint of genuine concern, but it was heavily overshadowed by a look of sheer determination. Just what she was determined to do or say, Janice wasn't sure. But the possibilities caused her hands to tremble again.

Janice had to clear her throat to speak. "I was just going to go turn in." She took a step toward the hallway but so did Carla, only she stepped toward her.

"Why?" She angled her head slightly, as if truly curious. She tossed her keys onto the coffee table while remaining focused on Janice. "It's a little early for you, isn't it?"

"I'm tired." Janice swallowed as Carla came closer, moving like a predator keenly focused on its prey.

"You don't look tired." She stepped into her path. "You look upset. Frazzled. You looked the same at Maurine's. Is something wrong?"

"No." But she turned her head as she said it, unable to hold Carla's intense gaze. "I just—got tired."

Carla came closer. Carefully, she took the glass from her hand and set it on the end table. She tried to do the same with the wine, but Janice wouldn't let go.

"No, I need this," Janice said, once again looking into her eyes.

"No, you don't," Carla said softly.

"I do. I—want it."

"No, you don't." She gently eased the bottle from her grip and placed it next to the glass.

Janice sidestepped to reach for it, but Carla stilled her with a slight grasp of her arm.

"You don't need it, Janice. And you don't really want it."

Her voice and demeanor were smooth and sure as if she could see everything there ever was to Janice. Every thought, every feeling, every fear. Every.... desire. Just like she'd insisted she could back at the barbecue at Maurine's. Was it possible that she really could? Could someone really know her so well?

Being seen like that so easily and for the very first time in her life, caused a sudden panic in her. There was nowhere to hide, no way to deny. She was now fully exposed and being held captive by the gaze of the most beautiful, alluring predator a poor, helpless prey like herself had ever encountered. Any attempt to try to form an escape plan or any other sort of complex or rational thought were futile. Her mind was melting, along with the rest of her body, save for her poor panicked heart, which was still careening.

Carla seemed to sense it and she drew even closer, now only mere inches away. Janice could smell the faint scent of her cologne, feel the slight caress of her breath and see the thrum of her pulse in her neck. Her close proximity at that moment was having such a strong effect on her, Carla might as well have been touching her.

Janice tried to speak, one last-ditch effort to say or do anything to somehow break the overwhelming spell. But the power of Carla's gaze seemed to smother her voice, allowing for only a meek noise of helplessness to escape.

"Were you going to say something?" Carla asked.

Janice was finding it hard to breathe. "I—don't know. I don't know what to say other than good night."

Carla smirked. "How about the truth, Janice?"

Oh God. Not again. I can't fight it.

Her racing heart plummeted to her feet.

"The truth?"

"Yes. How about, instead of me telling you what it is you really want, you tell me?"

"I—" How could she say it? What were the right words? How does someone reach into their own chest, grab hold of their beating heart and offer it someone else, hoping against hope that they really want it and won't tear it to pieces?

"It's not the wine you really want, Janice. And it's not sleep." She lightly ran her fingers up and down Janice's arm, teasing her skin like the touch of a feather.

Blood pounded in Janice's ears and heated her entire body. She shook her head, feeling completely out of control and unable to put voice to any of the sporadic thoughts and feelings coursing through her.

"I know you're scared. I am too. But I came here to tell you that I'm willing to move past my fear. I came here hoping that you'll be willing to do the same."

Janice held her chest, convinced she was going implode. Carla had just taken away the very last excuse she had for the continued denial of her feelings.

"You're still not going to say it, are you?" Carla asked. She moved her hand from her arm and grazed her cheek just before she cupped her jaw.

Janice shuddered and she knew Carla felt it by the sudden flash of hunger she saw in her eyes and by the deep and sultry way in which she spoke, like the predator she'd been emulating, who at long last was about to devour its prey.

"Then how about instead of you saying it, or me saying it, I just show you what it is you want? What it is you need."

Janice struggled to keep breathing. To remain standing. To remain fucking conscious as Carla carefully leaned in, skimmed her thumb across Janice's lower lip and then slowly, so very slowly, brought her mouth to hers and kissed her.

The kiss was warm, soft, and so incredibly gentle and seeking of permission that Janice felt faint. Carla was introducing her to her own desire, taking her hand and guiding her into the depths of her innermost self and yet she was still considerate and careful, making sure she was willing to take that next step alongside her. And she asked her again and again with each delicate, deliberate move of her mouth, lightly pressing her lips into Janice's, seeking and caressing and tasting and waiting.

With every single touch and careful collision of their lips, a scorching of yearning and desire began to burn hotter and fiercer deep inside Janice. Every cell seemed to burst aflame with life and need and they all cried out for more, demanded more. Made her feel like she was going to die if she didn't get more. So, she clung to her, grabbing fistfuls of her shirt, and kissed her back, desperate to taste more of her, desperate to feel more of the moist heat of her mouth. Her response brought out a primal sounding noise in Carla and she quickly tugged on her hips to meld their bodies together just like their mouths.

They were fused. In unison. Exploring. Giving. Receiving. And when Carla carefully sought with her tongue, Janice welcomed her, never before having wanted the feel of that slick velvet against her own so badly. And the way Carla kissed her, so passionately and yet so controlled, as if she wanted it to last, as if kissing Janice was the most meaningful and sacred thing in her entire existence. As if she knew it meant just as much to Janice as well.

Janice was grateful and she knew she forever would be, because she had absolutely no control left in her. Carla's kisses had splayed her wide open and every thought, feeling, and desire she'd had for her were now pulsing out of her. There was no stopping it. And no way in hell she wanted to stop it.

She pulled on Carla's shirt, to hold her closer, tighter, and answered her tongue with the hungry thrust of her own. Carla groaned and eagerly deepened the kiss, lowering her hands to her buttocks where she, too, held her tighter. They kissed wildly then. Fervently. And every stroke of Carla's tongue sent a rush of heat to Janice's throbbing center, causing a newfound aggression to take precedence. And suddenly she was clawing at Carla's back and trying to grind herself against her thigh.

Carla tore her mouth away and held her face. She panted as she stared into her with eyes as wild as their kisses.

"Is this what you want, Janice?" she asked. "Is this what you really want? Because if you aren't completely sure, tell me now. Tell me now before I lose the very last of my reason and inhibition."

Janice hung from her, limp and clinging like a woman drunk on desire. Drunk on Carla Sims. The distant sound of fireworks boomed in the night, as if in sync with her madly beating heart.

"I want it. I want you."

Janice saw her words penetrate. Carla's body tensed and her jaw flushed with a tinge of red just before it flexed. Her eyes however, her eyes softened with what could only be heartfelt emotion.

This woman really cares for me.
How could I have not seen it?
Why have I been so afraid?

"You're sure?" Carla continued, her voice now strained and raspy, as if what she was saying truly affected her. "Because if we continue and I—if we do what it is I've been dying to do with you, to you—everything will change. Everything. There won't be any going back."

Janice let go of her shirt and reached up to her own face where Carla was holding her and rested her hand on Carla's.

"I only want to go forward. With you."

Carla closed her eyes. And when she opened them they were glistening with tears.

"Are you okay?" Janice felt emotion tighten her throat as well. Carla merely smiled.

"Yes. And you're about to see just how okay I really am." She lowered her hands and cupped Janice's ass and lifted her in one quick motion. Janice wrapped her arms and legs tightly around her, so turned on she feared she might climax from the firm press of Carla's body between her legs alone.

"Where are we going?" Janice asked, already hungrily massaging her fingers into Carla's hair at the base of her skull.

Carla spun and continued through the living room.

"To the place I've dreamt about taking you for far too long now."

"Where's that?"

"Your bed."

Chapter Twenty-two

Carla set Janice down gently on the end of the bed. Then she stroked her face with her thumbs, dipped in for a long, sweet, soft kiss, and straightened. Janice grabbed her hand as she started to pull away.

"Where are you going?"

"Not far."

She released her hand and turned and left the room. She entered Janice's study and turned on the stereo, finding Janice's seductive sounding playlist she'd come to enjoy. The music came to life and she adjusted the volume, already feeling stirred by the erotic beats. Satisfied, she crossed back into Janice's room and found her leaning back on her hands, with her beautiful legs crossed, watching and waiting with an obvious sensual curiosity. The quiet confidence she now exuded sent fluttering, aimless butterflies free inside Carla and she realized she hadn't been nervous with a woman in years. Surprisingly, the nervousness only excited her and made her more attuned to the moment and the incredible night she was about to share with this incredible woman.

She lit the thick candle on the dresser and watched the flame envelop the wick just as she'd watched the flame dance against the angles of Janice's face not that long ago. Then she rounded the bed to the nightstand where she unplugged the house phone and extinguished the light. She didn't want anything disturbing them. And if she could have, she would've taken Janice thousands of miles away to nowhere just to ensure she could spend the next few hours with her alone. But as things stood, this was the best she could do.

She returned to Janice and lost her breath at the sight of her on that big, beautiful bed, waiting for her as the candlelight hungrily moved along her body. Carla held out her hand and helped her stand. She touched her face, and Janice, too, lost her breath as they stared into each other's eyes.

"I'm going to go slow, okay?" Carla said. "So, if I do anything you don't like, or you feel uncomfortable in any way—"

"Carla." Janice shushed her with a finger pressed to her mouth. "Please, stop."

Janice lowered her finger and slowly ran it down the column of Carla's neck as she spoke.

"I want you to do whatever you want."

"But I want to be sure—"

"No." She shook her head. "I'm already sure, Carla. And I'm already pretty sure I'm going to like everything you have in store for me." The corner of her mouth lifted in that coy, playful manner of hers. It immediately stoked the growing fire of Carla's libido. "So, please," Janice said softly as she wrapped her arms around Carla's neck once again. "Just shut up and make love to me."

Carla was incredulous, never having experienced such desire from a woman's demand.

Just shut up and make love to me.

She wanted to close her eyes to savor not only the words, but the sight of Janice standing before her, beckoning. But she couldn't bear to look away. The moment felt too surreal. It meant too much. She had to take it all in. Every last bit of it.

Carla eased her fingers into Janice's hair at the nape of her neck and pulled her closer. She looked into her eyes for as long as she could before her longing to kiss her sweet lips once again won out. She inched into her slowly, hoping for that ability to savor. But once she felt her hot mouth on hers, she completely lost it. The universe itself was quickly thrown to the wayside as they kissed, expressing everything they felt about one another with a hunger they'd had to endure day after torturous day. Now they could feast. And feast they did. Only breaking for quick half seconds to garner breath before delving back in. Janice had come alive in her arms and her strength and aggression were as surprising as they were arousing. When she wasn't knotting her hands in Carla's hair, she was clinging and clawing at her back like she couldn't enough of her. And when Carla sucked on her lower lip and Janice responded by taking hers with her teeth, Carla groaned and forced herself to pull away.

"Janice—you—" she panted. "Oh my God, I've never wanted anyone so badly."

"Me neither." She twisted a handful of Carla's shirt at her abdomen. "I'm so turned on I can't hardly stand. Is this—how it feels? How real desire for another feels?"

Carla absently fingered her lip. It was still tingling from Janice's sensual nibble.

"Yes, Janice. It is. When it's right. But the way I'm feeling now, with you, I'm beginning to wonder if anyone I've ever been with before was right. Because even I'm embarking on new territory here."

"But at least you got to feel, to experience. I've been sleepwalking through life, not having met anyone who could do this to me. And then, there was you. Right in front of me. All along. You announced that you were gay and my whole world tilted. You woke me up, Carla. And I haven't been able to get you off my mind since. Now I know why. I want you, Carla Sims. I fucking *want* you."

Carla slowly helped Janice release the grip on her shirt. Then she reached for the hem of Janice's halter top and eased it up and over her head. She stood there in her white bra, chest heaving with excited breath, her eyes burning wild. Carla ran her fingers along her collarbone and slipped them under the straps of the bra to lower them from her shoulders. She bent and kissed her there, lightly, softly, where the straps had been and Janice took in tiny, audible gasps of air.

Carla kissed her way down her chest and paused to graze the back of her fingers across her covered nipples. Janice shook and then she cried out softly when Carla covered her erect nipples with her mouth and plied them with kisses through the fabric.

"Carla," she pleaded. "Oh God, you don't know what that's doing to me."

"Oh, but I do," Carla said as she reached back and unfastened her bra. She eased it from her body and tossed it aside like she had done with her shirt. Then she leaned down next to her ear and whispered, "I'm going to make you feel so good, baby."

She again skimmed the back of her fingers down her chest to her bare breasts. She traced them around and around her nipples, causing them to bunch and harden with a hunger for touch, driving Janice completely mad. At long last, she gave in and grazed her erect buds while she vigorously fed on the delicate skin of her neck. Janice's body shuddered beneath her and her soft cries grew louder and evolved into desperate pleas. She gripped Carla's wrists as if she were somehow trying to control the insane pleasure her fingers were creating.

Janice nibbled her neck, relishing the feel and taste of her skin.

"I don't know what's more beautiful," she said again into her ear. "The reactions of your heavenly body or sounds of sheer pleasure coming from your soul."

"Oh, dear sweet God, Carla," she let out, sinking her fingernails into Carla's wrists. "I can't take it it feels so good."

"You can take it, baby. You'll be surprised at how much pleasure you can take." She kissed her way back down and held Janice firmly as she first teased her awakened breasts with her breath and then saturated them with her mouth. Janice hissed and cried out, knotting her hands in Carla's hair. Carla felt her legs try to buckle twice, but she held her tight as she continued her sensual assault. Janice's cries and frenzied clawing caused Carla's own body to begin to scream for touch. It had been a very long time since she'd felt the heavy pulse of her flesh nestled between her legs. But this pulse, this new one beating for Janice was so fierce and so strong the throbbing resonated throughout her body. From head to toe, she thrummed, craving for touch. To give it and receive it. Because she was quickly learning that giving to Janice felt like Janice was giving to her. Like she was mirroring Carla's touch and caress back onto her. Only those mirroring touches weren't near enough. They were teases, grazes, meant to awaken, to stir.

And they were succeeding.

She gave Janice one last, long round of heavy tonguing and kisses and then rose to speak yet again in her ear. The raging need of her own body had so aroused her thoughts, she almost couldn't find her voice to get the words out.

"I've got to touch you," she said, feeling heady at the sweet shampoo scent of her hair. "I've got to feel you."

"You are," Janice said, still breathless.

"No," Carla said. "I want to feel you somewhere else." She traced her hand down her middle to the waistline of her shorts. She hurriedly unfastened them and eased them open. The smooth plains of Janice's stomach quivered as Carla lingered at the edge of her panties. "I want to feel you here, Janice," she said, slowly lowering her hand inside the front of her cotton panties. Janice let out a shaky breath and held tightly to her, as if she knew her legs would most likely give at any moment.

And when Carla sank her hand in farther and found her slick, silky center, Janice did indeed buckle as Carla groaned with delight.

"No, no, no," Carla said, pressing her hand into her lower back for better support. "You can't go down yet, baby. Not yet. I want you to stand here and feel my touch. Feel the way my fingers slide into your folds, glide along your most sensitive spot, searing you with pleasure. I want you to feel that. I want you to stand here in my arms and feel that until you literally cannot stand here with me anymore."

Carla licked her ear and sucked on her lobe as her hand began to work her, massaging her cleft until it was slick and swollen with an eagerness for her continued attention. Janice's cries and pleas increased as her weak but electrified body moved against her, desperate and demanding.

"I can't believe how good you feel," Carla said, her face burning with pent desire. "You're so wet. So silky hot. It's like you can't get enough. Like you've never been touched before."

"I haven't," Janice said. "Not like this."

"I don't believe you," Carla said. "No one has touched you here?"

Janice made a noise and jerked as another obvious shot of pleasure came over her. "No. With Chuck—no. There wasn't much foreplay."

Carla stilled and Janice would've collapsed if Carla had not braced her.

"I don't understand," Carla said. "How in the hell did he keep his hands off you? More importantly, *why* in the hell did he keep his hands off you?"

Janice seemed at a loss for words. "I don't know. I guess it was me. There was something wrong with me."

"No, Janice. It wasn't you. I know with every ounce of my being that it wasn't you. Especially now. Now that I've seen you, kissed you, touched you, and witnessed the way you react. I mean, Jesus Christ. You're—fucking incredible. No, my dear, sweet woman, it most certainly was not you."

Carla slowly slid her hand from her panties and pressed a finger to her chin, not liking the sadness that seemed to have come over her.

"You haven't always blamed yourself for that have you?"

She wouldn't meet her gaze.

"Hey," Carla said softly.

"Chuck wasn't a bad lover. I don't think. He just—wasn't into me, I guess. And I wasn't into him."

"He was a fool. Or crazy. Or both." She tipped her chin again and this time Janice looked at her.

"You absolutely take my breath away," Carla said, lost in her eyes. "So much so, that I've forgotten what I was going to say. So, I think I'm going to have to do what I did earlier and skip trying to express my desire with words and just get back to showing you." She kissed her. Softly. Delicately. "How does that sound?"

"I don't have any complaints so far."

Carla laughed and scooped her up quickly and deposited her on the bed. She crawled up to her, kissed her passionately, until Janice was moaning into her and tearing at her shirt. Carla sat up, ripped off her top, and stripped off her bra. She was about to lean down for another kiss, but Janice stopped her by reaching out to touch her breasts. She did so tentatively, with light, curious fingers that gently skimmed and caressed. Carla found herself inhaling sharply at the sensations being brought to life in her nipples. She tried to remain still, seeing how much Janice was enjoying herself in touching her, but despite closing her eyes and steadying her breathing, the pleasure was too much and her desire for Janice won out.

Chapter Twenty-three

I'm dreaming.
I must be.

I've imagined this moment so much I can't tell whether it's really happening or not.

Janice was having trouble accepting reality. The moment was just too good to be real. Carla was right there next to her in the glow of candlelight, breathing hard, her small, taut breasts sharp with excitement, pebbling at her touch.

And her skin, oh dear Lord, her skin. So unbelievably soft beneath her fingers Janice had gasped right along with her at first contact. Now, as she continued to caress and explore, Carla's body had tightened with gooseflesh and she was beginning to tremble with her every stroke. As much as touching this goddess before her and eliciting such responses was exciting her, it was the way she was looking at her that was so profoundly moving.

Janice never, ever could've imagined the powerful, raw desire and deep, meaningful emotion she was seeing in her right then.

This could not possibly be a dream.

It was real.

She was real.

"Oh, my God," Janice said aloud as Carla once again crawled atop her and began to devour her neck and tease her ear with raspy whispers of desire.

"I love the way you smell, the way you feel and the way you taste. Your skin, your lips, your tongue. But I want more. I want to know what you taste like…" She shifted and lowered her hand to press against the flesh between Janice's legs. "Here," she said.

Janice moaned and arched slightly as both the words and massage of her hand infiltrated.

"Let me guess, no one has ever kissed you here either," Carla said, moving downward, brushing her lips and breathing upon her body as she went, before coming to rest at the waistline of her shorts.

"No."

Carla pulled down her open shorts and freed them from her legs. Then she maneuvered herself between her legs where she began teasing her sensitive inner thighs just as she had the rest of her.

Janice jerked and twitched, unable to remain still. Her body was reacting on its own accord, like it was one giant nerve ending, dangerously exposed and Carla was toying with it.

"Carla," she pleaded. "You're—killing me."

Carla kept on, making pleasurable noises of her own as she worked, winding Janice up, priming her for what was to come. When she finally moved her mouth to Janice's center and began kissing her through her panties, Janice jolted, her head and shoulders coming up off the bed, her hands clinging to Carla's head.

"Oh God!" She let out. "Wha—Oh, Jesus, God."

"Feel good, baby?"

"Mm, yes. I—it's—"

"Almost unbearable?"

Janice was straining, staring down at her, holding desperately to her.

"Hmm?" Carla said as she teased her some more.

"Ye-yes." Janice struggled to swallow. "Yes."

"It gets better," she said. "You won't believe how much better." She hovered above her a few seconds, then gave her a wicked grin and full on kissed her through her panties, urging her tongue against her aching clit.

Janice cried out and came up farther off the bed, the exposed nerve ending of her body now completely stimulated.

"Carla," she rasped. Carla pressed harder, deeper, the saturation of the heavy heat of her mouth now as equally affecting as her eager tongue. "Carla," Janice let out again, clenching her eyes as her arms burned and trembled from their desperate grip.

Carla moaned and slowed to a stop. Janice, with her eyes still clenched and her pulse on overdrive, tried to catch her breath.

"Janice," Carla said. "Janice, open your eyes, baby."

Janice looked at her.

To her surprise, Carla pushed away from her and crawled from the bed. The absence of her between her legs was felt at once and Janice made a small noise of protest, unsure what was happening.

"Come here," Carla said, reaching out for her hand. She brought Janice to a stand and led her to the side of the bed where she pulled back the covers and rearranged the pillows. Then she faced her, lightly touched her cheek, and knelt to carefully remove her panties. She grazed her with her fingernails as she came back up and then quickly removed her own remaining clothes.

Janice could make out the firm, etched contours of her body and she burned with a hunger and need so powerful, she was sure she was about to burst into flames. And yet, as overwhelming as the sight of her nude body was, Janice couldn't tear her gaze away from her eyes. For they were locked on to hers, reflecting everything Janice was thinking and feeling and searing it right back into her. They were connected, communicating, sharing. Without a single word.

Carla reached out, pulled her closer. Hot skin against hot skin, solidifying the connection.

"Lie down," Carla said, leading her onto the bed.

Janice relaxed back onto the pillows and smoothed her hands over the cool satin like she did each and every night.

"I'm never going to forget the way you look right now," Carla said. "Lying there on those shimmering sheets, looking up at me like you've been waiting for me to make love to you your entire life."

"I have," Janice said. "I've waited so long."

Carla touched her leg and traced up to her inner thigh. Janice sighed and welcomed her further by easing her legs apart.

"You touched me like this, didn't you?" Carla asked. "It came to me as I was driving here tonight. I recalled a lot of things tonight actually. Things you've said, their meaning somehow missed by me. And I remembered your touch. Like this. On my leg. And I remembered how badly I wanted it, how I begged you for it. But mostly, and more importantly, I remembered how badly you wanted to give it to me. You did want it badly, didn't you?"

"It took everything I had to stop."

"I'm sorry I missed those moments with you. I'd give anything to get them back."

"I'm sorry I couldn't share those things with you when you weren't drunk on wine."

Carla climbed onto the bed, settled on top of her and maneuvered herself between her thighs.

"Next to those apologies, I wish there was some way to make it up to one another."

"Oh, I think we can come up with something. Like maybe we should try our very best to make up for lost time."

"That could be fun. When should we start?"

"Right now."

"Now?"

Janice laughed and held her tightly. "Yes, before any more time passes us by."

"Yes," Carla said. "I don't want to waste another second." She kissed her deeply, claiming her with long, slick, probes of her tongue. Janice answered with a soft noise of approval and the running of her nails up and down Carla's back. Janice kept the scratches purposefully slight at first. But then slowly, and coinciding with their kiss, she increased the pressure. Until finally her fingernails penetrated enough to make Carla arch and groan. The thrill of her reaction was head spinning, but it was the aggression that came over her face that got to Janice the most. It was the same look she'd seen in her earlier when she'd lightly bitten her lip. Now it had returned, roaring to the surface and Janice knew that this time it wouldn't settle for anything short of absolute satisfaction.

"Oh, fuck, Janice," she said, staring down at her like a pacing, caged lion, hell-bent on breaking free. "How do you know how to get to me? How? Are you even aware of what you're doing to me?"

"I am now." She felt herself smirk and she opened herself more, loving the way Carla's body felt pressed tightly against her.

Carla seemed to understand, and she rocked into her, sliding her thigh along Janice's offered center.

"You're so wet," she whispered. "So blessedly wet."

Janice lifted her hips to match her rhythm, dying for the contact. She ran her nails along her spine again and into her hair where she began to graze her scalp. Carla closed her eyes, obviously affected and she kissed her again, plunging her tongue into her over and over while fucking her with her body. And then, as Janice dug and clawed more at her skin and scalp, Carla tore away and slid down between her legs and without warning or any further hesitation, took Janice in and fed.

The hot, wet heat of her mouth on her most sensitive, sacred flesh sent a tidal wave of the most insane pleasure she'd ever felt right up through her body and into her brain where it saturated and pulsed, and attempted to squeeze every last bit of ecstasy it could from those pleasure inducing chemicals. It was a mission that seemed endless, rocketing through her continuously, filling her so full of erotic bliss, she was sure she was going to lose consciousness.

But conscious she remained, feeling every last sensation Carla and her overly generous mouth gave to her, seemingly unaware that she was edging Janice toward the cliff of ultimate euphoria. Seemingly unconcerned that her continuing would surely cause Janice to fall off the side of that cliff and lose herself completely, maybe never to return again.

Janice had to tell her. She was approaching the cliff fast, Carla all but shoving her toward it. She finally found the ability to once again form words and tried to tell Carla what was happening. But Carla just laughed, sinister-like, which confirmed that she was very much aware after all and that she wasn't about to let up.

Janice begged and pleaded with her, head thrashing, limbs shaking, hands clinging. But Carla wouldn't stop. And the pleasure kept coming. Faster, harder, heavier, hotter. Burning holes right through her brain while setting the rest of her afire.

Words she'd never spoken before came from her. Sounds she didn't know she could make birthed from deep inside. Beads of sweat on her chest and abdomen reflected the candlelight and dampened her hair. The silk of her sheets made love to her back as she writhed and Carla, Carla branded her own feelings into her with long, intense looks from her fiery irises, lit up with that predatory look Janice had seen in her earlier.

The predator was now satiating itself on its prey.

"You're loving this," Janice said, staring back into her, watching as she was bringing her to the brink of heaven and beyond.

Carla closed her eyes and broke away just long enough to say, "I'm fucking loving it."

With the penetration of that statement, an overwhelming need and desire to do the same to Carla with her own mouth slammed through her and she suddenly understood.

And as Carla reattached to her and flicked and swirled her heavenly tongue on and around her aching clitoris, and more pleasure surged through her, Janice knotted her hands in her hair and spoke of her need.

"Oh, dear God, Carla, I can't wait to do this to you."

She heard Carla groan and felt her focus and punish her clit, pulsing her slick tongue against it and a raging inferno tore through her body and pushed beneath her skin.

With her most powerful desire having been spoken aloud, Janice angled her chin upward and cried out into the night as all the hot, sultry pleasure Carla was giving her, finally gathered and then exploded, shoving her over the edge of that cliff, sending her down, down, down into the beautiful land of erotic paradise, until her body and mind slowed, coming to rest on a floating cloud, where everything she'd just felt and experienced settled upon her bare skin like a warm, all-knowing, all-comforting blanket.

When she returned to the present and opened her eyes and saw those honey-glowing eyes looking down at her, and felt that familiar hot skin against hers, she realized that all-knowing, all-comforting blanket was Carla Sims.

Chapter Twenty-four

Janice awoke with a start, confused. She reached out but only felt the cool satin of the sheets where she'd expected Carla to be. Her heart leapt to her throat as she realized her absence.

She sat up and rubbed her face, trying to further awake. The candle that had burned for hours, bearing witness to their sighs and lustful confessions now flickered with waning light. As Janice recalled some of those sighs and confessions and what had caused them to be voiced, her own inner wick was reigniting, despite the fact that it had burned just as long and bright as the one on her dresser. The passage of time and spent energy may have led to a slower dance of flame, now buried deep in the barrel of wax inside herself and the candle, but nevertheless, both wicks still burned.

She crawled from the bed and didn't bother with a robe before heading down the hallway. Light from the lamp in the living room guided her on her quest to find Carla. But the couch and love seat were empty and her den dark and vacant. Shuffling noises in the kitchen, however, caught her attention as did a slant of bright light. She leaned against the doorjamb and crossed her arms, amused.

Carla, clad only in her cotton panties and the gray cotton bra she slept in, stood in front of the open refrigerator, digging through the contents.

"Hungry?"

She turned quickly with her hand to her chest and saw Janice grinning.

"Funny. Very funny. You know I think initiating a heart attack is considered murder in some states."

Janice couldn't help but laugh. "Yeah, well, not in this one."

"So, you would walk away scot-free then?"

"'Fraid so."

"Criminal," she said, turning back to the fridge to retrieve two bottles of water and the covered plate of fruit and cheese they often kept handy to snack on. She nudged the fridge closed with her hip and walked toward her.

"How about you? You hungry?" she asked, now with a grin of her own.

Janice allowed herself to look her up and down, unabashedly taking her time. "Mm, I think so."

Janice saw her face flush. "You're blushing."

Carla edged past her. "No, I'm not."

Janice followed her into the living room and watched her set her goods down on the coffee table. Then she sat in her usual spot and uncovered the plate and quickly popped a small cube of cheese in her mouth. She grinned as she chewed, now taking her turn in looking Janice up and down.

"Care to join me, Professor?"

"Professor? That's new."

"It's who you are, isn't it?"

"It is."

"So, Professor, and yes, I'm going to call you that from now on because it's who you are and honestly, it sounds really hot and it turns me on. Would you like to join me for a post-midnight snack?" She opened one of the water bottles without missing a beat and took a hearty drink. Some dripped down her chin and she flinched, probably from the chill and wiped it away with the back of her hand. "Guess I was a little thirsty."

Janice stared, unable to tear her gaze away from her wet mouth.

"You said you were hungry," Carla said, reaching for a strawberry. She took a bite and again liquid ran down her chin, this time dark pink juice from the strawberry. She cussed and hurriedly tossed the strawberry back onto the plate and wiped her chin with her fingers.

As if in a trance, Janice crossed to her.

"Did I get it?" Carla asked as Janice came to stand next to her.

Janice reached down and touched her stained lips. Then she ran her thumb across her chin.

"No," she said. "You didn't get it."

Carla tried to touch her, but Janice caught her hand and pushed it away. Carla looked at her in confusion and started to question her, but Janice held her jaw and then knelt and covered her mouth with hers, aggressively consuming her, sucking the strawberry off her so hard, Carla made a high-pitched noise of surprise and desperation. But Janice didn't stop, couldn't stop. She took her lips between her own again and again, sucking and then licking. And then she attacked the rim of her mouth and chin. Nothing had ever tasted so good.

"Janice," Carla managed, gripping her arm. Janice could hear her confusion and her weariness at where this was headed. She was used to being in control. And up until now she'd been in control. She'd made love to Janice for hours, barely letting her breathe, much less recover before she'd started in again. She hadn't even let her out of the bed until Janice had finally managed to outmaneuver her and make a mad dash to the bathroom just so she could pee.

Well, now it was her turn. And Carla wasn't going to stop her. Not this time.

Yearning now for so much more than the taste of her strawberry coated mouth, Janice shoved on her shoulders, pushing her back into the love seat.

"Janice," she tried again.

"Shut up." She went down on her knees and started tugging on her panties.

"Janice, wha—"

"I said, be quiet," Janice said, still tugging. "Lift your hips," she commanded.

"What are you—"

Janice burned a hard stare into her. "I told you I'm hungry. Now shut up and lift your hips."

Carla visibly swallowed and complied. Janice tore her underwear from her and threw it back over her shoulder. Then she caught sight of the bra. "This too. It needs to go." She forced it up over her head and tossed it, too, aside. "I want to see all of you," she said, running her fingers down her body. "I want to watch your skin dampen with sweat and your muscles strain and constrict as I make love to you with my mouth."

"Janice, Jesus," Carla whispered.

Janice lowered herself and wrapped her hands under her thighs and up to her pelvis edging her closer. Then, as Carla said her name yet again, Janice attacked her inner thighs, inched her even closer and then sank her mouth into her flesh. The moist, salty taste of Carla hit her the same second as Carla's throaty cry. Both instantly set off a frenzy inside her and she went insane. Literally lost herself totally and completely, with nothing but the primal need to consume Carla surging through her. She was like an animal, driven by instinct alone, as if she needed her to survive. And her cries, her heavenly cries, were like the life force that made her heart beat, that fueled her raging fire, insisting and ensuring that she keep going, keep wanting, keep needing.

And she did. Relentlessly. Quickly finding Carla's favorite spot and assaulting it with heavy swirls of her tongue and long, firm sucks with her lips. Driving Carla mad, until the sheen of sweat she'd longed to see on her body appeared and her muscles writhed beneath her tanned skin as she clawed at Janice, just as she'd clawed helplessly at Carla while writhing like a mad woman against her satin sheets, convinced she would never experience anything as fucking good as what she was then.

But now she was proving herself wrong.

Because this, the taste of Carla. The fucking feel of her flesh, like the silk covering her bed only softer, slicker, hotter, matched what she'd felt earlier when Carla's mouth was devouring her.

To say she understood what Carla had felt doing this to her would not come close to being sufficient. She not only understood. She felt it in her bones. And Carla's confession, telling her that she fucking loved doing it, didn't do justice to how she felt as Carla called out to her, shuddered into her and pulled and clung and clawed at her, so overcome with pleasure Janice knew she had gone beyond reality.

No, Janice didn't just fucking love doing it.

She'd fucking kill to do it.

As if she'd heard her thoughts, Carla fell back against the cushions, shook her head from side to side and began mouthing unintelligible words as her hips began to thrust, eager for more of Janice. Janice pressed into her harder, circled her tongue around and around and then rested fully on her clit, assaulting it while keeping it smothered. Carla's clenched eyes flew open and she came up off the back cushions.

"Janice," she pleaded. "Janice, fuck. Oh fuck. I'm gonna—oh God, I'm com—I'm fucking coming."

She arched, taut breasts and open mouth aimed at the ceiling and let out the deepest, throatiest cry Janice had ever heard. A cry that lasted longer than any pair of human lungs could possibly be capable of. And yet it went on and on as Carla's entire body froze with strain and her grip on Janice's head fiercely locked, unwilling to let her escape until her flesh had taken all the pleasure it could possibly stand.

Giving to her, watching her and feeling her at that moment, was the most magnificent thing Janice had ever experienced. And she wished, wished more than anything, she could stay there with her, frozen in time, just like her body. But eventually her cry faltered and her body went limp and Janice gently pulled away. She saw the flush of her cheeks, the deep red of her blood filled lips and the deep but easily seen emotion in her heavy lidded eyes and Janice now wished for *that* to be the moment she could freeze in time.

For there had never been anything more beautiful in existence.

Janice slowly stood and brushed the backs of her fingers along Carla's face.

"I don't want this night to ever end," she said. "But I know it has to."

Carla took hold of her hand and kissed it. "Come here." She pulled her down and Janice straddled her, lost once again in her eyes. "Don't think about anything else. Just us. Right here, right now."

She shifted and reclined them onto the cushions, holding Janice tight.

"Okay?" She kissed her hand again.

Janice swallowed, doing her best to force the rising emotion down.

"Okay."

"Good," Carla said softly. "Now be quiet and kiss me."

Janice laughed softly at the emulating of her own bossiness. The feel of Carla's lips silenced her, though, and with that tender, sensual kiss, everything slowly righted itself once again.

If only for the moment.

A moment Janice was determined to enjoy.

Chapter Twenty-five

Carla woke but her mind was still far too foggy with sleep to understand why. Her eyes slowly opened, and the reason why became apparent, shining directly upon her face. A bright wedge of sunlight had snuck in through the side of the window and, instinctively, her hand shot up to her brow for protection as she slipped from the bed to quickly adjust the curtain.

The sudden movement was too much for her exhausted brain and body, though, and she stumbled back into the covers for more rest. The fatigue, however, did little to douse the smile that came when she snuggled into Janice from behind and lost herself in the scent of her hair and the incredible warmth and softness of her creamy skin. She felt so damn good in her arms, Carla easily melted, and the heavy pull of sleep easily lured her in again.

She dreamt of Janice's warmth and rhythmic breathing. Of distant knocking and calling voices. All of it swam together in her slumbering mind, somehow making sense. But Janice's stirring began to rouse her, and when she spoke, Carla was already struggling to regain focus.

"Did you hear something?" Janice asked, squeezing her hand in hers. Sleep was still clinging to her tightly as well. Her voice was riddled with it and her words slurred some.

"Hmm?"

"Thought I heard something."

Carla held her tighter. "Like what?"

But then Carla heard it too and they both stiffened. There was movement outside the bedroom door. In the house.

"What the—" Carla's words were stymied as she heard the door suddenly thrust open. Carla and Janice bolted upright and found Maurine standing just inside the door. A horrible noise of shock and surprise came from her just before she stifled it with the smack of her palm over her mouth.

Carla blinked, trying to make sense of her presence, but Maurine's eyes remained wide open with obvious disbelief.

"Maurine," Janice said, yanking the sheet up to cover their bodies.

Maurine spoke behind the cover of her hand, as if she couldn't move it away from her mouth.

"I've been trying to call. Was worried about why you both left last night. I—" She shook her head. "You didn't answer the door. I got scared. Used my key." She searched both their faces as if desperate to find something, anything, that would disprove what she was seeing, what she was thinking. When she didn't seem to find it, she turned away like the sight of them was too awful to continue to take in.

"Maurine," Janice said again. Carla heard the panic in her voice. She reached to comfort her, but Janice swatted her away. "It's not what it looks like."

Carla looked at her with her own sense of shock. "It isn't?"

Janice ignored her. "I—this—"

Maurine in turn, ignored Janice. Instead, she faced them and aimed a hate-filled stare at Carla.

"How could you, Carla Marie Sims? My best friend? My very best friend? It wasn't enough for you to have everything else? Your expensive, fancy education, your steady job that you love, and your hip, progressive life in Phoenix that you left all of us for. Left Mama for. Because we just ain't good enough for you are we, Carla? You got to have more. You got to have better. You got to have whatever it is you want, no matter how it affects anyone else."

Carla shoved her way out from under the covers and stood next to the bed. She was so hurt and so angry her hands were balled into tight fists at her side.

"You're way out of line, Maurine."

Maurine scoffed. "Me? I'm out of line? I didn't seduce your best friend, Carla." She narrowed her eyes. "That's why you wanted to stay here, isn't it? So, you could get close to her and—"

"And what?" Carla seethed. "Worm my way in? Brainwash her? Work these, what, incredible gay magic powers you're implying I have? That I just all of a sudden one day woke up and decided, you know what? I think I'll go seduce Janice. Just for the hell of it. And of course, she'll give in and sleep with me, because I'm that good. I'm that powerful. So powerful are my skills that I easily tricked her into having wild, passionate, mind-blowing, soul-shattering sex with me all night long. Tricked her into enjoying every second of it." She clenched her jaw, her breathing now quick and ragged. "Do you know how fucking ridiculous you sound? But honestly, I don't know why I'm surprised. I know why you're saying these things. It's because your insane, irrational accusations are a lot easier for you to believe and deal with than the truth. Because you can't handle the truth."

"And what's that, Carla? That Janice, my very best friend in the whole world, that I've known forever, is suddenly a damn lesbian?" She laughed, shook her head. "She ain't gay, Carla. I would know something like that."

"Like you did me?"

"I didn't know about you because you didn't tell me. You kept it secret. Hid it."

"And no one else could possibly do the same?"

"Janice wouldn't do that. She would tell me."

"Would she?"

"Yes, she would."

"Why, because you're so calm and understanding and supportive? You're certainly proving that now, aren't you?"

"She ain't gay, Carla. She was married. To a man. You just took advantage of a lonely, vulnerable woman."

"I see. It's all me. The evil homosexual swooped in and corrupted yet another unsuspecting soul." She laughed. "My God, you are ridiculous."

"I'm just saying what I see."

"No, you're not. You're refusing to accept what you're seeing. Twisting it into something you can deal with. And apparently, demonizing me, your own niece, is what you're willing to stoop to to do it. When all you really have to do is talk to your best friend. The very person you claim to be so close to and know so well. But you won't even do that. You won't even allow her to speak. Because you don't want to hear it. So, you'd rather just tell her how she feels in a selfish, all-knowing, self-righteous sort of way rather than give her a chance to be heard, to be herself for the first time in her life."

Maurine crossed her arms over her chest. "I'm saying what I'm saying because I know her, Carla. I've known her all her life. And I know her a whole lot better than you. But, whatever. I'll listen. Janice, if you want to tell me how you feel, I'm all ears." But before she faced Janice, she looked at Carla with disgust. "For God's sake, put some clothes on."

"Why? You worried you're suddenly going to want a woman? I must have some serious fucking powers in your mind."

"Get over yourself, Carla." She looked to Janice. "Well?"

Janice shook her head, her mouth open but void of words.

"God, Maurine, you're not exactly being a beacon of understanding and support."

"I'm listening."

Carla sighed.

"Well, Janice? Am I right? Or is Carla?"

"Maurine," Carla said.

"I—" Janice said. "This is all happening so fast. I'm—I—"

Carla knew she was panicked, but she felt the sting of betrayal nonetheless in her reticence to admit how they felt about one another. And Maurine's hard demeanor that implied an extreme lack of empathy or willingness to understand obviously wasn't lost on Janice. She just kept stammering and staring at Maurine with wild eyes while clutching the sheet like a woman terrified to let go for fear of losing everything.

Maurine pushed out a breath. "See, Carla? She's all tore up. She's a wreck. She isn't gay. You've got her all mixed up and confused and now she feels so guilty she's scared to say anything."

Carla pleaded with Janice, now knowing the only way to reach Maurine was for Janice to say something. Otherwise, Maurine was going to create an excuse for all of it. And Carla couldn't let that happen. *They* couldn't let that happen. Janice couldn't let that happen. Could she?

But Janice wouldn't hold her gaze and she wouldn't say anything other than how this was all happening so fast.

"You should go now, Maurine," Carla said. "You barging in here like this has caused a lot of chaos. We all need some time to cool down."

Maurine didn't seem to take her request lightly. "I'll leave. But I'm not the one who should be going. You're the one who should go. Go back to Phoenix where you belong. And get the fuck out of here before you cause any more trouble."

"You get the fuck out, Maurine," Carla said. "You weren't invited."

"Carla!" Janice said.

Maurine looked to Janice. "You're going to let *her* kick me out of *your* house? Fine. I was leaving anyway. I've seen enough to make me sick for several lifetimes."

She turned and stalked out of the bedroom. Janice jumped from the bed and gave chase, bedsheet clutched to her chest, trailing along behind her.

"Maurine, wait. Mo, don't go, Mo!"

Carla could hear them talking but she couldn't make out what was being said. She quickly dressed, anger still boiling in her belly. The nerve. The fucking nerve of Maurine to march in there with her assumptions and accusations and then insist that she's the one who really knows how Janice feels.

Who does she think she is?

Deep down she knew why Maurine was behaving the way she was. She was scared. Shocked and scared. She'd already felt threatened by Janice and Carla's friendship, as if that would somehow diminish the close friendship she and Janice had, and then she walks in on this. She must be beyond terrified of losing Janice now. From her viewpoint, she'd just been horribly betrayed.

Even so, she shouldn't have reacted like she did.

But honestly, Carla knew she'd reacted rather poorly herself with some of the things she'd said.

She sat at the foot of the bed and slipped on her shoes. She buried her head in her hands, trying to fend off an impending headache and heard the front door slam. A few seconds later, she heard a car peel out. When she looked up Janice was standing in the room, eyes and cheeks red and wet with tears.

Carla tried to go to her, but Janice held out her hand, stopping her.

"No, Carla. No. Just—"

"Just what?" She took another step. Janice moved away. "Janice."

"No. You've done enough."

"Me? What the hell did I do? I just reacted, Janice. I was just as thrown as you were."

"You told her to get the fuck out of my house for one thing."

"I was standing up for us, Janice. She was insulting and attacking us."

"I don't need protecting, Carla. And she wasn't attacking me."

"Oh, she wasn't, was she? Telling us both how it is *you* feel isn't insulting? Accusing me of seducing you like I had some sort of sinister plot, like you are some kind of stupid and naive and helpless little woman isn't insulting? She was seriously out of line, Janice. And I did what needed to be done. I stood up for us."

"Yeah, well, I don't need you to. I don't want you too."

What?

Carla held up her palms. "Okay, don't worry, I won't. You want to continue to stand in silence and let someone else tell you who you truly are, then you go ahead. I, however, will not. I refuse. And I thought you—I thought you were strong enough to refuse too."

"Well, I guess I'm not, Carla. Okay? I guess I'm not strong and brave and willing to face off with my lifelong best friend when she's obviously shocked and overwhelmed and confused."

"She was shocked, yes. But she wasn't confused. She saw. She knew. She understood. She just refused to accept it. And that's her problem, not ours."

"No, it's *my* problem, Carla. Not ours. Mine. You've had years to come to terms with who you are and the freedom to do so in your own time and way. Me—I'm—this is new and I'm here, surrounded by everyone I've ever known and loved and they don't get this. I don't have the luxury of being three thousand miles away to give a damn whether or not they do or ever will."

"What are you saying?"

She shook her head. "I'm saying I'm not like you. I can't just blurt out how I feel. I can't just come out."

"You can, Janice, but you won't. And that's been the issue all along, hasn't it? That's why you fought your feelings so hard and tried to keep them hidden. But you couldn't, could you? Because they were eating you alive inside. And my being here, being so close only made it worse, didn't it? Now I wonder, though, had I not felt for you and been so inquisitive, would you ever have let any of this out? Or would you have continued on with your big secret, living a loveless, passionless life, just like you did with your husband?"

"That's not fair."

"It's the truth though, isn't it? If I'm wrong, tell me."

"Sometimes the truth needs to be brought to light carefully, considerately. Not shoved in someone's face. Especially when it might hurt them."

"You're referring to Maurine, once again dancing around yourself. But what about you, Janice? What about your pain? Why does your hurting come second to everyone else's?"

She looked away.

"When are you going to put your feelings first? Insist on your own happiness? Haven't you waited long enough?" Carla stood before her. Reached out and gently touched her face. "Hiding who you are...it's no way to live, Janice. I speak from experience."

"It's not that simple for me."

"No, it's not easy. But it beats the alternative. Wouldn't you rather face your fears and come out the other side to live in happiness, instead of letting those fears win out and keep you in misery?"

"Of course. I want happiness. I want you—I just—don't think I can have it."

"Why? Because you're scared?"

She looked at her. "Yes, because I'm scared. And because you—"

Carla waited. "Because I what?"

She shook her head. "Nothing."

"Tell me."

"It doesn't matter. Just think what you want."

"Are you really that scared and worried about everyone's reaction or are you using it as an excuse to avoid having to admit to and accept the truth yourself?"

"That was mean, Carla."

"It wasn't meant to be. It just seems to be very difficult for you to admit your feelings. And even more difficult for you to act on them."

"You don't know," she said. "You don't know me."

"Janice, I've seen it. Think about how hard it was for you to confess your feelings for me? To even act on them? You fought it like hell, even when it was plainly obvious, and I tried my very best to make you feel comfortable enough to do so. Jesus, Janice, I had to literally grab you and kiss you before you would admit it. To me, and I think, to yourself. Because *having* the feelings is one thing. You can hide them and keep them to yourself. But *admitting* them and acting on them? That's a whole other ball game isn't it? Because you can't take back words and actions. Once they're out, they're out. And that scares you."

Janice was quiet and Carla felt helpless at the sadness and defeat that resonated from her. It broke her heart.

"What can I do?" she asked softly. "How can I help, Janice? I'll do anything. Just, tell me. You want me to go talk to Maurine? Apologize for telling her to get out? I will."

"No. No don't do that. Just—"

"Yes?"

"I need to be alone."

Carla felt her body deflate like the words had pierced her new little world of happiness. She questioned her, desperate for clarification. Desperate to hear that she didn't really mean what

Carla feared she meant. "For what, a few hours? I can do that. I can take the truck and—"

"No, Carla," she said, staring into her with teary eyes. "Not for a few hours. Not for the day. For...for..."

Carla swallowed, the pain so sharp it was clawing at her throat as it tried to escape.

"Okay." She dropped her hand and backed away. She didn't know how, but her body somehow managed to make it to the doorway. She braced herself on the frame, growing weaker by the second. Still, she turned, needing to say one last thing before she dragged her tattered self from Janice and her home once and for all.

"For what it's worth," she said, her voice strained. "I would've continued to protect you. Not because you're helpless, but because I—love you. Even though that scares the shit out of me to feel and to say. But I'm feeling it. And I am saying it. I love you. And when you love someone you stand by their side and do your very best to support and protect them. I would've done that, Janice. I would've fought like hell for you. For us. And I never would've stopped. I never would've regretted doing so. Not ever."

She left her alone then and walked into the spare bedroom to pack her things. She heard Janice close her door and she was sure she heard what sounded like crying. But she didn't try to go to her. Not even when her heart and head screamed at her to. Because she couldn't do what she wanted. She had to do what Janice wanted.

And what Janice wanted, was for her to leave her alone.

Chapter Twenty-six

The doorbell rang for what seemed like the hundredth time the past week. But Janice didn't jerk with alarm at the threat of intrusion like she had previously. Instead, she remained where she was, spread out like a sorry sack of rotten potatoes on her couch, staring absently at a muted television screen. She thumbed the remote and scrolled through the channel menu, searching for something, anything that would hold her interest, while knowing all the while that what she was really searching for, she'd never find on a television, in her home, or anywhere in North Carolina for that matter. No, what she was seeking, she'd already found. But, thanks to her, it was now three thousand miles away.

The doorbell rang again and then gave way to knocking. She heard Maurine calling out for her, but she remained where she was, unaffected. Maurine began to pound. Call louder. Janice continued to stare at the television, her heart rate barely pulsing, pushing her blood along at the bare minimum.

She didn't even shift her gaze to the door when she heard Maurine insert the key and unlock the bolt. Nor did she when Maurine clamored inside, slammed the door behind her and stood at the end of the sofa with her hands on her hips and a pissed off look on her face.

"So, what, now you're deaf as well as depressed? What in the Sam Hill is going on with you?"

Janice considered not answering. She really didn't have the strength or the will. But she knew Maurine wouldn't leave if she didn't speak.

"Nothing," she said. It was true. There was literally nothing going on in her world.

"Oh, kiss my ass, will ya?" She crossed to the coffee table and started collecting the remnants of food containers and dishes that had collected from the past several days. "And since when are you such a slob?"

Janice shrugged.

Maurine took an armload into the kitchen and made way too much noise than was necessary for the job at hand. She was upset. And for some reason she didn't think Janice had noticed. So she was doing her best to make sure she heard it.

She marched back into the living room and continued straightening the table. She stacked the magazines, most of them issues of *Arizona Highways* and *Desert Living* that Janice had often perused through dreaming of a life in the southwest. That dream still tugged at her, something she couldn't seem to get past. Only now, when she thumbed through those magazines and saw the pictures of the beautiful desert sunsets and landscapes and the homes nestled against mountains, she could do nothing but imagine Carla there, living in that palm-treed paradise, going on with her life without her. And that was just too much to bear.

Even so, when Maurine finished stacking the magazines and picked them up, Janice panicked.

"What are you doing?"

"I was just going to put them away."

"No. Leave them."

"But the table's so cluttered."

"Leave them."

She frowned and returned them to the table. "You can't possibly be looking at all of them," she said under her breath.

"Actually, I can hardly stand to look at any of them anymore. But I want them there."

"Fine." She started in on the books and Janice sat up and snapped at her.

"Don't touch the books."

Startled, Maurine stared at her like a puppy that had just been admonished for the first time. "Okaay. You gonna tell me you can't read them either but for some reason want them right where they are?"

"I read them," she said defiantly.

"All of them?" There were nearly two dozen.

"Sometimes I'm in the mood for different things. I like having a choice." What she really did was return to well-known sections and reread them, needing whatever particular emotion that individual book and section invoked. She used to do that to reexperience the excitement she'd felt at the buildup and eventual release of passion between the two main characters. But now, when she reread those well-worn pages, she was often brought to tears. Nevertheless, she kept returning to those books, desperate for the rekindling of what she'd felt with Carla, even if it clenched her heart and made her cry. To lose those books, even just the sight of them, made her feel like she would lose Carla and what they'd shared.

Maurine threw up her hands and sighed. She rounded the table to settle on the love seat. Janice almost bit into her for sitting there, in Carla's spot, but she caught herself. Maurine didn't seem to notice her unease.

"When's the last time you cleaned?" She was glancing around, frowning once again.

Janice shrugged.

Maurine stood.

"What are you doing now?" Janice asked, and not very politely.

"I'm going to dust and run the vacuum."

"No."

"No?"

"You heard me."

"Janice, what is wrong?" She returned to her seat. "Are you still upset over the whole Carla thing?"

Janice flinched, unable to help it.

"I told you I didn't tell no one. I never will. It's over. You can forget about it."

Janice closed her eyes. She prayed for strength to fight back the tears that were still so painfully close to the surface. For the strength not to tear into her best friend, who, though she meant well, was slicing up her insides with every word.

"Has Carla called? Is that what's wrong? She's bothering you?"

Oh God, why does she have to keep saying her name? Please, make it stop.

"No," she croaked. "I haven't heard from her."

But that wasn't completely true. She'd received a post card day before yesterday. On the front was a beautiful photograph of a desert landscape at night. Complete with silvery sand, deep, purple, serrated mountains, dark cacti and hundreds of stars against a midnight blue sky. On the back, written in the elegant script she knew to be Carla's, were the words *Every night sky I see, regardless of where I may be in the world, still makes me think of you. Love, The Stargazer.*

She'd crumpled to the ground right there next to the mailbox after she'd read that and sobbed uncontrollably. And the sobbing had continued for the rest of that day and the next, sometimes racking her body so hard she cried not only in emotional anguish, but in physical pain. She'd sobbed until she could sob no more. Until there was nothing left inside. Nothing but empty space. And that emptiness, surprisingly, felt fucking wonderful.

But now Maurine was intruding upon it, forcing shit back inside her and stirring it all up, chasing away the numbness that had so mercifully accompanied the emptiness.

Damn her. Hasn't she done enough?

"Good, I told her to leave you alone. The last thing you need is her—"

Janice leaned toward her. "You did what?"

Maurine blinked at her. "I told her to leave you alone."

"When?"

"When she came by on her way to the airport. She wanted to talk, but I didn't want to, and I told her so. And I told her to leave you alone. That she'd done enough to upend your life and that if she cared about you at all, she'd leave you be."

Janice pushed herself up and ran her nails through her scalp, trying, now extremely hard not to rage at her best friend. There had been times when Maurine had upset her growing up, times when she'd even hurt her feelings. But Janice had always kept her anger in check and eventually given her the benefit of the doubt and forgave. Lately, however, Maurine's behavior had begun to bother her in a way she couldn't brush off and forget about. Her immaturity and "icing out" of both her and Carla in recent weeks had gotten under her skin and festered like a splinter. Now, with her aggressive insertion into their relationship and her ignorant insistence that she knew what was best for her, that splinter might as well have been a log. A huge, jagged, bacteria-laden log, spreading its infection throughout her body from beneath her skin.

Janice couldn't take it anymore.

This was going to end.

Now.

She was ready to cut off her own limb if need be to rid herself of the splinter.

"Anyway, she's gone, back to Phoenix. So you can move on." Maurine sat in silence, as if waiting for Janice to speak. When she didn't, she slapped her thighs. "So, let's get started. The first thing we need to do is get you in the shower and get you out of this house."

"I don't want to leave," Janice said, her voice barely controlled and beginning to quiver.

"You've been holed up in here for days."

"I've been out. I've driven around, gone to the store, spoken to people. And I don't want to go out again."

"Why?"

"Because it's all still the same!" she said, unable to hold back any longer. "The landscape, the homes, the old buildings in town, the goddamned people who still think, say, and do the same goddamned things. It's all the same and I've finally had my fill. I just can't take it anymore." It was how she'd been feeling for the past three years. It was why she'd taken such an interest in Arizona. It had also been the one other thing she hadn't wanted to face. This was where she was born, where she grew up, where she lived and loved. So she didn't understand why it no longer felt like home. Admitting that to herself caused so much guilt she'd fought it almost as much as she'd fought her feelings for Carla. Because to admit that this no longer felt like home, would mean somehow betraying the ones she loved.

Sitting there in her house, swallowed up in loneliness and depression, however, was no way to live. If she didn't face the truth, that's how things would continue. Because there was just no way she'd be getting over Carla and her dreams of Arizona by simply carrying on. She might be able to get up and eventually go to work every day when the time came, but every night she'd come back to this loneliness and depression. If she continued to do that, then Carla would be right. She'd keep wasting her life away, pretending everything was fine.

She tried to explain it to Maurine.

"It's like waking up to the same painting hanging on your wall day after day. You loved the painting when you picked it out and hung it, and you love it now. But you're ready for something different. You want to look at other paintings, see other landscapes. And maybe, just maybe, you'll find another painting that you love just as much, and you'll want to wake up to it every morning instead. It doesn't mean you love the old painting any less. You just want a different experience, a different view."

"Okaay," Maurine said softly. "So, what are you going to do? Stay in here and grow like a fungus on your couch? Or read your life away?" She reached for a book. "Getting lost in these?"

Janice didn't even bother to worry about what she was holding in her hand. She was too busy trying to get her to understand without verbally tearing her apart.

"Maurine, you aren't getting it. I'm saying the exact opposite."

She didn't seem to hear her. "Janice, what happened with Carla wasn't your fault. You don't need to feel guilty and beat yourself up about it. You don't need to hide away in here."

"You're not hearing me."

"Carla, she—"

"Enough about Carla!"

Maurine's eyes were wide with alarm.

"Okay, calm down."

"It wasn't her fault," Janice continued, unimpeded. "What happened…it wasn't all her."

"What do you mean? She—"

"I was there too." She ran her hand through her hair, frustrated. "Damn it, Maurine. Stop blaming her for everything. She didn't do anything wrong. She didn't do anything I didn't want."

Maurine stared at her.

"What—you mean—you're saying—"

"That I liked it?" She stared right back into her. "That I wanted it? Wanted her?"

The color drained from Maurine's face.

"Yes, Maurine, I did. I wanted it. I wanted her. I wanted her more than I've ever wanted anything in my life. And I'll tell you something else. I didn't just like it. I loved it. Making love with her surpasses everything. Everything. I couldn't have even dreamed, imagined how incredible it was. And believe me I tried. I tried for the last three years."

"You don't mean that. You're—"

"I'm not confused. I'm not vulnerable. I'm gay, Maurine."

Maurine looked as though she'd been smacked. "But you—"

"Just because I was with a man doesn't mean I'm not gay. I loved him, yes. But there was no passion. No desire. Only a friendship. An understanding of sorts. And that, I now know, is not a loving, romantic relationship. That is not happiness."

"And Carla…is?"

"Yes. I've been the happiest I've ever been this summer. And she's the reason why."

Maurine stared down at the table and then her gaze shifted to the back of the book in her hand. Her eyes widened again and then closed.

"This book is about two women. You're reading…gay…"

"Lesbian romances. I've been reading them for a couple of years now."

Maurine's eyes flew open as if she'd just heard her reference to time. "Years? How could it have been years? How did this—when did you—"

"It started the night Carla came out."

"And she said she didn't influence you when she obviously did. And you're telling me not to be upset with her?"

"Listen. Okay? I need you to really listen." She took a breath and started in, confessing things she'd never thought she'd be able to confess. Not even to Maurine.

"When Carla told us she was gay, something happened inside of me. I was immediately struck and…excited. My heart raced and my skin burned, and I couldn't stop looking at her. It was like I had been jolted awake, jolted to attention. And there she was. Right in front of me. This woman I had known for as long as I can remember, whom I always had love for and admired and thought beautiful, suddenly came to life in front of me. Almost like a blooming flower. One I had never seen fully open before. She was captivating. And hearing that she was attracted to women and wanted to be with women, well, that just sent me over the edge. I got lost in delirium imagining that. And eventually, got lost in delirium imagining her being with me."

Maurine glanced away and it seemed difficult for her to speak. "You didn't tell me."

"How could I? I wasn't even sure what exactly was happening. I was as surprised and confused by my feelings as you are now. Even when I figured things out and halfway understood my feelings, I knew you wouldn't take it well. And I knew why. I'm your best friend. Carla is your niece. We're both women. I didn't expect you to just accept it."

Janice softened her tone. "And the way you react to news you don't like, didn't encourage me to confide in you. I feared you shutting me out, rejecting me. I feared losing you."

Maurine turned toward the window. "I understand," she said. "I can see why you'd be afraid to come to me." She sighed and laughed a little. "And here I've been scared that you and Carla's closeness would lead to your rejection of me. I feel so stupid, now. I've been acting like such a jerk."

She met Janice's gaze. "I'm sorry for that, Jay Jay. I am. But honestly, I'm still not sure how to take this. Or even what to say. It's like I just walked in on you and Carla in bed all over again. I feel like I don't know you, or even if I ever really did." She shook her head. "I don't mean that in a bad way. I just—I thought we were best friends."

"We are."

"Then I should've known. Whether you were able to tell me or not."

"What would you have done had you known sooner?"

"I don't know."

"Understand? Be supportive?"

She sighed. "I wish I could say yes, but I'd be lying. Truth is...I woulda freaked out. I guess that means I'm not such a good friend after all. Because I'm sitting here, taking this in and really hearing you but I still can't make this feel okay."

"Do you love me?" Janice asked.

Maurine sniffled as if tears were going to come. "Yes."

"Right now, after everything I've just told you?"

"Yes."

"Do you love Carla?"

Her face clouded but with what looked like anguish and guilt rather than anger.

"Yes."

"I do too, Maurine. I'm in love with her."

"Are you...sure?"

"Yes. And she loves me."

Maurine grew quiet and Janice gave her some time to process. "And we both love you," Janice finally said.

"Carla's angry. She has every right to be. I hurt her."

"She still loves you. She always will. Just as I will. Whether you choose to accept me for who I am or not. I love you. Rain or shine."

"Lord," she said as she stood and came to sit next to her. "I can't sit here and let my feelings ruin what we have. This ain't about me." She opened her arms and pulled Janice into a firm hug and kissed her cheek repeatedly. "I got to quit thinking about my own feelings so much." She gripped her arms tightly and looked at her with deep sincerity. "I'm still in shock and all and I'm still trying to make sense of this and exactly how it is I feel about it, but that don't mean I can't love and support you."

Janice fell into her, relief and heartfelt love completely washing over her.

"You don't know how much what you just said means."

Maurine held her and rubbed her back. "Maybe not. But if it means anything close to what you mean to me, then I know it's a whole hell of a lot."

"Thank you," Janice said, as she began to cry.

"You don't need to thank me," Maurine said, her voice finally giving way to tears as well. "That's what friends are for."

CHAPTER TWENTY-SEVEN

Janice sat swaying quietly in the old porch swing nestled deep in the back of Mamie's carport. She'd retreated to the swing often as a child when she'd needed a break and some alone time from play with her boisterous cousins. The spot was a peaceful reprieve and she'd contemplated many things from that old swing. She reckoned that's what had drawn her there now.

She gave herself a gentle push with her foot, content with the lulling of the continued swaying. The afternoon was hot and sticky, but she was oblivious, lost in her thoughts and the comfort of the dark, cool carport. Nothing but her, the swing, and the daddy longlegs lounging in his web in the corner.

But the door to the house opened and changed all that.

"I thought that was your car I seen sitting in the driveway," Mamie said, easing open the screen door. "Whatcha doin' sitting out here, sugar?"

"Just thinking."

Mamie seemed to consider that for a moment. "You come all this way to sit in my swing and think?"

Janice shrugged. "I guess I did, yes." She took in the lush lawn and the bushes and trees beyond the driveway, remembering how she and her cousins ran barefoot through it all, chasing each other and laughing on long summer days just like this one. She smiled at the memory and watched as a wasp ducked under the roof and disappeared into its nest in the upper corner of the carport. It seemed she and the daddy longlegs weren't the only living occupants after all. She looked back to Mamie, who, in turn, was watching her. Janice tried to explain something she didn't quite understand herself. "I was driving through town, thinking about old times, thinking about now, searching for answers. But I didn't find any. So, I kept driving, kind of lost as to where I might find them, and I ended up here."

"You finding any?"

"No. Only memories."

"Maybe that's where your answers lie."

Janice couldn't see how. All she knew was that the memories had been and still were surrounding her, spilling into her mind everywhere she looked, filling her up with their bitter sweetness, causing her to laugh one second and cry the next. The process was becoming relentless and she'd never expected it to carry on for more than two days.

"I heard your friend left," Mamie said. "That Sims girl. Went back to Arizona."

Janice swallowed hard, wondering just what all she'd heard. The sudden panic made her wince and she cursed herself for it, knowing she shouldn't be so worried about what people knew and what they thought. It seemed to be a habit, one she knew well from having to hide for so long. Breaking it would be a struggle, but she was determined to try.

"Carla," Janice clarified, bringing on more pain. "Yes, she went home." She touched her throat, feeling as though her voice would soon fail her.

After another long moment, Mamie edged the door open farther. "Why don't you come on inside and sit a spell and talk to your old Mamie? Sometimes talking things through helps you find your way."

Janice stood and crossed to the door. She and Mamie embraced as she stepped inside and the feel of her familiar warmth and softness almost made her cry. Mamie seemed to notice. She closed the door and reached for her face.

"Lord, child, you look like you got the world itself on your shoulders."

Janice teared up but couldn't bring herself to speak.

Mamie held her and studied her carefully with her lively eyes. She'd always been able to see Janice, to sense things about her when no one else could. She was intuitive.

Just like Carla said I was.

She got choked up at the thought of her.

Mamie, saw that reaction too. She touched her shoulders, her face drawn with obvious concern.

"Why don't you go sit down?" She walked with Janice to the couch.

"Where are you going?" Janice asked as she walked away and bypassed her recliner.

"I thought you might like a glass of tea."

Janice shook her head. "No, thank you. I'm not thirsty right now."

"It ain't about thirst, sugar. It's about comfort." She disappeared into the kitchen and returned with a glass of iced tea. She gave it to Janice and then headed for the hallway. Janice chose not to ask after her that time and instead sipped her drink.

She found Mamie to be correct. The tea tasted damn good and she felt her spirits lift a little. She looked out the window and got lost in her thoughts again. She was so disconnected from her present surroundings; she didn't even notice when Mamie reentered the room. She had sat down next to her before she could fully grasp her presence once again.

"I got something for you," she said, patting the lid to an old shoebox.

"For me?"

"Uh-huh. You're the only one of all the young'uns in my life who I think can truly appreciate this. I always thought you might be, but I put off sharing it with you, waiting for you to come into your own. It seems now that maybe I waited too long. I hope that ain't the case. But either way, this is yours now. Maybe it can still help in some way. Maybe it can help ease that torment I can see a-brewing in your eyes."

She handed Janice the box.

Janice smoothed her hand across the top, having no idea what could possibly be inside.

"Go ahead, child. Open it," Mamie said, squeezing her arm.

Janice removed the lid and found a box full of old photographs and letters. She sifted through them, curious, but didn't see anything or anyone in the photos that looked familiar. Confused, she held one of the photos up for closer inspection.

"Who is this?" she asked, looking closely at what appeared to be two happy women, sitting on a low, concrete ledge, legs dangling in front of them, arms entwined, and laughter on their faces.

Mamie scooted closer, smiling, and pointed to the woman on the left.

"That's your great-aunt Gale."

Janice stared harder. "That's Aunt Gale?"

"Sure is."

"She looks so young. So...happy."

"She was," Mamie said. "Both."

Janice studied the woman next to her. She was just as attractive as Gale, but noticeably different in appearance. Gale had her hair set, dark lipstick on, and a dress that form-fit to her body. The woman next to her was all natural. From her free-flowing hair, to her makeup-free face, to her casual shirt and pants. Her femininity was still clearly evident, even if it wasn't in her choice of clothes. And even those she wore to fit her own style, with the sleeves to her shirt rolled up at the cuff showing the sinewy strength to her lean forearms. Her shirt was only buttoned halfway up, leaving the collar and a great deal more open, showing off her graceful looking chest and neckline. A very thin necklace hugged her neck, its charm, one that looked like a small heart, rested in the hallow of her throat.

Her whole ensemble had Janice's pulse racing as she continued to look back between her aunt and the woman, her eyes glued to their entwined arms and laughing faces.

"That there is Liza," Mamie said.

"Liza," Janice whispered.

"She was the friend of Gale's I was telling you about."

Janice ran her finger along the photo, already knowing, before Mamie had even said a word, that this was the woman she'd spoken of before. This was Great-Aunt Gale's special someone. She didn't have to wonder much at all as to just how special she was to Gale. Love and joy exuded from them both along with a sense of their deep connection.

"I remember," Janice said. She touched Liza's face, feeling her own connection. "Did I ever meet her? She seems so familiar."

"No, sugar. Liza died many years ago. Long before you was born. She died before her time."

Janice looked at her. "Why?"

Mamie shifted as if uncomfortable. "It ain't a pretty story."

Janice touched her arm. "Mamie? Please tell me."

Mamie stared out the window before she finally nodded. "One night Gale and Liza went out looking for a drink. They had to drive a spell, seeing as how this is a dry county and all and they found a popular old hole-in-the-wall full of smoke, liquor, and wild people. They was all sorts of things that went on there, such as gambling and things like that. But that never stopped Gale and Liza. It was like they was drawn to places and people like that from time to time. They loved the freedom they felt there in those places I reckon. And most of the time, they enjoyed themselves and let loose. But this one night, things didn't turn out so well.

"Seems there was a man there who didn't like how comfortable Gale and Liza was with each other. And he made it known. Spouted off. Liza mouthed off back at him, and he didn't take too kindly to that. So he got it in his head to go after Gale. He sauntered up to her and came on to her and started putting his hands all over her. Gale tried to push him away, but he wouldn't let her go. Liza went plum crazy and managed to get him off her, but they fell to the floor, fighting. Only..." She paused, her eyes glazed with sadness, focused somewhere beyond the room. "He was the only one to get up when it was over. Liza never did."

She dropped her head and stared at her hands.

"He had stabbed her. Right in the heart."

Janice covered her mouth. She trembled at both Mamie's obvious pain and the awful pain Gale must've gone through in losing Liza.

"That is so terrible, Mamie. I'm so sorry."

Mamie nodded. "It was. Gale was never the same. She never got over Liza." She looked up at her. "Ever."

Janice gripped Mamie's hand. Mamie squeezed hers in return.

"That's why I'm giving this to you. Because I see your aunt Gale in you. And I think, now that you seen those photos, that you do too."

Janice was speechless. Her heart raced with anguish from her aunt's despair, love from the familiar passion she must've felt for Liza and comfort in the form of recognition. Of feeling a connection with a woman she hadn't really known at all. A kindred spirit.

"And I think the reason Liza seems so familiar to you is because…well, because she's a lot like your friend."

Janice smiled before she could stop herself. She tried to cover it with her hand.

But Mamie gently pulled her hand away.

"Carla Sims is your Liza."

Janice's breath hitched and she tried to cover her mouth again, this time to try to stave off tears. But Mamie wouldn't let her. She kept hold of her hand, kept their gaze locked.

"You don't got to be afraid, sugar. Not with me. I knew about your aunt Gale even before she did. I was the one who told her she was in love with Liza. And that she outta quit fighting it and just be with her. Because there was no doubt that Liza was in love with Gale. She fell for Gale the second she saw her the summer Liza moved to town."

She smiled softly. "And now, after all these years, I'm sitting here telling you the same thing. Hoping you'll quit fighting it. You are in love with Carla Sims. I knew it the second I asked you about her. When you was sitting right here on this couch. You couldn't hide it, not from me. Because when I looked at you that day, when we was talking about Carla, I saw the way your eyes was a-shining and that little smile of yours kept reappearing. I saw the way you blushed, the way you fidgeted. Sugar, I saw my sister. She was in you, staring right back at me.

"And when I heard Carla had left and that you was all tore up, well, I knew for sure then. I just kept hoping and waiting for you to come around. I figured at some point you would."

She brushed her hand across Janice's cheek. "Quit fighting it, child. And go be with her. She's your someone special and when you got someone like that, you can't take it for granted." She nodded toward the photo. "They'd tell you the same thing. Be together while you can. For as long as you can. You don't want to have any regrets and you don't want to feel like you didn't get enough time."

She patted her leg, took the photo, set it in the box, and closed the lid.

"Take Gale and Liza with you. Look at their photos. At their faces. See the love. Read their letters and feel the love. You do that, sugar, and you won't have any more trouble in finding those answers you're after. This town, these people, they're all in your heart and in your mind. You can call upon them anytime, just like you did today. You don't got to be here to do that."

Hot tears streamed down Janice's face. She hugged Mamie so hard she protested, but Janice didn't ease up. She held tight and sobbed into the sweet scent of her neck.

Mamie soothed her and stroked her back. "It's okay, sugar. It's okay. You can let it all go now. Just let go and let love do its thing. You been waiting long enough."

"I'm just so scared," Janice said, pulling back. "Not so much of everyone knowing, I mean, I'm still not exactly relaxed over it or anything. But I'm getting there. I'm more scared of seeing Carla. Of telling her how I feel about her. I was—I told her to leave, Mamie. That was my response to her telling me she loves me. She would have every right to slam the door in my face."

"She told you she loves you?"

"Yes. And so much more. And I—I was a coward. I pushed her away. I can't bear the thought that I've lost her forever. It's just too terrifying."

"That's how you know you got to go tell her. Your fear. You being afraid is how you know your feelings are real. That they are strong and deep and worth more than anything. If they wasn't that deep and meaningful, you wouldn't be so scared. If you ain't doing things that scare you from time to time, then you ain't living. That's what my Mama used to say."

She wiped Janice's tears with the backs of her fingers.

"It's about time you started living, sugar."

Janice gripped her hands. "As always, Mamie. I think you may be right."

Chapter Twenty-eight

Carla turned off the steaming flow of water with her toe, satisfied with the increased warmth of her bath water. She'd been soaking long enough for the water to cool, but rather than climb out and face another night going to bed alone, where she'd no doubt spend hours chasing sleep that just wouldn't come, she'd topped off the tub with more hot water, content to remain where she was, where at least the temperature of the water could heat her body. Her insides however, and that spot just behind her sternum, the place that had recently been reanimated and filled to the brim with light and love, had stilled and gone dark, as if it had been unplugged. Nothing, it seemed, could penetrate the chill that now resided there.

She sank farther into the bath, submerging her shoulders and the back of her head, the water flowing around her ears. Her eyes fell closed and she tried to relax her mind, hoping it would follow her body and give in to the massage of the heated water. But so far it was refusing and even the muffled, womb-like sound in her ears wasn't enough to help. Her varied attempts to block out the world, which had grown more significant with the passing of days, continued to fail.

Nadine, unfortunately, had noticed and she'd been blowing up her phone since she'd returned home. It wasn't like Carla hadn't tried to move on and go on with her life with a good attitude and a smile on her face. She'd spent time with friends, gone out for meals and drinks, smiled, laughed, cried. She had done those things with every intention of carrying on. But her attempts had fallen flat. Her friends hadn't bought into it. Her despair was just too deep to mask. Nadine had said her sadness orbited her, surrounding her like a bubble, somehow fixed to her like the pull of a magnet. Carla had argued with her, but arguing with Nadine was pointless, especially when Carla knew she was right. So, instead of battling with her and instead of feigning off the overly concerned looks from her friends, she'd started staying at home and avoiding everyone altogether.

At least at home she was free to wallow in her misery. That is, when Nadine wasn't dialing her number every other hour. She'd remedied that though and given Nadine her own ring tone. She could better avoid her calls, and more importantly, she could stop jumping up with a rush of hope and excitement, thinking it might be Janice, only to be crushed with disappointment.

Though she knew it was probably pointless, she'd also assigned a ring tone for Janice, wanting to be sure she'd know it was her if she called. But the song she'd chosen, "At Last" by Etta James, had yet to play anywhere other than her mind where it seemed to repeat continuously. She could even hear it now. In the bath. Under the water. Like it was somewhere in the distance.

She opened her eyes, something sounding off, different. The same line of the song was repeating. She sat up. Listened.

Nothing. She rubbed her face, confused. She thought about slipping down into the water again, but Etta James called out. This time clear as a bell. Close by. She scrambled from the tub, slid into her satin robe, and hurried into her bedroom. She scooped up her phone, her motionless and cold heart suddenly careening and beating with fire, saw Janice's name on the screen, and answered.

"Hello?"

Silence.

Her heart stopped. Dead stopped in the center of her chest. It actually caused pain and she could feel the fire it had beat through her begin to cool.

"Janice? Hello, are you there?"

Please, be there.

"Hi." The greeting was soft, almost shy. But it was her. It was Janice.

Carla nearly buckled with relief. "Hi."

"I—are you home?"

Carla blinked. "Yeah. I'm at home."

"Oh. Are you busy?"

"No, I can talk."

"That would be—nice. I would like that. Only—"

Carla waited, her hesitation threatening to cause a panic. "Only, what?"

"I—I would like to do it in person."

Carla palmed her forehead. "I would like that too, but don't you think talking like this is better than nothing?"

"No," she said. "No, I don't. It's not good enough. I want to talk to you in person."

Carla pushed out a breath and ran her hand through her damp hair. "Janice, what do you want me to do? Come back? To talk?"

Dear God, I will. I'll do it. If you say yes, I'll book the next flight. It may be crazy but so is how I've been feeling here without you.

"No, I don't want you to do anything."

Carla clenched her eyes.

"Wait, no, that's not entirely true. There is one thing I need you to do."

"What's that?"

The doorbell rang, echoing throughout the house.

Carla opened her eyes.

Janice spoke.

"I need you to answer your door."

The phone fell from Carla's hand. She stared at the doorway to her bedroom in disbelief. The doorbell rang again. She ran into the hallway, sprinted across the tile and through the living room. The runner bunched as she slammed to a stop at the front door. She tried to catch her breath as she rested her forehead on the doorframe.

Could she really be here? Could she?

She quickly tied the belt to her robe, unlocked the door, and pulled it open slowly, afraid to find the front entry vacant, to feel that crush of disappointment she'd been trying so hard to avoid. But as the door edged farther open, Carla felt that rush of hope and excitement she'd felt with nearly every ring of her phone.

For Janice was really there, right next to her potted cactus, smiling shyly.

"Hi."

Carla struggled to speak. "Uh, hi. Hi. Hello."

"I was hoping we could talk. In person."

Carla pushed on the door. "Of course. Yes. I—come in."

Janice moved and Carla saw her luggage. Her throat tightened. She hadn't packed light. She wanted to cry. She swallowed it down, trying not to anticipate anything, but failing completely.

She stepped out into the night and grabbed her luggage.

"I can get it," Janice said.

"Don't even try," Carla said. "You're on my turf now. And yes, I know you want to say I told you so about my going out of my way for you, just as you said I would, but I wouldn't do that either if I was you." She set the luggage inside and turned. "That would be dangerous at the moment." She smiled and welcomed her inside. Janice entered the house and quietly looked around, like she was taking everything in but didn't want to be too obvious about it.

"Your home, it's very rustic but colorful. It's beautiful."

Carla closed the door and carried her bags into the living room.

"Most everything you see was made in Mexico. Furniture, rugs, artwork. I got lucky with some of them, bought them at a local store I loved that had to close down. The rest, I picked up over the years. But I can't take credit for the decorating and arranging. That's all my friend Nadine's doing."

"These, what are these?" Janice asked, staring at one of her decorated walls.

"Sugar skulls."

"Sugar what?"

Carla laughed and started to explain but Janice moved away from the wall, shaking her head.

"Maybe you can fill me in later."

There was very little light in the room, some spilling in from the window above the door from the porch light and some spilling in from the hallway. But Carla could see her face, see the fine, delicate features and the milky white of her skin. She could also see the worry in her eyes and the fidgeting of her hands.

In fact, the dim light was doing very little to hinder her sight and there was nothing at all hindering her other senses.

"You smell so good," Carla said, unable to keep that particular realization to herself. Janice appeared to be wound tighter than a top and Carla hoped her confession wouldn't send her running for the door.

"So do you. Like your cologne, but more subtle."

"Body wash," Carla said.

"You were in the shower," Janice said. "I noticed that you're… wet."

"Bath," Carla clarified.

"I hope I didn't interrupt."

"You did, actually."

"Oh, I'm sorry, I—"

"Don't be. I'd much rather be standing here with you than soaking all alone in the tub." She smiled at her again, hoping to ease her anxiety. But Janice rang her hands and only offered a weak smile in return.

"Would you like to sit down?" Carla motioned toward the couch. "Or maybe something to eat or drink?"

"No," Janice said. "I need to—talk."

"You don't want to at least sit down?"

"No. I just need to say some things and I don't want to get too comf—"

She's not planning on staying. At least not here, not with me.

"Okay," Carla said.

Janice seemed to be waiting for her to say more. When she didn't, she suddenly started in.

"I'm sorry, Carla," she blurted. "I never should've treated you the way I did. I never should've told you to go. It wasn't what I really wanted. Not at all. I was scared, like you said. I reacted with fear. I didn't think I could face being gay, or face telling anyone else. Maurine's reaction that day brought those fears to life and

I—panicked. And I pushed you away because of that. I'm so sorry. I know I hurt you. And if you can't forgive me, I understand. I wouldn't blame you. I hope you can. Hope you will. But regardless, I came all this way to apologize to you. Because at the very least I owed you that."

She stopped just as suddenly as she'd started. She'd stopped fidgeting too but now she was trembling.

"You don't owe me anything."

"I do."

"You apologized and that's enough. You're scared. I'd be a bold-faced liar if I denied understanding that. Coming out is not easy for some people. Even in this day and age and I probably shouldn't have pushed you. So, I apologize as well. You didn't have to come all this way to apologize to me, but your doing so is a testament to who you really are, Janice. You're something special, so please don't continue to beat yourself up because you're scared."

She opened her mouth. Closed it. "I was scared. But—I'm not scared of that anymore."

"You're not?"

"No. I've told quite a few people here recently, so, of course, I'm sure the entire county knows by now." She smiled and Carla responded like a wilted flower that had just been shined upon by the sun.

"I wouldn't doubt it." Carla took a step toward her, drawn to her like she very well was the sun and she needed her warmth and light to live, to exist. "Are you sure you wouldn't like to sit down? Now that you've got that off your chest? Relax a little."

She shook her head. "No—I. There's one more thing."

What else could there possibly be? Why does she still look like she's going to bolt at any second?

"And I *am* scared to tell you this."

Carla took another step, wanting to reach for her. "You don't have to be afraid."

"Please." She held out a hand, stopping her. "Carla, I—" She glanced away. But then she looked back at her and stared directly into her eyes. "Carla, I love you. I'm in love with you. No, not just in love. I'm madly, deeply, crazy, in love with you. And I really came all this way to tell you *that*. I wanted to look into your eyes and say it. Because I need you to know it's true, despite the way I acted when you told me the same. I love you. And I'm scared saying it, of telling you, because you have every right to turn me away, to say it's too late, that I've hurt you too badly. I'm so scared you're going to do that that I'm standing here shaking like a leaf and—"

Carla crossed to her, reached out and cupped her face and conquered her mouth with her own, kissing her long, and deep and slow, until Janice made a noise of surrender and threatened to collapse where she stood.

Carla kissed her for what felt like an eternity, drinking her in, every last delicious drop, having longed for the feel of her, for the taste of her. She kissed her until she, too, felt like she might weaken and fall with her to the floor.

"You don't have to be afraid," Carla breathed as she finally pulled her lips from hers. "I could never turn you away. I've done nothing but ache for you like a part of me had broken away and been left behind in North Carolina. I've never ached like that in my life."

Janice clung to her robe, as if she needed to for strength.

"You're not hurt? Upset?"

"Yes, I was torn to pieces, Janice. And I was upset with myself for falling for you. For giving my heart away again when I'd promised myself I wouldn't. But I was never angry at you. And the more I thought about things and tried to convince myself to be angry and cynical and curse love all over again, I realized I couldn't. Not this time, even though my heart had gone cold and dark in my chest. I just couldn't do it and I couldn't figure out why until I picked up my phone with the anticipation of hearing your voice and my heart suddenly jump-started back to life as if it had never stopped. Everything you evoke in me, every feeling, every thought, every desire, it all came rushing back and the familiarity of its return felt so good as it flooded into and filled all those dark, empty places inside. And when I opened that door and saw you standing there, I knew I'd never feel this way about anyone else, ever again. This is all you, Janice," she said touching her own heart. "I love you beyond what I thought possible."

"Yes," Janice said. "I understand because my love for you goes beyond everything and anyone else. It goes beyond me. I know that now. I know that nothing I fear is worth losing you over. Nothing." She kissed her neck, creating a trail down to the dip at her collarbone. Carla felt her breathe deeply as she paused there. "I have missed you so much," she said. "I thought I'd never get to kiss you right here again, in my favorite spot, where I could rest my head and breathe in your scent for eternity."

Carla shuddered as she placed more tiny kisses on her awakening skin, this time creating a trail that led into the satin edge of her robe, which she carefully pushed open farther to kiss along her shoulder. She was sparking her desire, one purposely delivered delicate kiss after another.

Carla hurried to speak.

"I almost cried when I saw your luggage and saw that you hadn't packed light. My heart leapt, hoping it meant you had come with the intention of staying a while. Now, with what I just heard you say and with what you're doing to me with your mouth, I'm about to either cry all over again or lose control and ravish you. So, please, tell me you're here to stay for a while. That you're going to stay a while."

"I am."

"With me?"

Janice touched her cheek. "If you'll have me."

Carla closed her eyes. "Oh, my God, yes." She opened them and took her in as if seeing her for the very first time. She picked her up. "I'll definitely have you." She turned, ready to carry her away. "But you get to choose where. Because I don't think I can wait until we reach the bedroom. To me the couch is looking pretty damn good. But I'll go wherever you want. It's your call."

Janice grinned. "The bedroom."

Carla groaned. "You're evil." She carried her down the hallway to the bedroom and released her by the bed. Janice stood before her, the shyness in her gone, grin still on her face.

"My bed isn't near as romantic as yours," Carla said.

"As long as it has you in it, it is." She reached up, touched her face again. "But the bed isn't what I had in mind."

"No?"

She pushed on her shoulders. "No. Because I'm feeling a little like you. Like I can't wait. Like I don't want to wait. Like I don't want to go slow." She backed her to the wall. "I want to touch you now. Feel your body now." She tugged on her belt and forced open her robe. She grazed her hand up her thigh. "You smelling so good, all wet from your bath, that robe clinging to you. I may have come here to apologize and to tell you I love you, but I was seriously tempted to throw all that to the wayside and have you first. I'm surprised I didn't jump you at the door, scared or not. That's how badly I want you."

She leaned in, kissed her neck again, and teased her between her legs with her fingertips.

"Because taking you right then and there was what I really wanted to do. And I think now I'm going to be all about doing what I want. Especially when it comes to you."

Carla saw the flash of hunger in her eyes, heard how her words were dripping with determined desire.

"I'm so fucking turned on I'm speechless. Motionless." She swallowed hard. "I'm helplessly yours, Janice."

"Good. Because I'm about to make another one of my dreams come true."

She slid her hand into her aching flesh and just as Carla cried out, she took her mouth with hers and devoured her audible pleasure, as if eliciting it with her fingers weren't enough. She had to taste it as Carla expelled it.

And she kept on, giving and then consuming, with seemingly no intention of stopping. Carla couldn't resist, couldn't plead for sweet mercy, not even when she began to quiver, and her legs began to buckle, and she was sure she was going to slide down the wall. Janice didn't let up, and Carla, whether she feared falling or not, had no choice but to completely relent, body and soul and give herself to the woman she loved.

To the woman who, she now wholeheartedly believed, loved her.

Chapter Twenty-nine

Janice set the large gift box she was carrying on the table in front of Carla. She tried, but she couldn't hold back the smile that was intent on spreading across her face. The last two weeks had somehow even surpassed what they'd shared in North Carolina. Their time together in Carla's home and when they managed to force themselves out of the bed to go out, had been filled with emotion, passion, and discovery. Janice had shared things with Carla that she'd never shared with anyone else. She told her how she felt, how she'd struggled with her attraction to her, caught up in both fear and overwhelming excitement. She'd done her best to answer the questions Carla had asked again, this time while Janice was curled up in her arms. She'd told her about her avid interest in Arizona and how she'd been reading about it for months, until her curiosity and interest had evolved into wanting to experience it firsthand. But she'd convinced herself it was just a dream knowing she would most likely love Arizona, based on what she'd seen and learned, and the mere possibility of that had consumed her with guilt. How could she leave the place that had always been her home? How could she leave Maurine and her other loved ones?

"What's this?" Carla's eyes were that deeper shade of gold that Janice now knew to be reticent of sleep. She was completely clueless to her beauty as she sat running her hand through her hair which was mussed from sleep and other certain activities. Activities that had caused Janice to run *her* hands through her hair, tangling and tugging, pleading and insisting. Her smile grew as she thought about yet another shared night of unbridled passion. Carla sitting there looking so sweet in her confusion, wearing nothing but her gray cotton sleep bra and matching shorts had Janice suddenly eager for a repeat of the night before.

How long will we be able to wait today? An hour? Possibly two, before we have to touch each other again? Two would be a record.

"A present," Janice said. "I thought for sure the wrapping and the big red bow would be a dead giveaway." She settled in across from her and rested her chin in her hand.

Carla gave her a look.

God, how I love her. Will it always be this good?

She thought about the future, near and far, and she was left feeling calm and assured, knowing that their love would grow and deepen. She imagined them waking next to each other and then coming home to each other at night. Nothing in the world sounded better and she knew Carla felt the same. She hadn't been able to hide her excitement when Janice had told her she'd resigned from her job, ready to step out into the world to see where the road took her. And Carla had brought up the future and their being together a few times since then, and Janice could tell she was testing the water. Janice had wanted to jump on her and bounce up and down and proudly declare that she wanted to be with her more than anything, but she'd held back, preferring to wait for the right moment. She had hopes that the right moment would present itself today. Maybe even very soon.

"I considered breakfast to be a gift," Carla said. "I didn't expect this."

"It's your birthday, Carla, and our last day together before you go back to work. So, breakfast was nothing. The gifts, this being one of them, will be plentiful and given throughout the day."

Carla raised her eyebrows.

"Don't argue with me, Sims. This is what I want to do to celebrate your birthday. I want to spoil you, show you how much I cherish you. Especially since this expert in literature seems to have trouble expressing her feelings through words alone."

"You're getting better. You're just not used to doing it, so it might take some time. And I told you to stop feeling so guilty about keeping everything inside. You were experiencing a lot while I was there, and most of it for the first time."

"Even so." She sighed. "Giving, like this, is something I know I'm good at."

"You give me plenty," Carla said. "More than enough."

"Will you just open the gift? You don't know how difficult it's been keeping it from you."

Carla tore away the paper and lifted the lid off the box. "No way." She seemed completely surprised, completely taken aback. "This—it's—I can't believe it. You're giving this to me?"

"Yes."

"Are you sure?"

"Carla, yes, I'm sure. I remember your reaction when you first saw it and from that moment on it became yours. I thought of you every second I spent finishing it, especially when you were right there, in the room next to me as I worked on it. It was made for you. I want you to have it."

Carla held the glossy, intricately painted chess pieces up and examined them, her face lit up in excitement and awe. "So, this was what was in that box that came soon after you arrived? The one you raced to the door for and wouldn't let me anywhere near? Even though it had *my* name and address on it?"

"Uh-huh."

"I'm glad you stayed," she said. "To intercept the box and give me the gift yourself."

She finally looked at Janice and appeared to be so moved she was on the verge of tears.

"Thank you."

"You're welcome."

"I don't know what else to say. I'm overwhelmed."

"Don't say anything. I'm content just sitting here watching you, basking in your happiness."

Carla rose and came to her side. She knelt and kissed her. "It's the best, most thoughtful gift anyone has ever given me. I can't even imagine you giving me any more."

"Well, whether you can imagine it or not, it's happening." She stood alongside her and led her by the hand to the living room. "Sit."

"Yes, ma'am."

Janice sat next to her and handed her the old shoebox she'd set on the coffee table. "This one isn't wrapped."

"Okay."

"It doesn't need to be. It represents something more than a birthday gift." She nodded toward the box, encouraging her to open it.

Carla removed the lid. "What is it?" She looked at her. "Do these belong to you?"

"They do now."

Carla picked up photo after photo.

"That's my great-aunt Gale," Janice said, pointing. "And that is Liza."

Carla studied the women closely, picture after picture.

"They were a couple," she eventually said. "They were in love."

"Yes," Janice whispered.

Carla smiled, wistful. "They were beautiful. And they look so happy."

"They were. But unfortunately, their time together was tragically cut short. Nevertheless, their love lives on." She reached in the box and held up some of the letters. "You can see a lot in the pictures," she said. "How close they were, how happy they were. But these tell you how they felt, what they thought, and just how much in love they really were."

Carla slowly took one and unfolded it. She read quietly. "Oh, my God."

"Uh-huh."

"Are they all like this?"

"If you mean deep, passionate and detailed, yes."

"This is—am I blushing? I feel like I should be blushing."

Janice laughed. "They, unlike me, certainly seemed to have no trouble in expressing themselves." She lightly touched her forearm. "I'm thankful that they could write so well, that they could tell each other how they felt because their feelings and their words helped put to voice just how much I feel for you. They said what I felt, what I wanted to say but wasn't able to. Their love gave me the strength to follow my heart. To come to you. To find my way...home."

Janice dipped her hand in her robe pocket and pulled out the gold necklace she'd brought with her. Carla eyed it and then eyed her. Janice unclasped it. "I want you to have this." She wrapped it around her neck and fastened it. "It's similar to the one Gale gave Liza. Like the one she's wearing in all the pictures."

Carla fingered the charm. "It's a heart."

Janice nodded. "It's my heart. You now officially have my heart, Carla Sims."

Carla placed the box back on the table. She slid her hand along Janice's neck and buried her fingers in her hair. "Then you're absolutely right. That box and everything it represents means so much more than any other gift ever could. It brought your feelings to light and it brought you to me." She leaned in and softly kissed her. "It brought you...home."

Janice began to tremble, like she had the night she'd arrived. Only now it wasn't from nerves or from fear of rejection. It was from being gently pulled in and enveloped in love.

"Please tell me you'll stay," Carla said. "Not just for a while. Or an extended visit. But for forever."

Janice smiled as a tear slid down her face. She nodded. "If you'll have me."

Carla grinned. "Oh, I'll have you." She tugged her closer, pulled her onto her lap. She traced her fingertip around Janice's heart. "This doesn't mean you'll be anything less than who you are or in any way devalue where you come from. It won't make you any less southern." She squeezed her. "Well, maybe a little. But only as much as you allow. Only as much as you want." She lightly poked her chest. "You'll still have plenty of that red mud flowing through your veins."

"I know. I realize that now. And I couldn't, even if I wanted to, deny how much I love it here."

"The desert, the dirt, and the heat?"

"Yep. Even the heat. I love it all. The raw, rugged beauty, the majesty of the purple mountains and the one other thing North Carolina doesn't have."

"What's that?"

"You."

"Oh, you're laying it on thick now, Carpenter."

Janice laughed and wrapped her arms around her neck.

Carla looked deep into her eyes and kissed her. And then she said the words Janice had only ever heard in her dreams.

"Then welcome home, baby. Welcome home."

The End

About the Author

Ronica Black lives in the desert Southwest with her menagerie of animals and her menagerie of art. When she's not writing, she's still creating, whether drawing, painting, or woodworking. She loves long walks into the sunset, rescuing animals, anything pertaining to art, and spending time with those she loves. When she can, she enjoys returning to her roots in North Carolina where she can sit back on the porch with family and friends, catch up on all the gossip, and relish an ice cold Cheerwine.

Ronica is a two-time Golden Crown Literary Society Goldie Award winner and a three-time finalist for the Lambda Literary Awards.

Books Available from Bold Strokes Books

A Love that Leads to Home by Ronica Black. For Carla Sims and Janice Carpenter, home isn't about location, it's where your heart is. (978-1-63555-675-9)

Blades of Bluegrass by D. Jackson Leigh. A US Army occupational therapist must rehab a bitter veteran who is a ticking political time bomb the military is desperate to disarm. (978-1-63555-637-7)

Guarding Hearts by Jaycie Morrison. As treachery and temptation threaten the women of the Women's Army Corps, who will risk it all for love? (978-1-63555-806-7)

Hopeless Romantic by Georgia Beers. Can a jaded wedding planner and an optimistic divorce attorney possibly find a future together? (978-1-63555-650-6)

Hopes and Dreams by PJ Trebelhorn. Movie theater manager Riley Warren is forced to face her high school crush and tormentor, wealthy socialite Victoria Thayer, at their twentieth reunion. (978-1-63555-670-4)

In the Cards by Kimberly Cooper Griffin. Daria and Phaedra are about to discover that love finds a way, especially when powers outside their control are at play. (978-1-63555-717-6)

Moon Fever by Ileandra Young. SPEAR agent Danika Karson must clear her werewolf friend of multiple false charges while teaching her vampire girlfriend to resist the blood mania brought on by a full moon. (978-1-63555-603-2)

Quake City by St John Karp. Can Andre find his best friend Amy before the night devolves into a nightmare of broken hearts, malevolent drag queens, and spontaneous human combustion? Or has it always happened this way, every night, at Aunty Bob's Quake City Club? (978-1-63555-723-7)

Serenity by Jesse J. Thoma. For Kit Marsden, there are many things in life she cannot change. Serenity is in the acceptance. (978-1-63555-713-8)

Sylver and Gold by Michelle Larkin. Working feverishly to find a killer before he strikes again, Boston Homicide Detective Reid Sylver and rookie cop London Gold are blindsided by their chemistry and developing attraction. (978-1-63555-611-7)

Trade Secrets by Kathleen Knowles. In Silicon Valley, love and business are a volatile mix for clinical lab scientist Tony Leung and venture capitalist Sheila Garrison. (978-1-63555-642-1)

Death Overdue by David S. Pederson. Did Heath turn to murder in an alcohol induced haze to solve the problem of his blackmailer, or was it someone else who brought about a death overdue? (978-1-63555-711-4)

Entangled by Melissa Brayden. Becca Crawford is the perfect person to head up the Jade Hotel, if only the captivating owner of the local vineyard would get on board with her plan and stop badmouthing the hotel to everyone in town. (978-1-63555-709-1)

First Do No Harm by Emily Smith. Pierce and Cassidy are about to discover that when it comes to love, sometimes you have to risk it all to have it all. (978-1-63555-699-5)

Kiss Me Every Day by Dena Blake. For Wynn Evans, wishing for a do-over with Carly Jamison was a long shot, actually getting one was a game changer. (978-1-63555-551-6)

Olivia by Genevieve McCluer. In this lesbian Shakespeare adaption with vampires, Olivia is a centuries old vampire who must fight a strange figure from her past if she wants a chance at happiness. (978-1-63555-701-5)

One Woman's Treasure by Jean Copeland. Daphne's search for discarded antiques and treasures leads to an embarrassing misunderstanding, and ultimately, the opportunity for the romance of a lifetime with Nina. (978-1-63555-652-0)

Silver Ravens by Jane Fletcher. Lori has lost her girlfriend, her home, and her job. Things don't improve when she's kidnapped and taken to fairyland. (978-1-63555-631-5)

Still Not Over You by Jenny Frame, Carsen Taite, Ali Vali. Old flames die hard in these tales of a second chance at love with the ex you're still not over. Stories by award winning authors Jenny Frame, Carsen Taite, and Ali Vali. (978-1-63555-516-5)

Storm Lines by Jessica L. Webb. Devon is a psychologist who likes rules. Marley is a cop who doesn't. They don't always agree, but both fight to protect a girl immersed in a street drug ring. (978-1-63555-626-1)

The Politics of Love by Jen Jensen. Is it possible to love across the political divide in a hostile world? Conservative Shelley Whitmore and liberal Rand Thomas are about to find out. (978-1-63555-693-3)

All the Paths to You by Morgan Lee Miller. High school sweethearts Quinn Hughes and Kennedy Reed reconnect five years after they break up and realize that their chemistry is all but over. (978-1-63555-662-9)

Arrested Pleasures by Nanisi Barrett D'Arnuck. When charged with a crime she didn't commit Katherine Lowe faces the question: Which is harder, going to prison or falling in love? (978-1-63555-684-1)

Bonded Love by Renee Roman. Carpenter Blaze Carter suffers an injury that shatters her dreams, and ER nurse Trinity Greene hopes to show her that sometimes love is worth fighting for. (978-1-63555-530-1)

Convergence by Jane C. Esther. With life as they know it on the line, can Aerin McLeary and Olivia Ando's love survive an otherworldly threat to humankind? (978-1-63555-488-5)

Coyote Blues by Karen F. Williams. Riley Dawson, psychotherapist and shape-shifter, has her world turned upside down when Fiona Bell, her one true love, returns. (978-1-63555-558-5)

Drawn by Carsen Taite. Will the clues lead Detective Claire Hanlon to the killer terrorizing Dallas, or will she merely lose her heart to person of interest, urban artist Riley Flynn? (978-1-63555-644-5)

Every Summer Day by Lee Patton. Meant to celebrate every summer day, Luke's journal instead chronicles a love affair as fast-moving and possibly as fatal as his brother's brain tumor. (978-1-63555-706-0)

Lucky by Kris Bryant. Was Serena Evans's luck really about winning the lottery, or is she about to get even luckier in love? (978-1-63555-510-3)

The Last Days of Autumn by Donna K. Ford. Autumn and Caroline question the fairness of life, the cruelty of loss, and what it means to love as they navigate the complicated minefield of relationships, grief, and life-altering illness. (978-1-63555-672-8)

Three Alarm Response by Erin Dutton. In the midst of tragedy, can these first responders find love and healing? Three stories of courage, bravery, and passion. (978-1-63555-592-9)

Veterinary Partner by Nancy Wheelton. Callie and Lauren are determined to keep their hearts safe but find that taking a chance on love is the safest option of all. (978-1-63555-666-7)

Everyday People by Louis Barr. When film star Diana Danning hires private eye Clint Steele to find her son, Clint turns to his former West Point barracks mate, and ex-buddy with benefits, Mars Hauser to lend his cyber espionage and digital black ops skills to the case. (978-1-63555-698-8)

Forging a Desire Line by Mary P. Burns. When Charley's ex-wife, Tricia, is diagnosed with inoperable cancer, the private duty nurse Tricia hires turns out to be the handsome and aloof Joanna, who ignites something inside Charley she isn't ready to face. (978-1-63555-665-0)

Love on the Night Shift by Radclyffe. Between ruling the night shift in the ER at the Rivers and raising her teenage daughter, Blaise Richilieu has all the drama she needs in her life, until a dashing young attending appears on the scene and relentlessly pursues her. (978-1-63555-668-1)

Olivia's Awakening by Ronica Black. When the daring and dangerously gorgeous Eve Monroe is hired to get Olivia Savage into shape, a fierce passion ignites, causing both to question everything they've ever known about love. (978-1-63555-613-1)

The Duchess and the Dreamer by Jenny Frame. Clementine Fitzroy has lost her faith and love of life. Can dreamer Evan Fox make her believe in life and dream again? (978-1-63555-601-8)

The Road Home by Erin Zak. Hollywood actress Gwendolyn Carter is about to discover that losing someone you love sometimes means gaining someone to fall for. (978-1-63555-633-9)

Waiting for You by Elle Spencer. When passionate past-life lovers meet again in the present day, one remembers it vividly and the other isn't so sure. (978-1-63555-635-3)

While My Heart Beats by Erin McKenzie. Can a love born amidst the horrors of the Great War survive? (978-1-63555-589-9)

Face the Music by Ali Vali. Sweet music is the last thing that happens when Nashville music producer Mason Liner, and daughter of country royalty Victoria Roddy are thrown together in an effort to save country star Sophie Roddy's career. (978-1-63555-532-5)

Flavor of the Month by Georgia Beers. What happens when baker Charlie and chef Emma realize their differing paths have led them right back to each other? (978-1-63555-616-2)

Mending Fences by Angie Williams. Rancher Bobbie Del Rey and veterinarian Grace Hammond are about to discover if heartbreaks of the past can ever truly be mended. (978-1-63555-708-4)

Silk and Leather: Lesbian Erotica with an Edge edited by Victoria Villasenor. This collection of stories by award winning authors offers fantasies as soft as silk and tough as leather. The only question is: How far will you go to make your deepest desires come true? (978-1-63555-587-5)

The Last Place You Look by Aurora Rey. Dumped by her wife and looking for anything but love, Julia Pierce retreats to her hometown, only to rediscover high school friend Taylor Winslow, who's secretly crushed on her for years. (978-1-63555-574-5)

The Mortician's Daughter by Nan Higgins. A singer on the verge of stardom discovers she must give up her dreams to live a life in service to ghosts. (978-1-63555-594-3)

The Real Thing by Laney Webber. When passion flares between actress Virginia Green and masseuse Allison McDonald, can they be sure it's the real thing? (978-1-63555-478-6)

What the Heart Remembers Most by M. Ullrich. For college sweethearts Jax Levine and Gretchen Mills, could an accident be the second chance neither knew they wanted? (978-1-63555-401-4)

White Horse Point by Andrews & Austin. Mystery writer Taylor James finds herself falling for the mysterious woman on White Horse Point who lives alone, protecting a secret she can't share about a murderer who walks among them. (978-1-63555-695-7)